The Triple Alliance

ITS TRIALS AND TRIUMPHS

HAROLD AVERY

1st WORLD
LIBRARY
Literary Society

The Triple Alliance

Harold Avery

© 1st World Library – Literary Society, 2004
PO Box 2211
Fairfield, IA 52556
www.1stworldlibrary.org
First Edition

LCCN: 2004091196

Softcover ISBN: 1-59540-642-5
eBook ISBN: 1-59540-742-1

Purchase *"The Triple Alliance"*
as a traditional bound book at:
www.1stWorldLibrary.org/purchase.asp?ISBN=1-59540-642-5

1st World Library Literary Society is a nonprofit organization dedicated to promoting literacy by:

- Creating a free internet library accessible from any computer worldwide.
- Hosting writing competitions and offering book publishing scholarships.

Readers interested in supporting literacy through sponsorship, donations or membership please contact:
literacy@1stworldlibrary.org
Check us out at: www.1stworldlibrary.org

The Triple Alliance
contributed by the Mahaney Family
in support of
1st World Library Literary Society

CONTENTS.

CHAPTER I.

A NEW BOY.

"What's your name?"

"Diggory Trevanock."

The whole class exploded.

"Now, then," said Mr. Blake, looking up from his mark-book with a broad grin on his own face - "now, then, there's nothing to laugh at. - Look here," he added, turning to the new boy, "how d'you spell it?"

Instead of being at all annoyed or disconcerted at the mirth of his class-mates, the youngster seemed rather to enjoy the joke, and immediately rattled out a semi-humorous reply to the master's question, -

"D I G, dig; G O R Y, gory - Diggory: T R E, tre; VAN, van; O C K, ock - Trevanock." Then turning round, he smiled complacently at the occupants of the desks behind, as much as to say: "There, I've done all I can to amuse you, and I hope you're satisfied."

This incident, one of the little pleasantries occasionally permitted by a class master, and which, like a judge's jokes in court, are always welcomed as a momentary relief from the depressing monotony of the serious business in hand - this little incident, I say, happened in the second class of a small preparatory school, situated on the outskirts of the market town of Chatford, and intended, according to the wording of a standing advertisement in the *Denfordshire Chronicle*, "for the sons of gentlemen."

This establishment, which bore the somewhat suggestive name of "The Birches," was owned and presided over by Mr. Welsby, who, with an unmarried daughter, Miss Eleanor, acting as housekeeper, and his nephew, Mr. Blake, performing the duties of assistant-master, undertook the preliminary education of about a dozen juveniles whose ages ranged between ten and fourteen.

On the previous evening, returning from the Christmas holidays, exactly twelve had mustered round the big table in the dining-room; no new faces had appeared, and Fred Acton, a big, strong youngster of fourteen and a half, was undisputed cock of the walk.

The school was divided into two classes. The first, containing the five elder scholars, went to sit at the feet of Mr. Welsby himself; while the second remained behind in what was known as the schoolroom, and received instruction from Mr. Blake.

It was while thus occupied on the first morning of the term that the lower division were surprised by the sudden appearance of a new boy. Miss Eleanor brought him into the room, and after a few moments' whispered conversation with her cousin, smiled round the class and then withdrew. Every one worshipped Miss Eleanor; but that's neither here nor there. A moment later Mr. Blake put the question which stands at the commencement of this chapter.

The new-comer's answer made a favourable impression on the minds of his companions, and as soon as the morning's work was over, they set about the task of mutual introduction in a far more friendly manner than was customary on these occasions. He was a wiry little chap, with bright eyes, for ever on the twinkle, and black hair pasted down upon his head, so as not to show the slightest vestige of curl, while the sharp, mischievous look on his face, and the quick, comical movements of his body, suggested something between a terrier and a monkey.

There was never very much going on in the way of regular sports or pastimes at The Birches; the smallness of numbers made it difficult to attempt proper games of cricket or football, and the boys were forced to content themselves with such substitutes as prisoner's base, cross tag, etc., or in carrying out the projects of Fred Acton, who was constantly making suggestions for the employment of their time, and compelling everybody to conform to his wishes.

Mr. Welsby had been a widower for many years; he was a grave, scholarly man, who spent most of his spare time in his own library. Mr. Blake was supposed to take charge out of school hours; he was, as every one said, "a jolly fellow," and the fact that his popularity extended far and wide among a large circle of friends and acquaintances, caused him to have a good many irons in the fire of one sort and another. During their hours of leisure, therefore, the Birchites were left pretty much to their own devices, or more often to those of Master Fred Acton, who liked, as has already been stated, to assume the office of bellwether to the little flock.

At the time when our story commences the ground was covered with snow; but Acton was equal to the occasion, and as soon as dinner was over, ordered all hands to come outside and make a slide.

The garden was on a steep slope, along the bottom of which ran the brick wall bounding one side of the playground; a straight, steep path lay between this and the house, and the youthful dux, with his usual disregard of life and limb, insisted on choosing this as the scene of operations.

"What!" he cried, in answer to a feeble protest on the part of Mugford, "make it on level ground? Of course not, when we've got this jolly hill to go down; not if I know it. We'll open the door at the bottom, and go right on into the playground."

"But how if any one goes a bit crooked, and runs up against the bricks?"

"Well, they'll get pretty well smashed, or he will. You must go straight; that's half the fun of the thing - it'll make it all the more exciting. Come on and begin to tread down the snow."

Without daring to show any outward signs of reluctance, but with feelings very much akin to those of men digging their own graves before being shot, the company set about putting this fearful project into execution. In about half an hour the slide was in good working order, and then the fun began.

Mugford, and one or two others whose prudence

exceeded their valour, made a point of sitting down before they had gone many yards, preferring to take the fall in a milder form than it would have assumed at a later period in the journey. To the bolder spirits, however, every trip was like leading a forlorn hope, none expecting to return from the enterprise unscathed. The pace was terrific: on nearing the playground wall, all the events of a lifetime might have flashed across the memory as at the last gasp of a drowning man; and if fortunate enough to whiz through the doorway, and pull up "all standing" on the level stretch beyond, it was to draw a deep breath, and regard the successful performance of the feat as an escape from catastrophe which was nothing short of miraculous. The unevenness of the ground made it almost impossible to steer a straight course. A boy might be half-way down the path, when suddenly he felt himself beginning to turn round; an agonized look spread over his face; he made one frantic attempt to keep, as it were, "head to the sea;" there was an awful moment when house, garden, sky, and playground wall spun round and round; and then the little group of onlookers, their hearts hardened by their own sufferings, burst into a roar of laughter; while Acton slapped his leg, crying, "He's over! What a stunning lark! Who's next?"

At the end of an hour and a half most of the company were temporarily disabled, and even their chief had not escaped scot free.

"Now then for a regular spanker!" he cried, rushing at the slide. A "spanker" it certainly was: six yards from the commencement his legs flew from under him, he soared into the air like a bird, and did not touch the ground again until he sat down heavily within twenty paces of the bottom of the slope.

One might have supposed that this catastrophe would have somewhat damped the sufferer's ardour; but instead of that he only seemed fired with a fresh desire to break his neck.

He hobbled up the hill, and pausing for a moment at the top to take breath, suddenly exclaimed, "Look here, I'm going down it on skates."

Every one stood aghast at this rash determination; but Acton hurried off into the house, and soon returned with the skates. He sat down on a bank, and was proceeding to put them on, when he discovered that, by some oversight, he had brought out the wrong pair. "Bother it! these aren't mine, they're too short; whose are they?"

"I think they're mine," faltered Mugford.

"Well, put 'em on."

"But I don't want to."

"But I say you must!"

"Oh! please, Acton, I really can't, I - "

"Shut up! Look here, some one's got to go down that slide on skates, so just put 'em on."

It was at this moment that Diggory Trevanock stepped forward, and remarked in a casual manner that if Mugford didn't wish to do it, but would lend him the skates, he himself would go down the slide.

His companions stared at him in astonishment, coupled

Harold Avery

with which was a feeling of regret: he was a nice little chap, and they had already begun to like him, and did not wish to see him dashed to pieces against the playground wall before their very eyes. Acton, however, had decreed that "some one had got to go down that slide on skates," and it seemed only meet and right that if a victim had to be sacrificed it should be a new boy rather than an old stager.

"Bravo!" cried the dux; "here's one chap at least who's no funk. Put 'em on sharp; the bell 'll ring in a minute."

Several willing hands were stretched out to assist in arming Diggory for the enterprise, and in a few moments he was assisted to the top of the slide.

"All right," he said; "let go!"

The spectators held their breath, hardly daring to watch what would happen. But fortune favours the brave. The adventurous juvenile rushed down the path, shot like an arrow through the doorway, and the next instant was seen ploughing up the snow in the playground, and eventually disappearing head first into the middle of a big drift.

His companions all rushed down in a body to haul him out of the snow. Acton smacked him on the back, and called him a trump; while Jack Vance presented him on the spot with a mince-pie, which had been slightly damaged in one of the donor's many tumbles, but was, as he remarked, "just as good as new for eating."

From that moment until the day he left there was never a more popular boy at The Birches than Diggory Trevanock.

"I say," remarked Mugford, as they met a short time later in the cloak-room, "that was awfully good of you to go down the slide instead of me; what ever made you do it?"

"Well," answered the other calmly, "I thought it would save me a lot of bother if I showed you fellows at once that I wasn't a muff. I don't mind telling you I was in rather a funk when it came to the start; but I'd said I'd do it, and of course I couldn't draw back."

The numerous stirring events which happened at The Birches during the next three terms, and which it will be my pleasing duty to chronicle in subsequent chapters, gave the boys plenty of opportunity of testing the character of their new companion, or, in plainer English, of finding out the stuff he was made of; and whatever his other faults may have been, this at least is certain, that no one ever found occasion to charge Diggory Trevanock with being either a muff or a coward.

One might have thought that the slide episode would have afforded excitement enough for a new boy's first day at school; yet before it closed he was destined to be mixed up in an adventure of a still more thrilling character.

The Birches was an old house, and though its outward appearance was modern enough, the interior impressed even youthful minds with a feeling of reverence for its age. The heavy timbers, the queer shape of some of the bedrooms and attics, the narrow, crooked passages, and the little unexpected flights of stairs, were all things belonging to a bygone age, of which the pupils were secretly proud, and which caused them to remember the place, and think of it at the time, as being in some way different from an ordinary school.

"I say, Diggy," exclaimed Jack Vance, addressing the new boy by the friendly abbreviation, which seemed by mutual consent to have been bestowed upon him in recognition of his daring exploit - "I say, Diggy, you're in my bedroom: there's you, and me, and Mugford. Mug's an awful chump, but he's a good-natured old duffer, and you and I'll do the fighting."

"What do you mean?"

"Why, sometimes when Blake is out spending the evening, and old Welsby is shut up in his library, the different rooms make raids on one another. It began the term before last. Blake had been teaching us all about how the Crusaders used to go out every now and then and make war in Palestine, and so the fellows on the west side of the house called themselves the Crusaders, and we were Infidels, and they'd come over and rag us, and we should drive them back. Miss Eleanor came up one night, and caught us in the middle of a battle. O Diggy, she is a trump! Blake asked her next day before us all which boys had been out on the landing, because he meant to punish them; and she laughed, and said: 'I'm sure I can't tell you. Why, when I saw they were all in their night-shirts, I shut my eyes at once!' Of course it was all an excuse for not giving us away. She doesn't mind seeing chaps in their night-shirts when they're ill, we all know that; and once or twice when for some reason or other she told us on the quiet that there mustn't be any disturbance that evening, no one ever went crusading - Acton would have licked them if they had. Acton's going to propose to Miss Eleanor some day, he told us so, and - "

"But what about the bedrooms?" interrupted Diggory; "have you given up having crusades?"

"Yes, but we have other things instead. We call our rooms by different names, and it's all against all; one lot come and make a raid on you, and then you go and pay them out. This term Kennedy and Jacobs sleep in the room above ours, and next to the big attic. They're always reading sea stories, and they call their room the 'Main-top,' because it's so high up. Then at the end of the passage are Acton, Shaw, and Morris, and they're the 'House of Lords;' and next to them is the 'Dogs' Home,' where all the other fellows are put."

A few hours later Diggory and his two room-mates were standing at the foot of their beds and discussing the formation of a few simple rules for conducting a race in undressing, the last man to put the candle out.

"You needn't bother to race," said Mugford; "I'll do it - I'm sure to be the last."

"No, you aren't," answered Vance. "We'll give you coat and waistcoat start; it'll be good fun - "

At this moment the door was suddenly flung open, two half-dressed figures sprang into the room, and discharged a couple of snowballs point-blank at its occupants. One of the missiles struck Diggory on the shoulder, and the other struck Mugford fair and square on the side of the head, the fragments flying all over the floor. There was a subdued yell of triumph, the door was slammed to with a bang, and the muffled sound of stockinged feet thudding up the neighbouring

Harold Avery

staircase showed that the enemy were in full retreat.

"It's those confounded Main-top men!" cried Jack Vance; "I will pay them out. I wonder where the fellows got the snow from?"

"Oh, I expect they opened the window and took it off the ledge," answered Diggory. "Look here - let's sweep it up into this piece of paper before it melts."

This having been done, the three friends hastily threw off their clothes and scrambled into bed, forgetting all about the proposed race in their eagerness to form some plan for an immediate retaliation on the occupants of the "Main-top."

"I wonder if they'll hear anything of the ghost again this term?" said Mugford,

"What ghost?" asked Diggory.

"Oh, it's nothing really," answered Vance; "only some-body said once that the house is haunted, and Kennedy and Jacobs say the ghost must be in the big attic next their room. They hear such queer noises sometimes that they both go under the bed-clothes."

"Do they always do that?"

"Yes, so they say, whenever there is a row."

"Well, then," said Diggory, "I'll tell you what we'll do: we'll go very quietly up into that attic, and groan and knock on the wall until you think they've both got their heads well under the clothes, and then we'll rush in and bag their pillows, or drag them out of bed, or something of that sort. You aren't afraid to go into the attic, are you?" he continued, seeing that the others hesitated. "Why, of course there are no such things as ghosts. Or, look here, I'll go in, and you can wait outside."

"N - no, I don't mind," answered Vance; "and it'll be an awful lark catching them with their heads under the clothes."

"All right, then, let's do it; though I suppose we'd better wait till every one's in bed."

The last suggestion was agreed upon, and the three friends lay talking in an undertone until the sound of footsteps and the gleam of a candle above the door announced the fact that Mr. Blake was retiring to rest.

"He's always last," said Vance; "we must give him time to undress, and then we'll start."

A quarter of an hour later the three boys, in semi-undress, were creeping in single file up the narrow staircase.

"Be careful," whispered Vance; "there are several loose boards, and they crack like anything."

The small landing was reached in safety, and the moon, shining faintly through a little skylight formed of a single pane of glass, enabled them to distinguish the outline of two doors.

Now it was a very different matter, when lying warm and snug in bed, to talk about acting the ghost, from what it was, when standing shivering in the cold and darkness, to put the project into execution. During the period of waiting the conversation had turned on haunted houses, and no one seemed particularly anxious to claim as it were the post of honour, and be the first to enter the big attic.

"Go on!" whispered Mugford, nudging Vance.

"Go on!" repeated the latter, giving Diggory's arm a gentle push.

The new boy had certainly undertaken to play the part of the ghost, and there was no excuse for his backing out of it at the last moment.

"All right," he muttered, "I'll go."

Just then a terrible thing happened. Diggory clutched the door-knob as though it were the handle of a galvanic battery, while Mugford and Vance seized each other by the arm and literally gasped for breath.

The stillness had been broken by a slight sound, as of something falling inside the attic, and this was followed a moment later by a shrill, unearthly scream.

For five seconds the three companions stood petrified with horror, not daring to move; then followed another scream, if anything more horrible than the last, and accompanied this time by the clanking rattle of a chain being dragged across the floor.

That was enough. Talk about a *sauve qui peut*! the wonder is that any one survived the stampede which followed. The youngsters turned and flew down the stairs at break-neck speed, and hardly had they started when the door of the "Main-top" was flung open, and its two occupants rushed down after them. As though to ensure the retreat being nothing less than a regular rout, Mugford, who was leading, missed his footing on the last step, causing every one to fall over him in turn, until all five boys were sprawling together in a mixed heap upon the floor.

Freeing themselves with some little difficulty from the general entanglement, they rose to their feet, and after surveying each other for a moment in silence, gave vent to a simultaneous ejaculation of "*The ghost!*"

"What were you fellows doing up there?" asked Kennedy.

"Why, we came up to have a joke with you," answered Vance; "but just when we got up to the landing, it - it made that noise!"

There was the sound of the key turning in the lock of Mr. Blake's door.

"*Cave!*" whispered Mugford.

"Tell him about it," added Vance; and giving Diggory a push, they all three darted into their room just as the master emerged from his, arrayed in dressing-gown and slippers.

"Now, then," exclaimed the latter, holding his candle above his head, and peering down the passage, "what's the meaning of this disturbance? I thought the whole house was falling down. - Come here, you two, and explain yourselves!"

"Please, sir," answered Kennedy and Jacobs in one breath, "it's the ghost!"

"The ghost! What ghost? What d'you mean?"

The two "Main-top" men began a hasty account of the cause of their sudden fright, taking care, however, to make no mention of the three hostile visitors who had shared in the surprise.

Mr. Blake listened to their story in silence, then all at once he burst out laughing, and without a word turned on his heel and went quickly upstairs. He entered the attic, and in about half a minute they heard him coming back.

"Ha, ha! I've got your ghost; I've been trying to lay him for some time past."

The jingle of a chain was distinctly audible; Mr. Blake was evidently bringing the spectre down in his arms! Diggory and Vance could no longer restrain their curiosity; they hopped out of bed and glanced round the corner of the door. The master held in his hand a rusty old gin, the iron jaws of which were tightly closed upon the body of an enormous rat.

"There's a monster for you!" he said; "I think it's the biggest I ever saw. He'd carried the trap, chain and all, right across the room, but that finished him; he was as dead as a stone when I picked him up. Now get back to bed; I should think you're both nearly frozen."

Diggory and Jack Vance followed the advice given to Kennedy and Jacobs, and did so rather sheepishly. They felt they had been making tools of themselves;

yet it would never have done to own to such a thing.

"What a lark!" said the new boy, after a few moments' silence.

"Wasn't it!" returned Jack Vance; "it's the best joke I've had for a long time. But we didn't pay those fellows out for throwing those snowballs; we must do it some other night. And now we three must swear to be friends, and stand by each other against all the world, and whatever happens. What shall we call our room?"

"I know," answered Diggory: "we'll call it 'The Triple Alliance!'"

CHAPTER II.

THE PHILISTINES.

The Triple Alliance, the formation of which has just been described, was destined to be no mere form of speech or empty display of friendship. The members had solemnly sworn to stand by one another whatever happened, and the manner in which they carried out their resolve, and the important consequences which resulted from their concerted actions, will be made known to the reader as our story progresses.

Poor Mugford certainly seemed likely to be a heavy drag on the association; he was constantly tumbling into trouble, and needing to be pulled out again by those who had promised to be his friends.

An instance of this occurred on the day following Diggory's arrival at The Birches. He and Vance had gone down after morning school into what was called the playroom, to partake of two more of the latter's mince-pies, and on their return to the schoolroom found a crowd assembled round Acton, who, seated on the top of a small cupboard which always served as a judicial bench, was hearing a case in which Mugford was the defendant, while Jacobs and another boy named Cross appeared as plaintiffs.

The charge was that the former was indebted to the latter for the sum of half a crown, which he had borrowed towards the end of the previous term, in separate amounts of one shilling and eighteen pence, promising to repay them, with interest, immediately after the holidays. The money had been expended in the purchase of a disreputable old canary bird, for which Noaks, the manservant, had agreed to find board and lodging during the Christmas vacation. Now, when the creditors reminded Mugford of his obligations, they found him totally unable to meet their demands for payment.

"Now, look here," said Acton, addressing the defendant with great severity, "no humbug - how much money did you bring back with you?"

"Well, I had to pay my brother before I came away for my share in a telescope we bought last summer, and then - "

"Bother your brother and the telescope! Why can't you answer my question? How much money did you bring back with you?"

"Only five bob."

"Then why in the name of Fortune don't you pay up?"

"Because I had to pay all that to Noaks for bird-seed."

"D'you mean to say that that bird ate five shillings' worth of seed in four weeks?"

"Well, so Noaks says; he told me he'd kept scores of birds in his time, but he'd 'never seen one so hearty at its grub before.' Those were the very words he used, and he said it was eating nearly all the day, and that's one reason why it looks such a dowdy colour, and never sings."

"Well, all I can say is, if you believe all Noaks tells you, you're a fool. But that's no reason why these two chaps should be done out of their money; so now, how are you going to pay them?"

"If they only wait till pocket-money's given out - " began Mugford.

"Oh no, we shan't!" interrupted Cross. "He only gets sixpence a week, and he's always breaking windows and other things, and having it stopped."

There seemed only one way out of the difficulty, and that was to put as it were an execution into Mugford's desk, and realize a certain amount of his private property.

"Look here," said Acton, "he must sell something. - Now, then," he added, turning to the defendant, "just shell out something and bring it here at once, and we'll have an auction."

The boy walked off to his desk, and after rummaging about in it for some little time, returned with a miscellaneous collection of small articles in his arms, which he proceeded to hand up one by one for the judge's inspection.

"What's this?"

"Oh, its a book that was given me on my birthday,

called 'Lofty Thoughts for Little Thinkers.'"

"Lofty grandmother!" said Acton impatiently.

"What else have you got ?"

"Well, here's a wire puzzle, only I think a bit of it's lost, and the clasp of a cricket belt, and old Dick Rodman's chessboard and some of the men, and some stuff for chilblains, and - "

"Oh, dry up!" interrupted Acton; "what bosh! Who d'you expect would buy any of that rubbish? Look here, we'll give you till after dinner, and unless you find something sensible by then, we shall come and hunt for ourselves."

"That's just like Mug," said Jack Vance to Diggory, as the group of boys slowly dispersed; "he's always doing something stupid. But I suppose as we made that alliance, we ought to try to help the beggar somehow."

They followed their unfortunate comrade to his desk, which when opened displayed a perfect chaos of ragged books, loose sheets of paper, broken pen-holders, pieces of string, battered cardboard boxes, and other rubbish.

"Look here, Mug, what have you got to sell? you'll have to fork out something."

"I don't know," returned the other mournfully, stirring up the contents of the desk as though he were making a Christmas pudding. "I've got nothing, except - well, there's this book of Poe's, 'Tales of Adventure, Mystery, and Imagination,' and my clasp-knife; and perhaps some one would buy these fret-saw patterns or this dog-chain."

He turned out two or three more small articles and laid them on the form.

"Are there any of these things you particularly wish to keep?" asked Diggory; "because, if so, Vance and I'll bid for them, and then you can buy them back from us again when you've got some more money."

"That's awfully kind of you," answered Mugford, brightening up. "I'll tell you what I should like to keep, and that's my clasp-knife and the book; they're such jolly stories. 'The Pit and the Pendulum' always gives me bad dreams, and 'The Premature Burial' makes you feel certain you'll be buried alive."

"All right; and did you bring a cake back with you?"

"Yes."

"Well, then, sell that first, and you can share our grub."

The auction was held directly after dinner. The cake fetched a shilling, and Diggory and Vance bid ninepence each for the book and pocket-knife; so Mugford came out of his difficulty without suffering any further loss than what was afterwards made good again by the generosity of his two comrades. They, for their part, made no fuss over this little act of kindness, but handed the book and clasp-knife over to Mugford without waiting for the money, and little thinking what an important part these trifling possessions would play in the subsequent history of the Triple Alliance.

The sale had not long been concluded, and the little community were preparing to obey Acton's order to "Come outside," when the latter rushed into the room finning with rage.

"I say," he exclaimed, "what do you think that beast of a Noaks has done? Why, he's gone and put ashes all over our slide!"

In their heart of hearts every one felt decidedly relieved at this announcement; still it was necessary, at all events, to simulate some of their leader's wrath, and accordingly there was a general outcry against the offender.

"Oh, the cad!" - "What an awful shame!" - "Let's tell Blake!" etc., etc.

"Who is Noaks?" asked Diggory. "Is he that sour-looking man who brings the boots in every morning?"

"Yes, that's so," answered Vance. "He hates us all - partly, I believe, because his son's a Philistine. I wonder old Welsby doesn't get another man."

"His son's a *what?*" asked Diggory; but at that moment Acton came marching round the room ordering every one out into the playground, and Jack Vance hurried off to get his cap and muffler without replying to the question.

Sliding was out of the question, and the "House of Lords" having amused themselves for a time by capturing small boys and throwing them into the snow-drift, some one remarked that it would be good fun to build a snow man; which proposition was received with acclamation, and all hands were soon hard at work rolling the big balls which were to form the base of the statue. As the work progressed the interest in it increased, the more so when Diggory suggested that the figure should be supposed to represent the obnoxious Noaks, and that the company could then relieve their feelings by pelting his effigy as soon as it was completed. Every one was pleased with the project, and even Acton, who as a rule would never follow up any plan which was not of his own making, took special pains to cause the snow man to bear some likeness to the original. He had just, by way of a finishing touch, expended nearly half a penny bottle of red ink in a somewhat exaggerated reproduction of the fiery hue of Noaks's nose, when the bell rang for afternoon school, and the bombardment had to be postponed until the following day.

It was no small trial of patience being thus obliged to wait nearly twenty-four hours before wreaking their vengeance on the effigy; still there was no help for it. The boys bottled down their feelings, and when at last the classes were dismissed, and the dux cried, "Come on, you fellows!" every one obeyed the summons willingly enough. There had been a slight thaw in the night, and the statue stood in need of some trifling repairs. Acton suggested, therefore, that the half-hour before dinner should be devoted to putting things to rights, and to making some small additions in the shape of pebbles for waistcoat buttons, and other trifling adornments.

Mr. Welsby kept the boys at the table for nearly a quarter of an hour after the meal was finished, talking over his plans for the coming term, and when at last he finished there was a regular stampede for the playground. Acton was leading the rush; he dashed through the garden doorway, and then stopped dead with an exclamation of dismay. All those who followed, as they arrived on the spot, did the same. Every vestige of the snow man, which had been left barely an hour ago standing such a work of art, had disappeared. Certainly a portion of the pedestal still remained, looking like the stump of an old, decayed tooth; but the figure itself had been thrown down, trodden flat, and literally stamped out of existence!

The little crowd stood for a moment speechless, gazing with woebegone expressions on their faces at the wreck of their hopes and handiwork; then the silence was broken by a subdued chuckle coming from the other side of the wall on their left, and every one, with a start and a sudden clinching of fists, cried simultaneously: "The Philistines!"

The words had hardly been uttered when above the brickwork appeared the head and shoulders of a boy a size or so bigger than Acton; a dirty-looking brown bowler hat was stuck on the very back of his head, and rammed down until the brim rested on the top of his ears; and it will be quite sufficient to remark that his face was in exact keeping with the manner in which he wore his hat. Once more everybody gave vent to their feelings by another involuntary ejaculation - "Young Noaks!"

The stranger laughed, pulled a face which, as far as ugliness went, was hardly an improvement on the one Nature had already bestowed upon him, and then pointed mockingly at the remains of the masterpiece.

His triumph, however, was short-lived. Jack Vance, as

Harold Avery

he left the house, had caught up a double handful of snow, which he had been pressing into a hard ball as he ran down the path, determining in his own, mind to be the first to open fire on the snow man. Without a moment's hesitation he flung the missile at the intruder's head, and, to the intense delight of his companions, it struck the latter fairly on the mouth, causing him to lose his precarious foothold on the wall and fall back into the road.

It needed no further warning to inform the Birchites that the Philistines were upon them, and every one set to work to lay in a stock of snowballs as fast as hands could make them. "Look out!" cried Kennedy. Young Noaks's face rose once more above the top of the wall, and the next moment a big stone, the size of hen's egg, whizzed past Diggory's head, and struck the garden door with a sounding bang.

"Oh, the cad!" cried Acton; "let's go for him."

The whole garrison combined in making a vigorous sortie into the road; but it was only to find the enemy in full retreat, and a few dropping shots at long range ended the skirmish.

"I say, Vance," exclaimed Diggory, "who are they? Who are these fellows?"

Now, as the aforesaid Philistines play rather an Important part in the opening chapters of our story, I propose to answer the question myself, in such a way that the reader may be enabled to take a more intelligent interest in the chain of events which commenced with the destruction of the snow man; and in order that this may be done in a satisfactory manner,

I will in a few words map out the ground on which this memorable campaign was afterwards conducted.

Take the well-known drawing of two right angles In Euclid's definition, and imagine the horizontal line to be the main road to Chatford, while the perpendicular one standing on it is a by-way called Locker's lane. In the right angle stood The Birches; the house itself faced the Chatford road, while behind it, in regular succession, came first the sloping garden, then the walled-in playground, and then the small field in which were attempted such games of cricket and football as the limited number of pupils would permit. There were three doors in the playground - one the entrance from the garden, another opening into the lane, and a third into the field, the two latter being usually kept locked.

Locker's Lane was a short cut to Chatford, yet Rule 21 in The Birches Statute-Book ordained that no boy should either go or return by this route when visiting the town; the whole road was practically put out of bounds, and the reason for this regulation was as follows:

At the corner of the playing field the lane took a sharp turn, and about a quarter of a mile beyond this stood a large red-brick house, shut in on three sides by a high wall, whereon, close to the heavy double doors which formed the entrance, appeared a board bearing in big letters the legend -

HORACE HOUSE,
Middle-Class School for Boys.
A. PHILLIPS, B.A., Head-master.

The pupils of Mr. Phillips had been formerly called by Mr. Welsby's boys the Phillipians, which title had in time given place to the present nickname of the Philistines.

I have no doubt that the average boy turned out by Horace House was as good a fellow, taking him all round, as the average boy produced by The Birches; and that, if they had been thrown together in one school, they would, for the most part, have made very good friends and comrades. However, in fairness both to them and to their rivals, it must be said that at the period of our story Mr. Phillips seemed for some time past to have been unusually unfortunate in his elder boys: they were undoubtedly "cads," and the character of the whole establishment, as far as the scholars were concerned, naturally yielded to the influence of its leaders.

It had been customary every term for the Birchites to play a match against them either at cricket or football; but their conduct during a visit paid to the ground of the latter, back in the previous summer, had been so very ungentlemanly and unsportsmanlike that, when the next challenge arrived for an encounter at football, Mr. Welsby wrote back a polite note expressing regret that he did not see his way clear to permit a continuation of the matches. This was the signal for an outbreak of open hostilities between the two schools: the Philistines charged the Birchites in the open street with being afraid to meet them in the field. These base insinuations led to frequent exchanges of taunts and uncomplimentary remarks; and, last of all, matters were brought to a climax by a stand-up fight between Tom Mason, Acton's predecessor as dux, and young Noaks. The encounter took place just outside the stronghold of the enemy, the Birchite so far getting the best of it that at the end of a five minutes' engagement he proclaimed his victory by dragging his adversary along by the collar and bumping his head a number of times against the very gates of Horace House. Unfortunately a rumour of what had happened got to the ears of Mr. Welsby. Mason was severely reprimanded, and his companions were forbidden, under pain of heavy punishment, to walk in Locker's Lane further than the corner of their own playing field.

"But who is young Noaks?" asked Diggory, as Jack Vance finished a hasty account of this warfare with the Philistines.

"Why, that's just the funny part of it," returned the other. "This Sam Noaks is the son of our Noaks, but he's got an uncle, called Simpson, who lives at Todderton, where I come from. This man Simpson made a lot of money out in Australia, and when he came back to England he adopted young Noaks, and sends him here to Phillips's school."

By this time the home forces had all struggled back into the playground. In one corner stood a wooden shed containing a carpenter's bench, a chest for bats and stumps, and various other things belonging to different boys. Acton, as head of the school, kept the key, and having unfastened the door, summoned his followers inside to hold an impromptu council of war and discuss the situation. There was a grave expression on each face, for every one felt that things were beginning to look serious. Mason, the only one of their number who had been physically equal to the leaders of their opponents, was no longer among them, and the enemy, evidently aware of their helpless condition, had

　　　　　　　Harold Avery

dared for the first time to actually come and beard them in their own den.

"What I want to know first is this," began Acton. "You can see by the footmarks that they came in through that door; of course it's always kept locked, and here's the key hanging up inside the shed. Now who opened it for them, and how was it done?"

"Perhaps it wasn't fastened," suggested Morris.

"Yes, it was," answered Kennedy excitedly. "I noticed that this morning, when we were picking up stones for the snow man's buttons."

"Then I tell you what it is," continued Acton solemnly: "some one here's playing us false, and my belief is it's old Noaks. D'you remember last term when Mason and Jack Vance and I made a plot for going down and throwing crackers into their yard? Well, they must have heard of it from some one; for they were all lying in wait for us behind the wall, and as soon as we got near to it they threw cans of water over us and pelted us with stones."

There was a murmur of suppressed wrath at the memory of the fate of this gallant expedition.

"Yes," added Shaw, "and I believe some one told them about this snow man."

"Well, one thing's certain," said Acton - "we must serve 'em out somehow for knocking it down. They evidently think now Mason's gone they can do what they like, and that we shall be afraid of them. Now what can we do?"

There was a silence; every one felt that a serious crisis had arrived in the history of the Birchites, and that unless some immediate steps were taken to avenge this insult they would no longer be free men, but live in constant terror of the Philistines; - every one, I say, felt that some bold action must be taken, yet nobody had a suggestion to make.

"Well, look here," said Acton, "something's got to be done. We must all think it over, and we'll have another meeting in a week's time; then if any one's made a plan, we'll talk it over and decide what's to be done."

"Jack," said Diggory two evenings later, "you know what Acton said about the Philistines; well, I've got part of a plan in my head, but I shan't tell you what it is till Wednesday."

CHAPTER III.

DISCOMFITURE OF THE PHILISTINES.

On Wednesday afternoon, as soon as dinner was over, Acton summoned his followers to attend the council of war which was to decide what reprisals should be taken on the Philistines for the destruction of the snow man. Every one felt the importance of a counter-attack, for unless something of the kind were attempted, as Acton remarked in his opening speech, "they'll think we're funky of them, and they'll simply come down here as often as they like, and worry us to death."

"Couldn't we tell Mr. Welsby?" suggested Butler, a timid small boy belonging to the "Dogs' Home."

"Tell Mr. Welsby!" cried half a dozen voices in withering tones; "of course not!"

It was well known by both parties that whenever the real state of affairs became known to their respective head-masters, the war would come to an abrupt termination; and the great reason why each side forbore to make any open complaint against the other was undoubtedly because every one secretly enjoyed the excitement of the campaign, and felt that a peace would make life rather dull and uninteresting.

"The thing that licks us," said Acton, "is what I was speaking about last week: somehow or other, they always seem to know just what we're up to, and it's no use our doing anything, because they're always prepared. Some one's acting the spy. I can't think it's any of you fellows, but I believe it's old Noaks. You see his son's there, and for some reason or other he seems to hate every one here like poison. Now, what are we to do?"

There was a silence, broken at length by Diggory Trevanock.

"I don't know what you think," he began, "but it seems to me it's no use making any plans until we find out who tells 'em to the Philistines. I should say that Noaks is the fellow who does it, but we ought to make certain."

"Yes, but how are we to do it?" asked Acton, laughing; "that's just what I want to know."

"Well, I've got a bit of a plan," returned the other, "only I should like to tell it you in private."

"All right," answered the dux; "come on outside. Now, then, what is it?"

"Why," said Diggory, "it's this (I didn't want the other chaps to hear, because then it'll prove who's the spy). You say the last time you went down to throw some crackers over the wall they were all lying in wait for you. Well, let you and me go into the boot-room when Noaks is at work there, and pretend to make a plan as though we were going to do it again to-morrow night; then two of us might go down and see if they're prepared. If so, it must have been Noaks who told them, because no one else knows about it. I'll go for one, and Jack Vance'll go for another. I'll tell him to keep it dark, and you can let us in and out of the door."

"Oh - ah!" said Acton, "that isn't a bad idea; at all events we'll try it."

The project was put into immediate execution. That same afternoon, just before tea, Acton and Diggory discussed the bogus plan in Noaks's hearing, while Jack Vance, having been admitted into their confidence and sworn to secrecy, willingly agreed to go out with Diggory and form the reconnoitering party which was to report on the movements of the enemy.

"I knew you'd come," said the latter; "and we'll show them what sort of stuff the Triple Alliance is made of."

On the following evening, as soon as tea was over, the two friends slipped off down into the playground, where they were joined a minute later by Acton, who, unlocking the shed, took down from the peg on which it hung the key of the door in the outer wall.

"You'll have plenty of time," he said, glancing at his watch, "and with this moonlight you'll soon be able to see if they're about. I'll keep the door, and let you in when you come back."

The next moment the two members of the Alliance were trotting down Locker's Lane. It was a bright, frosty night, and the hard ground rang beneath their feet like stone. They turned off on to the grass, lest the noise should give the enemy warning of their approach; and when within about a hundred yards of

Horace House, pulled up to consider for a moment what their plan of action should be, before proceeding any further.

"I don't see any one," said Jack Vance.

"Perhaps they are hiding," answered Diggory. "Look here! let's get into this field and run down on the other side of the hedge until we get opposite the gate."

The stronghold of the Philistines was silent as the grave. The two chums crouched behind a thick bush, and peering through its leafless branches could see nothing but the closed double doors, and a stretch of blank wall on either side.

"There's no one about," whispered Vance; "I don't believe old Noaks has told them."

"Wait a minute," answered Diggory. "I'll see if I can stir any of them;" and so saying, he knelt up, and cried in an audible voice, "Now, then, are you all ready?"

Diggory and Jack Vance dropped flat on their stomachs, for the words had hardly been uttered when the doors were flung open, and at least ten of the Philistines rushed out into the road with a yell of defiance. Many of them were bigger than Acton, and what would have been the fate of the two Birchites had they kept to the road instead of acting on Diggory's suggestion of advancing under cover of the hedge, one hardly dares to imagine.

"Hullo!" cried young Noaks, who had headed the sortie. "There's nobody here, and yet I'll swear I heard them somewhere."

"So did I," answered another voice; "they must have cut and run."

"There's no place for them to run to," returned Noaks; "they must be behind that hedge. - Come out of it, you skunks!"

A big stone came crashing through the twigs within a yard of Diggory's head. The two boys crouched close to the low earth bank and held their breath.

"They must be about somewhere," cried Noaks. "I knew they were coming, and I'm sure I heard some one say, 'Are you ready?' They're behind that hedge. We can't get through, it's too thick; but you fellows stop here, and I and Hogson and Bernard'll run down to the gate and cut off their retreat."

"What shall we do?" whispered Jack; "this field's so large they'll run us down before we get to the other hedge. Shall we make a bolt and chance it?"

Diggory was just about to reply in the affirmative, when help came from an unexpected quarter.

"What are you boys doing out here at this time?" cried a loud, stern voice. - "Noaks, what are you about down the road there? - Come in this moment, every one of you!"

"Saved!" whispered Jack Vance, in an ecstasy of delight as the Philistines trooped back through the double doors. "That was old Phillips. I hope he gives Noaks a jolly good 'impot.' That chap is a cad," continued the speaker, as they hurried back towards The Birches: "when he can't do anything else, he chucks stones like he did to-night. The wonder is he hasn't killed some one before now. I don't see how it's possible for the Philistines to show up well when they've got a chap like him bossing the show."

The bell for evening preparation was ringing as they reached The Birches, and only a very few hasty replies could be given to Acton's eager inquiries as they rushed together up the garden path. In the little interval before supper, however, the subject was resumed in a quiet corner of the passage.

"So it must have been old Noaks who told them," said Acton; "that's proved without a doubt. I vote we go and have a jolly row with him to-morrow morning."

"No, I shouldn't do that," answered Diggory; "don't let him know that we've found him out."

"Well, look here," answered Acton, thumping the wall with his fist and frowning heavily, "what are we going to do to get even with the Philistines? We can't go out and fight them in Locker's Lane; we're too small, and they know it. Young Noaks would never have dared to act as he did after they'd knocked our snow man down if Mason had been here. They think now they're going to ride rough-shod over us; but they aren't, and we must show them we aren't going to be trampled on."

"So we will," cried Jack Vance excitedly, "and that jolly quick!"

"But how?"

There was a moment's pause. "I'm sure I don't know," answered Jack sadly, and so the meeting terminated.

The fact of the insult, which had been put upon them by the destruction of their snow man, remaining unavenged, caused a sense of gloom to rest upon the Birchites, as though they already felt themselves suffering beneath the yoke of the conquering Philistines. Even the bedroom feuds were forgotten: night after night the "House of Lords" left the "Dogs' Home" in undisturbed tranquillity, and the occupants of the "Main-top" retired to rest without even putting a washstand against their door. One thought occupied the minds of all, and even Mugford, when asked on one occasion by Mr. Blake who were the conspirators in the Gunpowder Plot, answered absent-mindedly, "The Philistines!"

"Look here, you two," said Diggory one evening, as he scrambled into bed, "we three must think of some way of paying those fellows out for knocking down our snow man. It would be splendid if we could say that the Triple Alliance had done it, and without telling any one beforehand."

"So we will," answered Jack Vance; "that is if you'll think of the plan. I'm not able to make one, and I'm jolly sure Mugford can't."

The speaker turned over and went to sleep; but after what seemed half the night had passed, he was suddenly aroused by several violent tugs at his bed-clothes. Thinking it nothing less than a midnight raid, Jack sprang up and grasped his pillow.

"No, no, it's not that," said Diggory, "but I wanted to help you; I've got an idea."

"W - what about?" asked the other, in a sleepy voice.

"Why, how we can pay out the Philistines!"

"Oh, bother the Philistines!" grumbled Jack, and promptly returned to the land of dreams.

"I wonder where those fellows Vance and Trevanock are?" said Acton the following afternoon, as the boys were picking up for a game at prisoner's base. "And there's that dummy of a Mugford - where's he sneaked off to? he never will play games if he can possibly help it."

They set to work, and at the end of about twenty minutes were engaged in a most exciting rally. Acton had started out to rescue one of the prisoners, while Shaw had rushed forth to capture Acton. Morris left the base with similar designs on Shaw, and every one, with the exception of the den-keepers, seemed suddenly seized with an irresistible desire to do something. The playground was full of boys rushing and dodging all over the place, when suddenly everybody stood still and listened. Some one was pounding with his clinched fist at the door opening into Locker's Lane, and at the same time Jack Vance was heard shouting, "Let us in quick, or the Philistines'll have us!"

Acton ran to fetch the key, and the next moment the three members of the Triple Alliance dashed through the open door, which was hastily secured behind them, while a shout of baffled rage some little distance down the road showed that they had only narrowly escaped falling into the hands of the enemy. The pursuit, however, was evidently abandoned, and Morris, climbing on the roof of the shed, saw young Noaks and Hogson slowly retreating round the corner of the road.

The three friends certainly presented a striking appearance. Mugford's nose was bleeding, Jack Vance's collar seemed to have been nearly torn off his neck, while Diggory's cap was in his hand, and his hair in a state of wild disorder. Their faces, flushed with running, were radiant with a look of triumph, while all three, the unfortunate Mugford included, leaned up against the wall, and laughed until the tears ran down their cheeks.

"What have you fellows been up to?" cried Acton; "why don't you tell us?"

"Oh my!" gasped Diggory, "we've taken a fine rise out of the Philistines; they can't say we're not quits with them now!" and he went off into a fresh fit of merriment.

Shaw and Morris seized hold of Jack Vance, and at length succeeded in shaking him into a sufficient state of sobriety to be able to answer their questions.

"Oh dear," he said faintly, "I never laughed so much in my life before! Diggory ought to tell you, because he planned it all. We went very quietly down to Horace House, and found the double doors were shut. You know just what they're like, how the wall curves in a bit, and there's a scraper close to the gate-post, on either side, about a foot from the ground. We'd got an old play-box cord with us, and we tied it to each of the scrapers. The doors have a sort of iron ring for a handle, and through this we stuck a broken cricket-stump, and Mug and I held the two ends so that you couldn't possibly lift the latch on the inside. Then - but you go on, Diggy."

"Well, then," continued the other, "I scrambled oh to these two chaps' shoulders, and looked over the top of the door. We could hear some of the Philistines knocking about on the gravel, and I saw there were about half a dozen of them playing footer with a tennis-ball. I shouted out, 'Hullo! Good-afternoon!' They all stood still in a moment, and young Noaks cried, 'Why, it's a Birchite! - What do you want here, you young dog?' I couldn't think of anything else to say, so I said, 'I want to know if this is the bear-pit or the monkey-house.' My eye, you should have seen them! I dropped down in a trice, and they all rushed to the doors; but they couldn't lift the latch, because Mug and Jack were holding fast to the stump. We waited a moment, and then let go and ran for it. You may judge what happened next. It's a regular sea of mud outside those gates. They all came rushing out together, and I saw Noaks and Hogson go head first over the rope, and two or three others fall flat on the top of them. It was a sight, I can tell you!"

"Yes, but that wasn't all," interrupted Jack Vance. "Bernard, one of their big chaps, hopped over the rest and came after us. We ran for all we were worth, but he collared me. Mugford went for him, and hung on to his coat like a young bull-terrier, and got a smack on the nose; and just then Diggory turned, and came prancing back, and ran his head into the beggar's stomach, and that doubled him up, and so we all got away. But," concluded the speaker, turning towards his wounded comrade, "I never thought old Mug had so much grit in him before; he stuck to it like a Briton!"

A demonstration of the most genuine enthusiasm followed this warlike speech. Acton folded Diggory to his breast in a loving embrace, Shaw and Morris

Harold Avery

stuffed the door-key down Mugford's back, while the remainder of the company executed a war-dance round Jack Vance.

"My eye," cried the dux, "won't the Philistines be wild! Fancy upsetting them in the mud, and knocking Bernard's wind out! They won't be in a hurry to meddle with us again. Well done, Diggy!"

"It wasn't I alone," said the author of the enterprise; "we did it between us - the Triple Alliance."

"Then three cheers for the Triple Alliance!" cried Acton.

The company shouted themselves hoarse, for every one felt that the honour of The Birches had been retrieved, and that the day was still far distant when they would be crushed beneath the iron heel of young Noaks, or be exposed as an unresisting prey to the ravages of the wild hordes of Horace House.

CHAPTER IV.

THE SUPPER CLUB.

As this story is to be a history of the Triple Alliance, and not of The Birches, it will be necessary to pass over many things which happened at the preparatory school, in order that full justice may be done to the important parts played by our three friends in an epoch of strange and stirring events at Ronleigh College.

Diggory, by the daring exploit described in the previous chapter, won all hearts; and instead of being looked upon as a new boy, was regarded quite as an old and trusty comrade. Acton displayed marked favour towards the Triple Alliance, and was even more friendly with Diggory and Jack Vance than with his room and class mates, Shaw and Morris.

The Philistines seemed, for the time being, paralyzed by the humiliation of their mud bath, and for many months there was a complete cessation from hostilities.

It was perhaps only natural that in time of peace a brave knight like Acton should turn his thoughts from war to love-making, and therefore I shall make no excuse for relating a little experience of his which must be introduced as a prelude to the account of the formation of the famous supper club.

At the very commencement of the summer term it was plain to everybody that something was wrong with the dux; he seemed to take no interest in the doings of his companions in the playground, and only once roused himself sufficiently to bang Cross with a leg-guard for bowling awful wides at cricket.

At length, one afternoon, Diggory and Jack Vance on entering the shed found him sitting on the carpenter's bench, with his chin resting in his hand, and a most ferocious expression on his face.

"Hullo! what's up?"

Acton stared blankly at the new-comers until the question had been repeated; then he sat up and straightened his back with the air of one who has made a great resolve.

"I don't mind telling you two," he said. "You know I've said before that I meant some day to propose to Miss Eleanor. Well," he added, stabbing the bench with the gimlet, "I'm going to do it."

"I've saved five and ninepence," continued the speaker, "to buy a ring with, but I can't make up my mind whether I'd better speak or write to her. What do you think?"

"I should say," answered Diggory, after a moment's thought, "that the best thing would be to toss up for it."

"All right; have you got a coin?"

"No, but I think I've got a brass button. Yes, here it is. Now, then, front you speak, and back you write. There you are - it's a letter!"

"Well, now," said Acton, getting off the bench and sticking his hands deep in his trousers pockets, "what had I better say? I shall be fifteen in August; I thought I'd tell her my age, and say I didn't mind waiting."

"I believe it's the girl who always says that," answered Jack Vance, kicking a bit of wood into a corner.

"Then, again, I don't know how to begin. Would you say 'Dear Miss Eleanor,' or 'Dear Miss Welsby'? I think 'Dear Eleanor' sounds rather cheeky."

"I'll tell you what I should do," answered Diggory, who seemed to have a great idea of letting the fates decide these matters: "I should write 'em all three on slips of paper and then draw one."

"Well, I'm going to write the letter in 'prep' this evening, and let her have it to-morrow. Did you notice I gave her a flower this morning, and she stuck it in her dress?"

"Yes; but fellows are often doing that," answered Jack Vance, "and she always wears them, either in her dress or stuck up somehow under her brooch."

"Oh, but this was a white rose, and a white rose means something, though I don't know what. At all events, she'll have the letter to-morrow, and I'll tell you fellows when I give it her, only of course you mustn't breathe a word to any one else."

"All right: we won't," answered Diggory, "except to old Mugford, because he's one of the Alliance, and we've sworn not to have any secrets from each other, and he won't split."

That evening the Triple Alliance lay awake until a late hour discussing the situation. Mugford's opening comment was certainly worth recording, -

"I hope she'll accept him."

"Why?"

"Why, because if she does, I should think old Welsby'll give us a half-holiday."

It was evident at breakfast, to those who were in the know, that Acton was prepared for the venture. He was wearing a clean collar and new necktie, and ate only four pieces of bread and butter, besides his bacon.

"He's shown me the letter," whispered Diggory to Jack Vance; "only I promised I wouldn't say what was in it, but it ends up with a piece of poetry as long as this table!"

After morning school was the time agreed upon for the dux to cast the die which was to decide his future; and as soon as the classes were dismissed, Jack Vance and Diggory met him by appointment in one corner of the garden.

"I've done it," he said, looking awfully solemn. "She was in the hall, and I gave it to her as I came out. I say, how many *t's* are there in 'attachment'?"

Jack Vance thought one, Diggory said two; and the company then relapsed into silence, and stood with gloomy looks upon their faces, as though they were waiting to take part in a funeral procession.

At length a voice from the house was heard calling, "Fred - Fred Acton!" The dux turned a trifle pale, but pulling himself together, marched off with a firm step to learn his fate.

"She called him Fred," murmured Diggory; "that sounds hopeful."

"Oh, that's nothing," answered Jack Vance; "Miss Eleanor always calls fellows by their Christian names. There's one thing," he added, after a few moments' thought - "if she'd cut up rough over the letter, she might have called him Mr. Acton. Hullo, here he comes!" As he spoke Acton emerged from the house, and came down the path towards them; his straw hat was tilted forward over his eyes, and his cheeks were glowing like the red glass of a dark-room lamp. He sauntered along, kicking up the gravel with the toe of his boot.

"Well, what happened?" inquired Jack Vance.

No answer.

"What's the matter ?" cried Diggory; "what did she say?"

"Why, this!" answered the other, in a voice trembling with suppressed emotion: "she said I was a silly boy, and - and - *gave me a lump of cake!*"

If any one else had done it, the probability is Acton would have slain them on the spot. Diggory opened his eyes and mouth wide, and then exploded with laughter. "Oh my!" he gasped, "I shall die, I know I shall! Ha, ha, ha!"

Acton eyed him for a moment with a look of indignant astonishment; then he began to smile, Jack Vance commenced to chuckle, and very soon all three were laughing in concert.

"Well, I think it's rather unfeeling of you fellows," said the rejected suitor; "I can tell you I'm jolly cut up about it."

"I'm awfully sorry," answered Diggory, "but I couldn't help laughing. Cheer up; why, think, you won't have to get the ring now, so you can do what you like with that five and ninepence you saved. Why, it's worth being refused to have five and ninepence to spend in grub!"

"Ah, Diggy !" said the other, shaking his head in a mournful manner, "wait till you're as old as I am: when you're close on fifteen you'll think differently about love and all that sort of thing."

As has already been hinted, it was the failure of this attempt on the part of the dux to win the heart and hand of Miss Eleanor that indirectly brought about the formation of the famous supper club. About a week after the events happened which have just been described, Acton invited the Triple Alliance to meet the "House of Lords" in the work-shed, to discuss an important scheme which he said had been in his mind for some days past; and the door having been locked to exclude outsiders, he commenced to unfold his project as follows: -

"I've been thinking that during the summer term, and while the weather's warm, our two rooms might form a supper club. We'd hold it, say, once a week, when pocket-money is given out, and have a feed together; one time in your room, and the next in ours, after every one's gone to bed. You know I saved some money at the beginning of the term to buy an engagement ring with; but I don't want it now, so I'm going to spend the tin in grub, and if you like I'll stand the first feed."

There was a murmur expressive of approbation at this generous offer, mingled with sympathy for the unhappy circumstance which gave rise to it, and which was now an open secret.

"Oh," said Shaw, "that's a grand idea! I know my brother Bob, who's at a big school at Lingmouth, told me that he and some other chaps formed a supper club and held it in his study. It's by the sea, and they used to go out and catch shrimps; and they only had one old coffee-pot, that they used to boil over the gas; so they cooked the shrimps in it first, and made the coffee after. One night they only had time to heat it up once, and so they boiled the shrimps in the coffee; and Bob says they didn't taste half bad, and that they always used to do it after, to save time."

"Well, I propose that we have one," cried Morris.

The resolution was carried unanimously. Acton was elected president, and by way of recognizing the mutual interest of the Triple Alliance, Jack Vance was appointed to act as secretary, and it was decided to hold the first banquet on the following night.

"We can buy the grub to-morrow," said Acton; "but

there's one thing we ought to fetch to-day, and that is, I thought we might have, say, six bottles of ginger-beer. Then each man must take his own up to bed with him this evening, and hide it away in his box or in one of his drawers."

This was accordingly done, and, as it happened, was the cause of the only disaster which attended the formation of the club. For the first week in June the weather was unusually hot: a candle left all day in the "Main-top" was found drooping out of the perpendicular, and when the Triple Alliance retired to rest their bedroom felt like an oven. They were just dozing off to sleep, when all three were suddenly startled by a muffled bang somewhere close to them. In an instant they were sitting up in bed, rubbing their eyes with one hand and grasping their pillows with the other.

"Look out, they're coming!" whispered Jack Vance; "wasn't that something hit the door?"

"It sounded as if something fell on the floor," answered Diggory. "I wonder if anything's rolled off either of the washstands."

Jack Vance reconnoitred the passage, while Diggory and Mugford examined the room; but nothing could be found to account for the disturbance.

"It must have been the fellows in the 'Main-top.' I expect they dropped a book or upset a chair. Don't let's bother about it any more."

The following morning, however, the mystery was explained. The boys were hastily putting on their clothes, when Mugford, who had just thrown aside a dirty collar, gave vent to an exclamation of dismay, which attracted the attention of his two companions.

"Hullo! what's up?"

"Why, look here! If this beastly bottle of ginger-beer hasn't gone and burst in the middle of my box!"

The first meeting of the supper club was a great success. How ever Acton and his noble friends had managed to smuggle upstairs, under their jackets, a pork-pie, a plum-cake, a bag of tarts, and a pound of biscuits, was a feat which, as Jack Vance remarked, "beat conjuring."

Shortly after midnight the Triple Alliance wended their way to the "House of Lords," where they found the three other members quite ready to commence operations. The good things were spread out on the top of a chest of drawers, and the company ranged themselves round on the available chairs and two adjacent beds, and commenced to enjoy the repast.

"Ah, well," sighed Acton, with his mouth full of pork-pie, "I'm rather glad for some things that I didn't get engaged. It must be rather a bore having to spend all your money in rings and that sort of thing, instead of in grub; though I really think I'd have given up grub for Miss Eleanor."

"I wonder," said Morris, who was of a more prosaic disposition, "how it is that it's always much jollier having a feed when you ought not to than at the proper time. For instance, eating this pork-pie at a table, with knife and fork and a plate, wouldn't be a quarter the fun it is having it like we're doing now - cutting it with a razor out of Acton's dressing-case, and knowing that if we were cobbed we should get into a jolly row."

"Talking about rows over feeds," said Acton, "my brother John is at Ronleigh College, and I remember, soon after he went there, he said they had a great spree in his dormitory. One of the chaps had had a hamper sent him, and they smuggled the grub upstairs; and when they thought the coast was clear, they spread a sheet on the floor, and laid out the grub as if it were on a table-cloth. The fellow who was standing treat was rather a swell in his way, and among other things he'd got his jam put out in a flat glass dish. It was a fine feed, and they'd just begun, when they heard some one coming. They'd only just got time to turn out the gas and jump into bed before the door opened, and in came one of the masters called Weston. Well, of course, they all pretended to be asleep. But the master had heard them scrambling about, and he walked in the dark up the aisle between the beds, saying, 'Who's been out of bed here?' Then all of a sudden he stuck his foot into the glass jam-dish, and it slid along the floor, and down he came bang in the middle of all the spread. John said that when the gas was lit they couldn't help laughing at old Weston: he'd rammed one elbow into a box of sardines, and there was a cheese-cake stuck in the middle of his back. But oh, there was a row, I can tell you!"

This yarn produced others, and the time passed pleasantly enough, until full justice had been done to the provisions, and hardly a crumb remained.

"Phew! isn't it hot?" said Diggory; "let's open the window a bit. The moon must be full," he continued, as he raised the sash; "it's nearly as light as day. I can see all down the garden, and - hullo! quick, put the candle out!"

Every one started to his feet, and the light was extinguished in a moment.

"What is it - what's the matter?" they all asked. "There's some one in the playground," whispered Diggory, as the others crowded round him. "You see the door at the bottom of the garden; well, just when I spoke some one opened it and looked up at the house, and then shut it again. It must have been Blake, and he's seen our light."

"It can't be Blake," answered Acton; "he's gone to Fenley to play in a cricket match, and isn't coming back till to-morrow morning. Old Welsby went to bed hours ago; and, besides, what should either of them want to be doing down there at this time of night? You must have been dreaming, Diggy."

"No, I wasn't; I saw it distinctly. It must be old Blake. He's come home sooner than he expected, and I shouldn't wonder if he's going round by the road to take us by surprise."

"He can't do that," answered Acton, "because I've got the key of the shed, and the door-key's hung up inside."

Acton remained watching at the window while the others hastily cleared away all traces of the feast; the Triple Alliance retired to their own room, and nothing further was heard or seen of the mysterious visitor.

The next morning it was discovered that Mr. Blake had not returned from Fenley, and the five other members of the supper club were inclined to regard Diggory's vision of the midnight intruder as a sort of waking nightmare, resulting from an overdose of cake and pork-pie. Two days later Cross came into the school-room in a great state of excitement.

"Look here, you fellows," he exclaimed: "some one keeps taking away my things out of the shed, and not putting them back. Last week I missed a saw and two chisels, and now that brace and nearly all the bits are gone. It's a jolly shame!"

Carpentering was Cross's great hobby, and his collection of tools was an exceptionally good one, both as regards quantity and quality. Every one, however, denied having touched the things mentioned. A general search was made; but the missing articles could not be found, and at length the matter was reported to Mr. Welsby.

The latter was evidently greatly displeased on hearing the facts of the case. As soon as dinner was over he called the school together, and after standing for some moments in silence, frowning at the book he carried in his hand, said briefly, -

"With regard to these tools, there is a word which has never been used before in connection with any pupil at The Birches, and which I hope I may never have occasion to use again. I can hardly think it possible that we have a *thief* in the house. I am rather inclined to imagine that some one has removed the things and hidden them away in joke; if so, let me tell him that the joke has been allowed to go too far, and that, unless they are returned at once, a shadow of doubt will be cast upon the honour and integrity of all here present.

It is impossible for such large articles as a saw and a brace to be mislaid or lost on such small premises as these, and I trust that before this evening you will report to me that the things have been found. I have purposely allowed the key of the shed to remain in your own possession, feeling certain that your behaviour as regards each other's property would be in accordance with the treatment which one gentleman expects to receive from another. You may go."

There was little in the nature of a scolding in this address, and yet something in it caused every one to leave the room in a state of great excitement. Acton and Jack Vance especially fairly boiled with wrath.

"What old Welsby says is quite right," remarked the latter; "and until those things are found, we may all be looked upon as thieves."

The search, however, proved fruitless; and, what was worse, in turning over the contents of the shed, Acton discovered that a bull's-eye lantern belonging to himself had disappeared from the shelf on which it usually stood; while Mugford declared that a box of compasses, which he had brought down a few days before to draw a pattern on a piece of board, was also missing.

Directly after tea Acton button-holed Diggory, and taking him aside said, "Look here, I'm in an awful rage about these thing's being prigged, because, of course, I've got the key of the shed; and didn't you hear what old Welsby said about it? It looks uncommonly as if I were the thief. You remember what you said the other night when we had that feed, about seeing that man? D'you think there *is* any one who comes here at night and steals things?"

"Well, I'm certain I saw some one in the playground when I told you. It was a man; but whether he comes regularly and goes into the shed I don't know, but I think we ought to be able to find out."

"How?"

"Oh, some way or other; I'll tell you to-morrow." That night, long after the rest of the house were asleep, the Triple Alliance lay awake engaged in earnest conversation; and in the morning, as the boys were assembling for breakfast, Diggory touched Acton on the shoulder and whispered, -

"I say, we've thought of a plan to find out if any one goes into the shed at night."

"Who's 'we'?"

"Why, the Triple Alliance; we thought it out between us. Sneak out of the house directly after evening 'prep,' and meet me in the playground, and I'll show you what it is."

At the time appointed Acton ran down the path, and found Diggory waiting for him by the shed.

"Look," said the latter, "I've cut a little tiny slit with my knife in each door-post, about three feet from the ground, and I'm going to stretch this piece of black cotton between them. No one will see it, and if they go through the door, the thread will simply draw out of one of the slits without their noticing it, and we shall see that it's been disturbed. Jack Vance says that when he's been out shooting with his guv'nor he's seen the keeper put them across the paths in a wood to find out if poachers have been up them. Now unlock the door, and let's go inside."

In front of the bench, where the ground had been much trodden, there was a great deal of loose dust. Diggory went down on his hands and knees, and producing an old clothes-brush from his pocket, swept about a square yard of the ground until the dust lay in a perfectly smooth surface.

"There," he said, rising to his feet again; "we'll do this the last thing every night, and any morning if we find the cotton gone we must look here for footprints, and then we ought to be able to tell if it's a man or a boy."

"Don't you think we ought to tell Blake about that man you saw?" asked Acton, as they walked back to the schoolroom.

"Well, I don't see how we can," answered Diggory. "The first thing he'll ask will be,' Who saw him?' I shall say, 'I did;' and then he'll want to know how I saw the playground door from my bedroom window, which looks out on the road; and then the fat'll be in the fire, and it'll all come out about that supper."

Regularly every evening, as soon as supper was over, the two boys stole down into the playground to set their trap; but when morning came there was no sign of the shed having been entered. This went on for nearly a month, but still no result.

"I don't think it's any good bothering about it any more," said Acton; "the thief doesn't mean to come again."

"Well, we'll set it to-night," answered Diggory, "and that shall be the last time."

The following morning Acton was sauntering towards the playground, when Diggory came running up the path in a state of great excitement. "I say, the cotton's gone!"

Acton rushed down, unlocked the door of the shed, and went inside.

"Hullo!" he exclaimed, as Diggory followed; "*it is* some man. Look at these footprints, and hobnailed boots into the bargain!"

CHAPTER V.

CATCHING A TARTAR.

It was impossible for two boys to keep such an important discovery to themselves, and the shed was soon filled with an eager crowd, all anxious to view the mysterious footprints. The Triple Alliance gained fresh renown as the originators of the scheme by which the disclosure had been made, and it was unanimously decided that the matter should be reported to Mr. Blake.

The master cross-questioned Acton and Diggory, but seemed rather inclined to doubt their story.

"I think," he said, "you must be mistaken. I expect the piece of cotton blew away, and the foot-marks must have been there before. I don't see what there is in the shed that should make it worth any one's while to break into it; besides, if the door was locked, the thief must have broken it open, and you'd have seen the marks."

Certainly nothing seemed to have been touched, and as no boy complained of any of his property having been stolen, the subject was allowed to drop, and the usual excitement connected with the end of term and the near approach of the holidays soon caused it to be driven from every one's thoughts and wellnigh forgotten.

With the commencement of the winter term a fresh matter filled the minds of the Triple Alliance, and gave them plenty of food for discussion and plan-making. On returning to Chatford after the summer holidays, they discovered that all three were destined to leave at Christmas and proceed to Ronleigh College, a large school in the neighbourhood, to which a good number of Mr. Welsby's former pupils had been transferred after undergoing a preliminary course of education at The Birches. Letters from these departed heroes, containing disjointed descriptions of their new surroundings, awakened a feeling of interest in the doings of the Ronleigh College boys. The records of their big scores at cricket, or their victories at football, which appeared in local papers, were always read with admiration; and the name of an old Birchite appearing in either of the teams was a thing of which every one felt justly proud.

"I wish I was going too," said Acton, addressing the three friends; "but my people are going to send me to a school in Germany. My brother John is there; he's one of the big chaps, and is captain of the football team this season. I'm going to get the *Denfordshire Chronicle* every week, to see how they get on in the matches."

Early in October the goal-posts were put up in the field, and the Birchites commenced their football practice. Mr. Blake was a leading member of the Chatford Town Club, and although six a side was comparatively a poor business, yet under his instruction they gained a good grounding in the rudiments of the "soccer" of the period. The old system of dribbling and headlong rushes was being abandoned in favour of the passing game, and forwards were learning to keep their places, and to play as a whole instead of as individuals.

"Come here, you fellows," said the master, walking into the playground one morning, with a piece of paper in his hand; "I've got something to speak about."

The boys crowded round, wondering what was up.

"I've got hero a challenge from Horace House to play a match against them, either on our ground or on theirs. I think it's a pity that you shouldn't have an opportunity of playing against strangers. Of course they are bigger and heavier than we are, and we should probably get licked; but that isn't the question: any sportsman would sooner play a losing game than no game at all, and it'll be good practice. We always used to have a match with them every term; but some little time ago there seemed to be a lack - well, I'll say of good sportsmen among them, and the meetings had to be abandoned. I've talked the matter over with Mr. Welsby, and he seems willing to give the thing another trial."

An excited murmur ran through the crowd.

"Wait a minute," interrupted the speaker, holding up his hand. "Mr. Welsby has left it with me to make arrangements for the match, and I shall only do so on one condition. I know that since the event happened to which I referred a moment ago a decidedly unfriendly spirit has existed between you and the boys at Mr. Phillips's. Now an exhibition of this feeling on a football field would be a disgrace to the school. You must play like gentlemen, and there must be no wrangling or disputing. They are agreeable for a master to play on each side, so I shall act as captain. Anything that has to be said must be left to me, and I shall see you get fair play. Do you clearly understand?"

"Yes, sir."

"Very well, then, I'll write and say we shall be pleased to play them here on Saturday week."

The prospect of mooting the Philistines in the open field filled the mind of every boy with one thought, and the whole establishment went football mad. It was played in the schoolroom and passages with empty ink-pots and balls of paper, in the bedrooms with slippers and sponges, and even in their dreams fellows kicked the bed-clothes off, and woke up with cries of "Goal!" on their lips.

Mr. Blake arranged the order of the team, and remarking that they would need a good defence, put himself and Shaw as full backs. Acton took centre forward, with Jack Vance on his right, while Diggory was told off to keep goal.

At length the eventful morning arrived. Class 2 came utterly to grief in their work; but Mr. Blake understood the cause, and set the same lessons over again for Monday.

It was the first real match most of the players had taken part in, and as they stood on the ground waiting for their opponents to arrive, every one was trembling with excitement. The only exception was the goal-keeper, who leaned with his back against the wall, cracking nuts, and remarking that he "wished they'd hurry up and not keep us waiting all day." At length there was a sound of voices in the lane, and the next moment the enemy entered the field, headed by their under-master, Mr. Fox. Young Noaks and Hogson pounced down at once upon the practice ball, and began kicking it about with great energy, shouting at the top of their voices, and evidently wishing to make an impression on the spectators before the game began.

"I say," muttered Jacobs, "they're awfully big."

"Well, what does that matter?" answered Diggory, cracking another nut and spitting out the shell. "They aren't going to eat us; and as for that chap Noaks, he's all noise - look how he muffed that kick."

Mr. Blake tossed up. "Now, you fellows," he said, coming up to his followers, "we play towards the road; get to your places, and remember what I told you."

With young Noaks as centre forward, Hogson and Bernard on his right and left, and other big fellows to complete the line of hostile forwards, the home team seemed to stand no chance against their opponents. The visitors bowled them over like ninepins, and rushed through their first line of defence as though it never existed. But Mr. Blake stood firm, and kept his ground like the English squares at Waterloo. Attack after attack swept down upon him only to break up like waves on a rock, and the ball came flying back with a shout of "Now, then! Get away, Birches!" Twice the Horace House wing men got round Shaw, and put in good shots; but Diggory saved them both, and was seen a moment later calmly rewarding himself with another nut. Gradually, as the time slipped away and no score was made, the Birchites began to realize that being able to charge wasn't everything, and that their opponents could do more with their shoulders than with their feet, and soon lost control of the ball when bothered by the "halves." The play of the home eleven became bolder - the forwards managed a run or two; and though the Philistines had certainly the upper hand, yet it soon became obvious to them that it was no mere "walk over," and that victory would have to be struggled for.

Noaks and the two inside forwards evidently did not relish this state of things; they had expected an easy win, and began to show their disappointment in the increased roughness of their play.

At length, just before half-time, a thing happened which very nearly caused Mr. Blake's followers to break their promise.

Cross was badly kicked while attempting to take the ball from Hogson, and had to retire from the game.

There were some black looks and a murmur of indignation among the home team, but Mr. Blake hushed it up in a moment.

"I think," he said pleasantly, "that the play is a trifle rough. Our men," he added, laughing, "are rather under size."

Noaks muttered something about not funking; but Mr. Fox said, -

"Yes, just so. Come, play the game, boys, and think less about charging."

The loss of their right half-back was distinctly felt by

the Birchites during the commencement of the second half, and Diggory was called upon three times in quick succession to save his charge. He acquitted himself like a brick, and the last time did a thing which afforded his side an immense amount of secret satisfaction. He caught the ball in his hands, and at the same moment Noaks made a fierce rush, meaning to knock him through the goal. Diggory, with an engaging smile, hopped on one side, and the Philistine flung himself against the post, and bumped his head with a violence which might have cracked any ordinary skull. He came back scowling. A moment later Jack Vance ran into him, and took the ball from between his feet. Noaks charged viciously, and in a blind fit of temper deliberately raised his fist and struck the other player in the face.

"*Stop!*"

It was Mr. Blake's voice, and he came striding up the ground looking as black as thunder.

"I protest against that deliberate piece of foul play. I have played against all the chief clubs in the district, and in any of those matches, if such a thing had happened, this man would have been ordered off the ground."

There was a buzz of approval, in which several of the Philistines joined.

"You are quite right, Mr. Blake," answered Mr. Fox. "I deeply regret that the game should have been spoiled by a member of my team. - Noaks," he added, turning to the culprit, "put on your coat and go home; you have disgraced yourself and your Comrades. I shall see that you send a written apology to the boy you struck."

"Bravo!" whispered Acton; "old Fox is a good sort."

"Oh, they're most of them all right," answered Morris; "it's only two or three that are such beasts."

The game was continued. The loss of one man on each side made the teams equal in numbers, but the sudden calamity which had overtaken their centre forward seemed to have exerted a very demoralizing effect on the Philistines.

Their attacks were not nearly so spirited, and several times the Birchite forwards appeared in front of their goal.

Neither side had scored, and it seemed as though the game would end in a draw - a result which the home team would have considered highly satisfactory.

The umpire looked at his watch, and in answer to a query from Mr. Fox said, "Five minutes more."

"Look here, Acton," said Mr. Blake: "let me take your place, and you go back. Do all you can to stop them if they come."

The ball was thrown out of touch; Mr. Blake got it, and in a few seconds the fight was raging in the very mouth of the enemy's goal. Morris put in a capital shot; but the ball glanced off one of the players, and went behind.

"Corner!" cried Mr. Blake. "I'll take it. Now you fellows get it through somehow or other!"

"Mark your men, Horace House!" cried Mr. Fox. The next moment every one was shoving and elbowing with their eyes fixed on the ball as it flew through the air. It dropped in exactly the right place, and Jack Vance, by some happy fluke, kicked it just as it touched the ground. Like a big round shot it whizzed through the posts, and there was a rapturous yell of "*Goal!*"

The delight of the Birchites at having beaten their opponents was unbounded, and when, a short time later, the latter retired with a score against them of one to nil. Jack Vance was seized by a band of applauding comrades, who, with his head about a couple of feet lower than his heels, carried him in triumph across the playground, and staggered half-way up the steep garden path, when Acton happening to tread on a loose pebble brought the whole procession to grief, and caused the noble band of conquering heroes to be seen all grovelling in a mixed heap upon the gravel.

But it is not for the simple purpose of recording the victory over Horace House that a description of the match has been introduced into our story; and although the important part played by Diggory in goal and Jack Vance in the "fighting line" caused it to be an occasion when the Triple Alliance was decidedly in evidence and won fresh laurels, yet there are other reasons which make an account of it necessary, as the reader will discover in following the course of subsequent events. If Jack Vance had kicked the ball a yard over the bar instead of under it, the probability is that the following chapter would never have been written; while the public disgrace of young Noaks was destined to cause our three comrades more trouble than they ever expected to encounter, at all events on this side of

Harold Avery

their leaving school.

If the result of the match made such a great impression on the minds of the victors, it is only natural that it should have had a similar effect on the hearts of their opponents. Most of the Philistines would have been content to take their defeat as a sportsman should, but neither Noaks nor his two cronies, Hogson and Bernard, had any of this manly spirit about them; and smarting under the disappointment of not having won, and the knowledge that at least one of them had reaped shame and contempt instead of glory, they determined to seek a speedy revenge. As the three biggest boys in the school, they had little difficulty in inducing their companions to join in the crusade which they preached against The Birches, and the consequence was that the two schools were soon exchanging open hostilities with greater vigour than ever.

Now, although the Birchites had proved themselves equal to their opponents at football, they would have stood no chance against them in anything like a personal encounter. The other party were, of course, perfectly well aware of this fact, and waxed bold in consequence. Again and again, when Mr. Welsby's pupils were at football practice, and Mr. Blake happened not to be present, the enemy's sharp-shooter crept into ambush behind the hedge and discharged stones from their catapults at the legs of the players, while the latter replied by inquiring when they meant to "come over and take another licking." At other times these Horace House Cossacks swooped down on single members of the rival establishment, harrying them in the very streets of Chatford, and on one occasion had the audacity to lay violent hands on Jacobs, beat his bowler hat down over his eyes, and push him through the folding doors of a drapery establishment, where he upset an umbrella-stand and three chairs, had his ears boxed by the shop-walker, and was threatened with the police court if ever he did such a thing again! At length it became positively perilous for the weaker party to go beyond the precincts of their own citadel except in bodies of three or four together. All kinds of plans for retaliation were suggested, but still the Philistines continued to score heavily. At length, about the last week in October, a thing happened which raised the wrath of the Birchites to boiling-point.

Cross having received five shillings from home on the morning of his birthday, determined to celebrate the occasion by the purchase of a pork-pie, of which he had previously invited all his companions to partake. The latter were standing in the playground waiting for his return from Chatford, when they became conscious of certain "alarms without;" whoops and war-cries sounded somewhere down Locker's Lane, and ceased as suddenly as they had begun. The boys stood for some moments wondering what this could mean, and were just thinking of starting a fresh game of "catch smugglers," when there came a banging at the door. It was flung open, and Cross rushed into their midst, flushed, dishevelled, and empty-handed!

What words of mine can tell that tale of woe or describe the burst of indignation which followed its recital? Cross had unwisely decided to shorten his return journey by risking the dangers of Locker's Lane. He had been captured by a party of Philistines, who, under the leadership of Hogson, had not only robbed him of his pie, but had held him prisoner while they devoured it before his very eyes!

What this terrible outrage would have excited those who had suffered this cruel wrong to do in return - whether they would have started off there and then, burnt Horace House to the ground, and hung its inhabitants on the surrounding trees - it would be hard to say; as it was, at this very moment a counter-attraction was forced upon their attention by Morris, who came shouldering his way into their midst, saying, -

"Look here, you fellows, some one's stolen my watch and chain!"

It seemed as if a perfect shower of thunderbolts had commenced to descend from a clear sky upon the devoted heads of Mr. Welsby's pupils. Every one stared at his neighbour in mute amazement, and only Fred Acton remained in sufficient possession of his faculties to gasp out, -

"*What?*"

"It's true," continued Morris excitedly. "I didn't change for football yesterday afternoon, but before going into the field I hung my watch up on a nail in the shed, and stupidly forgot all about it until I came to wind it up last night. Then it was too late to fetch it, and now it's gone!"

"Look here !" cried Acton, glaring round the group with an unusually ferocious look, "who knows any-thing about this? speak up, can't you! We've had enough of this prigging business, and I'm sick of it!"

No one attempted to reply.

"Well," continued the dux, "I'm going straight off to old Welsby to tell him, and I won't keep the key of that place. Of course it makes me look as if I were the thief, and I won't stand it any longer."

The speaker turned on his heel and strode off in the direction of the house.

"Oh, I say," muttered Jack Vance, "now there'll be a row!"

Jack's prophecy was soon fulfilled. The watch and chain could not be found, and there was but little doubt that they had been stolen. Mr. Welsby called the boys together, and though he spoke in a calm and collected manner, with no trace of passion in his voice, yet his words made them all tremble. Miss Eleanor sat silent at the tea-table, with a shocked expression on her face; and Mr. Blake, when told of the occurrence, said sharply, "Well, we'd better have locks put on everything, and the sooner the better."

Acton produced his bunch of keys, and insisted that all his possessions should be searched, and every one else followed his example. The whole of the next afternoon was spent in a careful examination of desks and boxes, but with no result beyond the discovery that Mugford owned a cord waistcoat which he had 'never had the moral courage to wear.

There is one feature in the administration of justice by an English court which is unhappily too often overlooked in the lynch law of schoolboys, and that is the principle that a man shall be considered innocent until he has been clearly proved guilty. Smarting under a sense of shame which was entirely unmerited, every

Harold Avery

boy sought eagerly for some object on which to vent his indignation; it became necessary, to use the words of the comic opera, that "a victim should be found," and suspicion fell on Kennedy and Jacobs. The result of Diggory's trap seemed to show that the various thefts had been committed at night. It was agreed that the two occupants of the "Main-top" had special opportunity for getting out of the house if so minded; every other room had one or more fellows in it who had suffered the loss of some property; and lastly, Kennedy was known to possess a pair of hob-nailed fishing-boots, which he usually kept under his bed. The two boys indignantly denied the accusation when it was first brought against them, but the very vehemence with which they protested their innocence was regarded as "put on," and accepted as an additional proof of their guilt. The evidence, however, was not thought sufficient to warrant bringing a charge against them before the head-master, and accordingly it was decided to send them both to Coventry until some fresh light should be brought to bear upon the case.

To do full justice to the memory of Diggory Trevanock, he alone stood out against this decision, and incurred the wrath both of Acton and Jack Vance in so doing. He continued to affirm that it must be the man he had seen in the playground on the occasion of the first meeting of the supper club; and that the footprint in the dust had been a man's, and much larger than Kennedy's boot could have produced.

This outlawing of the "Main-top" and difference of opinion with Diggory spoiled all chance of games and good fellowship. Even the association of the Triple Alliance seemed likely to end in an open rupture, and very possibly might have done so if it had not been for an event which caused the members to reunite against the common enemy.

One half-holiday afternoon Mugford and Diggory had gone down to Chatford. It was nearly dark when they started to come back, and the latter proposed the short cut by Locker's Lane.

"I'm not afraid of the Philistines; besides, they won't see us now."

As they drew near to Horace House, a solitary figure was discovered standing in the shadow of the brick wall.

"It's young Noaks," whispered Diggory. "It's too late to turn back, but most likely he won't notice us in this light if we walk straight on."

They passed him successfully, and were just opposite the entrance, when three more boys sauntered through the doorway. A gleam of light from the house happened to fall on Diggory's cap and broad white collar, and immediately the shout was raised, "*Birchites!*"

There was a rush of feet, a wild moment of grabbing and dodging, and Mugford, who had managed somehow to shake himself free from the grasp of his assailants, dashed off at full speed down the road. After running for about two hundred yards, and finding he was not followed, he pulled up, waited and listened, and then began cautiously to retrace his steps. There was no sign either of his companion or the enemy; and though he ventured back as far as the double doors, which were now closed, not a soul was to be seen. He

Harold Avery

knew in a moment that his class-mate had been captured, but all hope of attempting anything in the shape of a rescue was out of the question. It was impossible for him single-handed to storm the fortress, and so, after lingering about for some minutes in the hope that his friend would reappear, he ran home as fast as he could, and bursting into the schoolroom, where most of his schoolfellows sat reading round the fire, threw them into a great state of consternation and dismay by proclaiming in a loud voice the alarming intelligence that Diggory had been taken prisoner, and was at that moment in the hands of the Philistines!

CHAPTER VI.

GUNPOWDER PLOT.

The news caused a profound sensation, the like of which had probably never been witnessed at The Birches before - no, not even on that memorable occasion when the intelligence arrived that Scourer, one of the past seniors, had ridden his bicycle through the plate-glass window of Brown's big crockery-shop, and was being brought home on a shutter.

All the boys threw down their books, and started to their feet. Acton and Vance banished from their minds all thought of the disagreement which had lately estranged them from their unfortunate school-fellow, and joined heartily in the general outburst of wrath and consternation.

The thought that Diggory, their well-beloved, was at that very moment languishing, a prisoner of war, in the hands of the Philistines was almost unbearable.

"What will they do with him?" - "Where have they put him?" - "How can we rescue the fellow?" were questions which everybody was asking, but no one could answer. It seemed altogether beyond their power to do anything, and yet there was not a boy who would not have given his dearest possession, were it a white rat or a stamp collection, if by parting with it he could have rendered some assistance to his ill-fated comrade.

"There's only half an hour before tea," said Vance, looking up at the clock; "if anything can be done, we must do it at once."

The precious moments sped away, but in vain did the assembly rack their brains for some plan of action which might in any way be likely to serve the purpose they had in view. The first wild suggestion, that they should go in a body and carry Horace House by storm, was abandoned as impracticable; in hopeless inactivity they stood watching the long hand of the clock creep up from six till twelve.

The first tea-bell had just finished ringing, when there was a sound of footsteps hurrying along the passage, the door burst open, and in rushed no other person than Diggory himself!

"Hullo! how did you get away?" - "What have they been doing?" - "How did you escape?"

"Oh, such a lark!" cried the boy. "They'll wish they'd never caught me! I'll tell you all about it after tea."

As soon as the meal was over, Diggory was seized, hurried up into the schoolroom, and there forced to relate his adventures.

"Well," he began, "they collared me, and dragged me through the gates and along into their playground. Noaks looked at me and said, 'Hullo, here's luck! This is the young beggar who tied that rope to the scrapers; I vote we give him a jolly good licking.' I told them that my father was a lawyer, and if any of them touched me he'd take a summons out against them for assault. That frightened Noaks, for you can see he's a regular coward, so he asked the others what they thought had better be done with me.

"'I know,' said Hogson. 'There's an old cow-shed in the field next to ours; let's shut him in and keep him there till after tea. He'll get a jolly row for being late when he gets back, and he won't dare to say where he's been; because I know it's against their rules to come anywhere near us, and Locker's Lane is out of bounds. If he does tell, we'll swear he was in the road chucking stones at the windows.'

"Some one said there was only a staple on the door of the shed, but Noaks said he'd fetch the padlock off his play-box, and so he did.

"Well, they took me across their playing field, and over the hedge into the next, and shut me up in this beastly old hovel. 'It's no use your making a row,' said Hogson, 'because no one'll hear you; and if you do, summons or no summons we'll come down and give you a licking.' After that they left me, and went back to the house; and as soon as they'd gone, I began to try to find some way of escape, but it was so dark inside the shed I couldn't see anything. Presently I heard a knocking on the boards. There was a wide crack between them in one place, and looking through it I could just make out that there was some boy standing there with what looked like a dirty apron over his trousers. I said, 'Hullo!' and he said, 'Hullo! what's up? who are you? and what have they been a-sticking of you in there for?'

"I told him, and asked him who he was, and it turned out his name was Joe Crump, and he's the boy who cleans the knives at Philips's. He happened to be knocking about when they took me prisoner, and he couldn't see who it was in the dark, and thought it might be his younger brother who comes on errands from the grocer's; the Philistines are always playing tricks on him.

"I said, 'Look here, Joe Crump, you let me out, there's a good chap.' But he wouldn't; he was afraid of what young Noaks would do to him. At last I gave him a shilling through the crack of the boards, and vowed I wouldn't say who'd done it, and then he undid the door. I fastened the padlock again, and threw the key into the hedge, for Noaks had left it in the keyhole; so now he won't be able to get his lock again unless he either breaks it or the staple, and they're both pretty tough. After that I got round through two other fields into the lane, and here I am."

The conclusion of Diggory's story was hailed with shouts of triumph. To imagine the disappointment of the Philistines when they discovered that the bird had flown, and the chagrin of young Noaks when he found that his play-box padlock was fastened to the door of the shed, was simply delightful; and Acton was so carried away that he once more fell on Diggory's neck, and pretended to shed tears of joy upon the latter's broad turn-down collar.

"But that's not all," cried the youngster, shaking himself free from his leader's embrace. "The best is this. I had a bit of a talk with Joe Crump before I came away, and he says that young Noaks is going to leave at the end of this term, and he's been telling the

Philistines that before he goes he means to do something that'll pay us out for his being sent off the field in that football match. Crump doesn't know what he means to do, but I made him promise, if he finds out, to come and tell me, and I'll give him another shilling. Then we shall be prepared."

"I say, Diggy," exclaimed Jack Vance, "you are a *corker!*" and the bell now commencing to ring for evening preparation, the meeting terminated.

It was an annual custom at The Birches for the boys to subscribe towards getting a display of fireworks, which were let off in the playground under the superintendence of Mr. Blake. The head-master himself gave a donation towards the fund, and allowed the boys to prepare the next day's work in the afternoon instead of in the evening.

This year, however, when Acton went, as usual, to the library to formally ask permission that the celebration should take place, he met with a terrible rebuff.

"No, Acton," answered Mr. Welsby; "as long as the school continues to be disgraced by these repeated thefts - as, for example, this recent instance of Morris's watch and chain - I do not feel inclined to allow the same privileges as before. There will be no fireworks this term."

As may be imagined, when the dux reported the result of his visit to head-quarters, the news created great excitement. The unfortunate occupants of the "Maintop," who were still in the position of scapegoats, were hunted round the place by an indignant mob, and fled, vainly protesting their innocence, from one shelter to another, until they finally escaped from the playing field into the open country, where they hid behind hedges for the remainder of the afternoon.

"Look here," exclaimed Jack Vance, as the Triple Alliance were wending their way from the playground to the house, "there's only one thing to be done, and that is, we must set Miss Eleanor on old Welsby's track. She'll make him alter his mind. Some one must go and ask her. - Acton, you're the man; you must do it!"

"I'm shot if I do!" answered the dux, turning round to face the trio, and walking backwards up the path; "why should I go more than any other fellow?"

"Why, because you've got such a way with you," returned Diggory. "She'd be sure to do it for you; why, the last time you spoke to her she gave you a lump of cake."

Acton seized the speaker by the neck and shook him like a rat. "You're the cheekiest little imp I ever came across," he said. "I've a jolly good mind to give you a good licking, only I don't believe you'd care tu'pence if I did!"

"Well, anyhow you've got to go," answered Diggory, calmly picking up his cap, which had fallen to the ground; "and if you're afraid to go alone for fear she should think it's another proposal, I'll come with you."

After some further discussion it was agreed that the thing should be attempted. The two boys found Miss Eleanor making cake, and the conference began by Diggory's having his ears boxed for picking plums out of the dough. But no one ever appealed to Miss Eleanor without being sure, at all events, of a patient hearing, and the following morning Mr. Welsby informed the school that he had been led to reconsider his decision regarding the fifth of November, and that they might have their display as usual.

Accordingly, the fireworks were ordered, and arrived soon after breakfast on the morning of the fourth. Miss Eleanor had a dread of gunpowder, and Mr. Blake sent Jack Vance to tell Noaks to carry the box as usual down into the shed.

"Humph!" growled the man, as the boy gave him the message. "It's a nice thing that I should have to fetch and carry all your fooling playthings for you; it's a pity you young gen'lemen can't do something for yourselves, instead of bothering me."

"Well, it isn't my orders," answered Jack; "it's Mr. Blake's."

"Mr. Blake's, is it? All right, I'll do it when I can spare the time."

When the boys came out at interval, the box was still lying about in the yard, although there were heavy clouds overhead threatening rain. Mr. Blake sent for Noaks, and a rather sharp passage of arms took place between them, which ended in the man's being told to leave what he was doing and carry the fireworks down to the shed.

"I believe he left them on purpose, in the hope they'd get wet," said Shaw. "He hates us all like poison, and I believe it's all because his son's at the other school.

D'you remember what a row he kicked up when he heard Acton say that the Philistines were cads for shooting at us with catapults?"

"Yes," answered Morris; "and if he hates us, he hates Blake a jolly sight worse. He's been like it ever since that football match; and he'll get sacked if he doesn't mind, for Blake won't stand his cheek much longer."

The purchase of fireworks had this year been more extensive than on any previous occasion, and every one was looking forward with great anticipation to the business of the following evening.

"I say, Diggy," cried Acton at the close of afternoon school, "I wish you'd run down into the playground and bring up that football flag that's got to be mended; I left it in the corner by the shed. I'd go myself, but I want to finish this letter before tea."

Diggory trotted off to fetch the flag, and Jack Vance, who was loitering about one of the passages, accompanied him down into the playground. It was very dark, the stars being hidden by heavy clouds.

"I say," exclaimed Diggory, "it'll be a splendid night for the fireworks if it's like this to-morrow. We must get - Hark! what's that?"

"I didn't hear anything."

"Yes, there was a sort of a rapping sound. Hush! there it is again."

Jack heard it this time. "It's some one knocking very gently against that door leading into Locker's Lane," he whispered.

They groped their way across the playground until they reached the wall. There was no mistake about it - some one was gently tapping with his knuckles on the other side of the door.

"Who's there?" asked Jack Vance.

"I want to speak to the young gen'leman who was locked up t'other day in the cow-shed," was the answer, given in a low voice which Diggory instantly recognized.

"I know him," he said; "it's Joe Crump. Here, give me a leg up, and I'll talk to him over the wall. - All right, Joe; I'm the chap."

"Well, if you are," answered the voice, "you'll remember you offered me a bob if I could find out and tell you when somebody was going to do something."

"Well, what's the news?"

"Give me the money first, and then I'll tell you."

Jack Vance fortunately had the required coin in his pocket, and Diggory dropped it into Joe Crump's cap.

"Well, the news is this," said the latter, speaking in the same low tone - "that there Noaks and Hogson are coming up here to-night just afore nine o'clock, and they're a-going to drown your fireworks."

"Drown our fireworks! why, what ever d'you mean? How do they know we've got any fireworks? and how can they get at them when they're all locked up?"

"I can't say," returned Crump, "so it's no use asking me. I only knows that Noaks is a-going to do it; 'drown 'em all in a bucket of water,' was what he said. Remember you promised to tell nothink about me, that's all. Good-night, mister!"

The stranger vanished in the darkness, and Diggory dropped down from the wall.

"Here's a pretty go!" he remarked. "What are we to do? there's no time to lose. Come on, Jack, let's go and tell Acton."

The latter was engaged on the closing sentence of his letter; but on hearing the intelligence which Diggory had to impart, he threw the unfinished epistle into his desk, and rose to his feet with an exclamation of astonishment.

"D'you think it's really true? or is this fellow, Lump or Bump or whatever you call him, trying to take a rise out of us, or telling lies to earn the shilling?"

"I don't think so," answered Diggory, "and I'll tell you why. For some reason or other, he's at daggers drawn with young Noaks and Hogson. I think they've knocked him about, and he's doing it to pay them out."

"But how did they get to know about our fireworks? and how do they reckon they're going to get them out of the shed? Look here, hadn't we better tell Blake?"

"We can't do that," answered Jack Vance, "or it'll get Diggy in a row. If he says anything about Joe Crump, it'll all come out about his having been in Locker's Lane when the Philistines caught him, and of course that's against rules."

"What time did he say they meant to come?"

"About a quarter to nine."

There was a silence which lasted for over a minute; then Diggory spoke.

"This is what I think we'd better do. If they come at all, they are certain to be here soon after half-past eight, because I heard Fox telling Blake on the day of the match that they go to bed at nine. We won't tell any one, but as soon as 'prep' is over we'll cut down into the playground, and when they come we'll kick up a row. They'll soon make tracks if they find they're discovered, and it'll be better than saying anything to Blake about it, and we shall have defeated them ourselves."

"All right," answered Acton. "But it'll look queer if we all three stop out from supper; two's enough. I'll go for one, and you and Vance toss up."

This suggestion was accepted with some reluctance, as both boys were anxious to take part in the adventure. Acton's word, however, was law, and eventually Diggory was chosen by fate to be his companion.

Directly after tea all the boys paid a visit to the shed; the door was securely locked, as also was the one leading into Locker's Lane, and it seemed impossible for the Philistines to carry out their evil designs upon the fireworks.

"I believe it's all bunkum," said Acton, as they strolled back towards the house. "However, we'll come down as we said, and just see if anything happens."

Three boys, at all events, did very little work that evening, for it was impossible to concentrate one's mind on Caesar or on French verbs with such an adventure looming in the near future. How would the Philistines get at the fireworks? Would they change their minds, and instead of drowning them apply a slow match and blow up the shed? or would it, after all, turn out to be only a false alarm, raised by the boy Crump for the sake of the promised shilling?

These and other thoughts filled the minds of the trio as they sat frowning at the books in front of them. The clock seemed to go slower and slower, until they really began to wonder whether it had stopped. At length the long hand reached the half-past. Mr. Blake yawned, put down his paper, and said, "Put away your work, and pass on to supper."

Acton and Diggory, both tingling with excitement, lingered behind until the rest had left the room; then, when the coast was clear, they slipped out into the garden, and hurried down the sloping path. It was considerably lighter than it had been before tea; the clouds had cleared away, and there were plenty of stars.

"Locked," muttered Acton, examining the shed. "Locked," he repeated, trying the door leading into Locker's Lane. "I don't believe there's anything in it. They might get over the wall if one gave the other a leg up, but then how's the last man to get back again?"

"Well, if there's nothing in it," answered Diggory, "how should Joe Crump have got to know we had any fireworks in the place? There must - Hush! what's that?"

There was a sound of footsteps coming down the path from the house. "*Cave!*" cried Acton. "It's Blake; let's hide!"

Several shrubs growing in the garden and overhanging the boarded partition threw one corner of the play-ground into deep shadow. The boys rushed into the angle, and, crouching down in the inky darkness, were at once hidden from the view of any one who might advance even to within a few feet of their hiding-place.

They had hardly time to conceal themselves, when a man, the outline of whose figure they could just make out in the gloom, came through the garden door, and, advancing a few yards, stood still, turning his head from side to side as though looking to make sure that the quadrangle was empty.

"He heard us talking," whispered Acton.

The new-comer having apparently come to the conclusion that he was alone, walked slowly across to the shed, halted in front of the door, and the next moment there was the sound of a key being fitted into the lock. At that instant Diggory, who had been craning his neck forward to get a better view of the intruder, suddenly gripped Acton's arm, and, putting his mouth close to the latter's ear, whispered, -

"*It isn't Blake; it's old Noaks!* Now keep quiet," he

added, as his companion made a movement as though he meant to rush out of their hiding-place; "let's see what he does."

"He's the thief who stole all those things!" answered Acton excitedly. "He must have another key, and he's going to bag something now."

Noaks (for certainly it was he) disappeared inside the shed; but in a few seconds he was out again, and once more stood waiting as though undecided what to do next.

Before the boys could have counted ten, there was a low whistle in the lane.

"They've come," whispered Diggory. "He's got the key of the door, and is going to let them in."

His words were speedily verified, and the next moment two more figures entered the playground, the object of their visit being at once made evident by the fact that one of them was carrying a bucket. It was too dark to distinguish their faces, but the short conversation which took place on their entry soon made them known to the two watchers.

"Now, then," said old Noaks, "if you're going to do it, just look sharp."

"Awful joke, isn't it, dad?" answered one of the new-comers. "Lend us a hand, and we'll dip 'em all in this bucket and put 'em back again."

"No, I shan't," returned the man. "I don't know nothink about it. It's your game, and all I promised was I'd open the door."

"Well, show us where the box is. - Come on, Hogson; don't make more row than you can help."

After a moment's hesitation and some muttered remarks about "that there Blake" and "them uppish young dogs," Noaks senior led the way across the gravel, and followed by the two Philistines entered the shed. Hardly had they crossed the threshold when Diggory started up, kicked off his slippers, crept swiftly and noiselessly as a shadow across the ground, and before his companion had time to realize what was happening, the door of the shed was slammed to and locked on the outside.

To describe exactly what followed would be well-nigh impossible, as even the principal actors themselves seemed to have but a confused recollection of the part they played. Those concerned, however, will probably never forget Diggory's bursting into the room as they sat finishing supper, and striking every one dumb with amazement by saying to Mr. Blake, "Please, sir, some fellows are stealing our fireworks, and I've locked them up in the shed." And there will still remain in their minds memories of a wild rush to the playground; of old Noaks being peremptorily ordered to "clear out," and on attempting to bandy words with Mr. Blake, being taken by the scruff of the neck and "chucked out;" of the two Philistines being conducted, under a strong escort, to Mr. Welsby's study; of a polite note being dispatched by the latter to Mr. Philips; and of the unmitigated delight of the Birchites when Hogson and Noaks junior were delivered over into the hands of Mr. Fox, and marched off by that gentleman to take their trial at Horace House. Every one was in high spirits.

Acton and Diggory were made to tell their story over twenty times. Kennedy and Jacobs were at once declared innocent, and instead of being looked upon as outcasts, came to be regarded as martyrs who had suffered in a good cause. Old Noaks was clearly the culprit. He volunteered no explanation as regarded his possession of a duplicate key to the shed door, and though no attempt was made to bring the charge home against him, there was little doubt as to his guilt, and he was dismissed the next morning.

The firework display came off the following evening, and was a great success. Every rocket or Roman candle that shot into the air seemed to attest the final triumph of the Birchites over the Philistines, and was cheered accordingly. I say final triumph, for the removal of young Noaks and Hogson from the rival school caused a great change for the better among the ranks of Horace House. The old feud died out, giving place to a far bettor spirit, which was manifested each term in the friendly manner in which the teams met for matches at cricket and football.

This sounds very much like the end of a story; but it is not, and for a connecting-link to join this chapter to those that follow, we will go forward for one moment into the future.

Nearly a year later Diggory and Jack Vance were sauntering arm in arm across one of the fives-courts at Ronleigh College.

"D'you remember," remarked the former, "how, that night we caught the Philistines bagging our fireworks, you said, 'Well, I should think now we've just about finished with young Noaks'?"

"Did I?" answered Jack, shrugging his shoulders. "My eye, I ought to have said we'd just begun!"

CHAPTER VII.

RONLEIGH COLLEGE.

The first two or three weeks of a new boy's life at a big school are, as a rule, a dull and uneventful period, which does not furnish many incidents that are of sufficient interest to be worth recording.

The Triple Alliance passed through the principal entrance to Ronleigh College one afternoon towards the end of January, with no flourish of trumpets or beat of drums to announce the fact of their arrival to their one hundred and eighty odd schoolfellows. They were simply "new kids." But though, after the fame they had won at The Birches, it was rather humiliating at first to find themselves regarded as three nobodies, yet there was some compensation in the thought that, just as the smallest drummer-boy can point to a flag covered with "honours," and say "My regiment," so, in looking round at the many things of which Ronleians past and present had just reason to be proud, they could claim it as "our school," and feel that they themselves formed a part, however small and insignificant, of the institution.

The crowd of boys, and the maze of passages, rooms, and staircases, were very confusing after the quiet, old-fashioned house at Chatford; but though in this world there is no lack either of lame dogs or of stiles, there is also a good supply of kindly-disposed persons who are ever ready to help the former over the latter, and our three friends were fortunate enough to fall in with one of these philanthropic individuals soon after their arrival.

The stranger, who was a youngster of about their own age, with a pleasant, good-natured-looking face, patted Diggory on the back in a fatherly manner, and addressing the group said, -

"Well, my boys, we're a large family at Ronleigh, but fresh additions are always welcome. How did you leave them all at home? Quite well, I hope? Um, ah! Just so. That's what Dr. Denson always says," continued the speaker, without waiting for any reply to his numerous questions. "You'll have to go and see him after tea. My name's Carton; what's yours?"

The three comrades introduced themselves.

"What bedroom are you in?"

"Number 16."

"Then you're in the same one as I and young Hart. Come for a stroll, and I'll show you round the place."

With Carton acting as conductor, the party set out on a tour of inspection. It was some time before the new-comers could find their way about alone without turning down wrong passages, or encroaching on forbidden ground, and getting shouted at by irate seniors, and ordered to "Come out of that!" But by the time they had finished their round, and the clanging of a big bell summoned them to assemble in the dining-hall for tea, they had been able to form a general idea as to the geography of Ronleigh College, and a brief account of their discoveries will be of interest to the reader.

Passing through the central archway in the block of buildings which faced the road, the boys found themselves in a large gravelled quadrangle surrounded on all sides by high walls, broken by what appeared at first sight to be an almost countless number of windows, while the red brick was relieved in many places by a thick growth of ivy.

"That's the gymnasium on the left," said Carton, "and above it are studies; and that row of big windows on the right, with the coloured glass in the top, is the big schoolroom."

Crossing the gravel they passed through another archway, in which were two folding-doors, and emerged upon an open space covered with asphalt, upon which stood a giant-stride and two double fives-courts.

This formed but a small corner of a large level field, in which a number of boys were to be seen wandering about arm in arm, or standing chatting together in small groups, pausing every now and then in their conversation to give chase to a football which was being kicked about in an aimless fashion by a number of their more energetic companions.

"The goal-posts aren't up yet," said Carton, "and this is only what's called the junior field; the one beyond is where the big fellows play. The pavilion is over the hedge there, with the flagstaff by the side of it. That's the match ground, and there's room for another game besides."

"Where do all the fellows go when they aren't out of doors?" asked Diggory.

"Well, the Sixth all have studies; then comes Remove, and those chaps have a room to themselves; all the rest have desks in the big school, and you hang about there, though of course, if you like, there's the gymnasium, or the box-room - that's where a lot of fellows spend most of their time."

"What sort of a place is that?"

"Oh, it's where the play-boxes are kept. Come along; we'll go there next."

They passed once more through the double doors, and were crossing the quadrangle, when a certain incident attracted their notice, unimportant in itself, but indicating a strong contrast in the manner of life at Ronleigh to what they had always been accustomed to at The Birches. A youngster was tearing up a piece of paper and scattering the fragments about on the gravel.

"Hi, you there!" cried a voice; "pick that up. What d'you mean by making that mess here?"

The small boy grabbed up the bits of paper, stuffed them in his pocket, and hurried away towards the schoolroom.

"Is that one of the masters?" asked Mugford.

Harold Avery

"No," answered Carton, "that's Oaks; he's one of the prefects. Don't you see he's got a blue tassel to his mortar-board?"

"But what's a prefect?"

"Whew!" laughed the other, "you'll soon find out if you play the fool, and don't mind what you're about. Why, there are fourteen of them, all fellows in the Sixth, and they keep order and give you lines, and all that sort of thing."

"Why, I thought it was only masters did that," said Jack Vance.

"Well, you'll find the prefects do it here," answered Carton; "and when they tell you to do a thing, I'd advise you to look alive and do it, for they don't reckon to speak twice."

The evening passed quickly enough. After tea came an interview with the head-master in his study, and then what was perhaps a still more trying ordeal - a long spell of sitting in the big schoolroom answering an incessant fire of questions such as, "What's your name?" - "Where d'you come from?" etc., etc.

At length the signal was given for passing on to bed, and the Triple Alliance were not sorry to gain the shelter of No. 16 dormitory.

The room contained seven other beds besides their own, two of which were as yet still vacant, waiting the arrival of boys who had not turned up on the first day. The remainder were occupied by a couple of other new-comers, and three oldsters, Carton, Hart, and Bayley.

It was very different from the cosy little bedrooms at The Birches; but the three friends were glad to be allowed to undress in peace and quiet, and had scrambled safely into bed some time before the prefect put in an appearance to turn out the light.

"I tell you what," said Hart, a few moments later: "you new kids may think yourselves lucky that you're in a quiet room for a start. I know when I came first there used to be christenings and all kinds of humbug."

"What was that?" asked Diggory.

"Why, fellows used always to christen you with a nickname: they stuck your head in a basin and poured water over you, and if you struggled you got it all down your back."

"Yes," continued Carton, "and they hid your clothes, and had bull-fights and all sorts of foolery. That was in *Nineteen*: old 'Thirsty' was the prefect for that passage, and he doesn't care tu'pence what fellows do. But Allingford's put a stop to almost all that kind of thing: he's captain of the school, and he's always awfully down on anything of that sort."

By the time breakfast was over on the following morning, Diggory and his two companions were beginning to recover a little from their first state of bewilderment amid their strange surroundings. They donned the school cap of black flannel, with the crest worked in silk upon the front, and went out to enjoy some fresh air and sunshine in the playground.

It was a bright, frosty day, and the whole place seemed full of life and activity. There was plenty to engage their attention, and much that was new and singular after their comparatively quiet playground at The Birches. But whatever there was to awaken their interest out of doors, a thing was destined to happen during their first morning school which would be a still greater surprise than anything they had yet encountered during their short residence at Ronleigh.

At nine o'clock the clanging of the big bell summoned them to the general assembly in the big schoolroom. They took their places at a back desk pointed out to them by the master on duty, and sat watching the stream of boys that poured in through the open doors, wondering how long it would take them to become acquainted with the names of such a multitude.

The forms passed on in their usual order, and the new boys were conducted to a vacant classroom, where they received a set of examination papers which were intended to test the amount of their knowledge, and determine the position in which they were to start work on the following day.

Jack Vance, Diggory, and Mugford sat together at the first desk, just in front of the master's table, and were soon busy in proving their previous acquaintance with the Latin grammar. Presently the door opened, and a voice, which they at once recognized as Dr. Denson's, said, "Mr. Ellesby, may I trouble you to step here for a moment?" None of the trio raised their eyes from their work. There was a muttered conversation in the passage, and then the door was once more closed.

The master returned to his desk, dipped his pen in the

ink, and addressing some one at the back of the room, inquired, -

"What did Dr. Denson say your name was?"

"Noaks, sir."

The Triple Alliance gave a simultaneous start as though they had received an electric shock, and their heads turned round like three weathercocks.

There, sure enough, at the back desk of all, sat the late leader of the Philistines, with a rather sheepish expression on his face, somewhat similar to the one it had worn when the marauders from Horace House had been ushered into Mr. Welsby's study.

Jack Vance looked at Mugford, and Mugford looked at Diggory. "Well, I'm jiggered!" whispered the latter, and once more returned to his examination paper.

At eleven o'clock there was a quarter of an hour's interval. Being still, as it were, strangers in a strange land, the three friends kept pretty· close together. They were walking arm in arm about the quadrangle, giving expression to their astonishment at this latest arrival at Ronleigh, when Diggory suddenly exclaimed, "Look out! here he comes!"

After so many encounters of a decidedly hostile nature, it was difficult to meet their old enemy on neutral ground without some feeling of embarrassment. Young Noaks, however, walked up cool as a cucumber, and holding out his hand said, -

"Hullo, you fellows, who'd have thought of seeing you

here! How are you?"

The three boys returned the salutation in a manner which, to say the least, was not very cordial, and made some attempt to pass on their way; but the new-comer refused to see that he was not wanted, and insisted on taking Mugford's arm and accompanying them on their stroll.

"I say," he continued, addressing Jack Vance, "were you at Todderton these holidays? I don't think I saw you once."

"The last time I saw you," returned Jack, in rather a bitter tone, "was when you came to spoil our fireworks, and we collared you in the shed."

Noaks clinched his fist, and for a moment his brow darkened; the next instant, however, he laughed as though the recollection of the incident afforded him an immense amount of amusement.

"Ha, ha! Yes, awful joke that, wasn't it? almost as good as the time when that fool of a master of yours, Lake, or Blake, or whatever you call him, had me sent off the field so that you could win the match."

"It was no such thing," answered Jack. "You know very well why it was Blake interfered; and he's not a fool, but a jolly good sort."

"Oh, don't get angry," returned the other. "I'm sure I shouldn't fly into a wax if you called Fox or old Phillips a fool. I got sick of that beastly little school, as I expect you did of yours, and so I made my uncle send me here. - Hullo! I suppose that's the bell for going back to work; see you again later on."

"I say," whispered Diggory, as soon as they had regained their seat in the examination-room, "I vote we give that chap the cold shoulder."

The following morning the three friends heard their names read out as forming part of the Third Form, to which their friend Carton already belonged. Young Noaks was placed in the Upper Fourth, and they were not destined therefore to have him as a class-mate.

The Third Form at Ronleigh had, for some reason or other, received the title of "The Happy Family." They certainly were an amusing lot of little animals, and Diggory and his companions coming into the classroom rather late, and before the entrance of the master, saw them for the first time to full advantage. Out of the two-and-twenty juveniles present, only about six seemed to be in their proper places.

One young gentleman sitting close to the blackboard cried, "Powder, sir!" and straightway scrubbed his neighbour's face with a very chalky duster. The latter, by way of retaliation, smote the former's pile of books from the desk on to the ground - a little attention which was immediately returned by boy number one; while as they bent down to pick up their scattered possessions, a third party, sitting on the form behind, made playful attempts to tread upon their fingers. Two rival factions in the rear of the room were waging war with paper darts; while a small, sandy-haired boy, whose tangled hair and disordered attire gave him the appearance, as the saying goes, of having been dragged through a furze-bush backwards, rapped vigorously with his knuckles upon the master's table, and inquired loudly how many more times he was to say "Silence!"

The entrance of the three new-comers caused a false alarm, and in a moment every one was in his proper seat.

"Bother it!" cried the small, sandy-haired boy, who had bumped his knee rushing from the table to his place; "why didn't you make more noise when you came in?"

"But I thought you were asking for silence, answered Diggory.

"Shut up, and don't answer back when you are spoken to by a prefect," retorted the small boy. "Look here, you haven't written your name on Watford's slate. - They must, mustn't they, Maxton?" he added, turning to a boy who sat at the end of one of the back seats.

"Of course they must," answered Maxton, who, with both elbows on the desk, was blowing subdued railway whistles through his hands; "every new fellow has to write his name on that little slate on Mr. Watford's table, and he enters them from there into his mark-book. I'm head boy, and I've got to see you do it. Look sharp, or he'll be here in a minute, and there'll be a row."

Diggory, Vance, and Mugford hastily signed their names, one under the other, upon the slate. There was a good deal of tittering while they did so; but as a new boy is laughed at for nearly everything he does, they took no notice of it, and had hardly got back to their places when the master entered the room, and the work began in earnest.

About a quarter of an hour later the boys were busy with a Latin exercise, when silence was broken by a shuffle and an exclamation from the back desk. "You again, Maxton," said the master, looking up with a frown. "I suppose you are determined to idle away your time and remain bottom of the class this term as you were last. I shall put your name down for some extra work. Let's see," he continued, taking up the slate: "I appear to have three boys' names down already - 'Vance,' 'Mugford,' and 'Trevanock.' What's the meaning of this? This is not my writing. How came these names here?"

"Please, sir," faltered Mugford, "we put them there ourselves."

"Put them there yourselves! What d'you want to put your names down on my punishment slate for? I suppose some one told you to, didn't they?"

"Please, sir," answered Diggory warily, "we thought we had to, so that you might have our names to enter in your mark-book."

There was a burst of laughter, but that answer went a long way towards setting the Alliance on a good footing with their class-mates.

"That young Trevanock's the right sort," said Maxton, "and so are the others. I thought they'd sneak about that slate, but they didn't."

Mr. Noaks, junior, on the other hand, was destined to find that he was not going to carry everything before him at Ronleigh as he had done among the small fry at Horace House, The Upper Fourth voted him a "bounder," and nicknamed him "Moke." After morning school he repeated his attempt to ally himself with his former foes, but the result was decidedly unsatisfactory.

Down in the box-room, a good-sized apartment boarded off from the gymnasium, Jack Vance was serving out a ration of plum-cake to a select party, consisting of his two chums and Carton, when the ex-Philistine strolled up and joined himself to the group.

"Hullo!" he said, "are you chaps having a feed? D'you remember that pork-pie we bagged from one of your kids at Chatford? Ha, ha! it was a lark."

"I don't see it's much of a lark to bag what doesn't belong to you," muttered Diggory.

"What's that you say?"

"Nothing for you to hear," returned the other. "I don't know if you're waiting about here to get some cake, but I'm sure I never invited you to come."

"Look here, don't be cheeky," answered Noaks. "If you think I want to make friends with a lot of impudent young monkeys like you, all I can say is you're jolly well mistaken," and so saying he turned on his heel and walked away.

"I say, Trevanock," said Carton, two days later, "that fellow Noaks has found a friend at last: he's picked up with Mouler. They'll make a nice pair, I should say. Mouler was nearly expelled last term for telling lies to Ellesby about some cribs."

Noaks certainly seemed to have discovered a chum in the black sheep of the Upper Fourth, and the Triple Alliance began to congratulate themselves that he would trouble them no further. In a big school like Ronleigh College there was plenty of room for everybody to go his own way without fear of running his head into people whom he wished to avoid. Our three friends, however, seemed fated to find in the person of Noaks junior a perpetual stumbling-block and cause of disquietude and annoyance. They had no sooner succeeded in setting him at a distance when an incident occurred which brought them once more into violent collision with the enemy.

The pavilion, which has already been mentioned as standing on the match ground, was a handsome wooden structure, surrounded by some low palings, in front of which was a small oblong patch of gravel. On the second Saturday morning of the term Noaks and Mouler were lounging across this open space, when Oaks, the prefect, emerged from the pavilion, carrying in his hand a pot of paint he had been mixing for the goal-posts, which were just being put up. On reaching the paling he suddenly ejaculated, "Bother! I've forgotten the brush;" and resting the can on the top of the little gate-post, hurried back up the short flight of steps, and disappeared through the open door.

"I say, there's a good cock-shy," said Noaks, nodding his head in the direction of the paint.

"Umph! shouldn't like to try," answered Mouler.

"Why not?"

Harold Avery

"Because Oaks would jolly well punch both our heads."

"Well, here's a new kid coming; let's set him on to do it. You speak to him; he knows me. His name's Mugford."

The two cronies both picked up a handful of stones, and began throwing at the can, taking good care that their shots should fly wide of the mark.

Mugford, who, as we have already seen, was not blessed with the sharpest of wits, paused for a moment to watch the contest. The paint had been mixed in an old fruit-tin, and at first sight it certainly seemed to have been put on the post for the sole purpose of being knocked off again.

"Hullo, you new kid!" exclaimed Mouler. "Look here, we want a chap for the third eleven next season - a fellow who can throw straight. Come along, and let's see if you can hit that old can."

It certainly looked easy enough, and Mugford, pleased at being taken some notice of by a boy in the Upper Fourth, picked up some pebbles, and joined in the bombardment. The second shot brought the tin down with a great clatter, and a flood of white paint spread all over the trim little pathway. At the same instant Oaks dashed down the steps boiling with rage.

"Confound you!" he cried; "who did that ?"

"I did," answered Mugford, half crying; "I thought it was empty."

"Thought it was empty! why didn't you look, you young blockhead?" cried the prefect, catching the small boy by the arm, while Noaks and Mouler burst into a roar of laughter.

Things would probably have gone hard with the unfortunate Mugford if at that moment a fifth party had not arrived on the scene. The new-comer, who, from the show of whisker at the side of his face and the tone of authority in which he spoke, seemed to be one of the masters, was tall and muscular, with the bronze of a season's cricketing still upon his cheeks and neck.

"Stop a minute, Oaks," he said. "I happened to see this little game; let's hear what the kid's got to say for himself."

In faltering tones Mugford told his story. Without a word the stranger stepped up to Mouler and dealt him a sounding box on the ear.

"There!" he said, "take that for your trouble; and now cut off down town and buy a fresh pot of paint out of your own pocket, and do it jolly quick, too. - As for you," he added, turning to Noaks, "get a spade out of that place under the pavilion and clean up this path. If you weren't a new fellow I'd serve you the same. Look out in future."

"And you look out too," muttered Noaks, glancing at Mugford with a fierce expression on his face as the two seniors moved off, "you beastly young sneak. The first chance I get I'll give you the best licking you ever had in your life."

"Old Mug is rather a fool," remarked Jack Vance to

Diggory a few hours later; "he ought to have seen through that. But we must stand by him because of the Triple Alliance. Noaks is sure to try to set on him the first chance he gets."

"Yes," answered Diggory; "look out for squalls."

CHAPTER VIII.

THIRD FORM ORATORY.

At the end of the first fortnight our three friends had begun to find their feet at Ronleigh, and the sense of being "outsiders" in everything was gradually wearing off as they grew more intimate with their schoolfellows.

Jack Vance and Diggory soon became popular members of "The Happy Family," and their loyalty to Mugford caused the latter's path to be much smoother than it probably would have been had he been compelled to tread it alone.

Carton turned out a capital fellow; Rathson, the small, sandy-haired boy mentioned in the previous chapter, and who generally went by the name of "Rats," took a great fancy to Jack; while Maxton repeated his assertion that young Trevanock was "the right sort," and as a further mark of his favour presented the new-comer with a moleskin of his own curing, which looked very nice, but, as "Rats" put it, "smelt rather fruity."

But it was not in the Third Form only that Diggory began to find friends; for by a lucky chance he was fortunate enough to make a good impression on the minds of the great men, who, as a rule, took no further notice of the small fry than to exact from them a certain amount of obedience, or in default a certain number of lines or other "impots."

One morning, soon after breakfast, a little group was gathered round Carton's desk in the big school-room, discussing the value of some foreign stamps, when a small boy came up to them, saying, -

"Is Trevanock here? Well, Acton wants you now at once in his study."

"Hullo," said Carton, looking up from the sheet of specimens in front of him - "hullo, Diggy! What have you been up to?"

"I haven't been doing anything," answered the other. "What do you think he wants me for?"

"I don't know, but it sounds rather like getting a licking. At all events, you'd better hurry up; prefects don't thank you for keeping them waiting. His is the third door on the right as you go down the passage."

Diggory hastened to obey the summons, wondering what it could mean. He found the door, and in answer to the loud "Come in!" which greeted his knock turned the handle, and found himself for the first time inside one of the Sixth Form studies.

It was a small, square room, and looked very cosy and comfortable with its red window-curtains, well-filled bookshelf, and many little knick-knacks that adorned the walls and mantelpiece. An array of silver cups, several photographs of cricket and football teams, and a miscellaneous pile of bats, fencing-sticks, Indian clubs, etc., standing in one corner, all spoke of the athlete; while carelessly thrown down on the top of a cupboard was an article for the possession of which many a, boy would have bartered the whole of his worldly wealth - a bit of worn blue velvet and the tarnished remnant of what had once been a gold tassel - the "footer cap" of Ronleigh College.

But it was not so much the furniture as the occupants of the study that attracted Diggory's attention. John Acton, a tall, wiry fellow, who looked as though his whole body was as hard and tough as whip-cord, was standing leaning on the end of the mantelpiece talking to another of the seniors, who sat sprawling in a folding-chair on the other side of the fire; while seated at the table, turning over the leaves of what appeared to be a big manuscript book, was no less a personage than Allingford, the school captain.

"I don't understand a bit what's coming to 'Thirsty,'" the football leader was saying. "I was rather chummy with him when we were in the Fifth, and he was all right then, but now he seems to be running to seed as fast as he can; and I believe it's a great deal that fellow Fletcher. - Hullo, youngster! what d'you want?"

"I was told you wanted to see me," said Diggory nervously.

"Oh yes. You were at The Birches, that school near Chatford, weren't you? Well, I want to hear about that love affair my young brother had with the old chap's daughter. - It was an awful joke," added the speaker, addressing his companions. "He was about fourteen, and she's a grown-up woman; and he was awfully gone, I can tell you. - How did he pop the question?"

"He wrote," answered Diggory. "We tossed up whether he should do that or speak."

There was a burst of laughter.

"Did you see the letter?"

"Yes."

"What did he say?"

"I can't tell you."

"Why not? don't you remember?"

"Yes; but he only showed me the letter on condition I wouldn't ever tell any one what was in it."

"Oh, that's all rot! you can tell me; I'm his brother. Come, out with it."

It was an awful thing to beard the lion in his den - for a new boy to face so great a personage as the football captain, and refuse point-blank to do as he was told. Diggory shifted uneasily from one foot to another, and then glancing up he became aware of the fact that Allingford was gazing at him across the table with a curious expression, which somehow gave him fresh encouragement to persist in his refusal to disclose the contents of his former friend's love-letter.

"I can't tell you," he repeated; "it was a promise, you know."

The Ronleigh captain laughed. "Well done," he said. "I wish some other fellows were a bit more careful to keep their promises. - Acton, you beggar, you swore you'd keep up this register for me, and there's nothing entered for last term."

"Oh, bother you, Ally!" exclaimed the other; "what a nigger-driver you are! - Hullo, there's the bell! - Here, kid, stick those two oranges in your pocket; go 'long!"

Diggory left the room, having gained something else besides the two oranges; for as he closed the door Allingford laughed again, and rising from his chair said, "He's a stanch little beggar; I think I'll keep an eye on him."

The subject of this remark hurried away, and had just joined the crowd of boys who were thronging into the big school for assembly, when some one took hold of his arm, and glancing round he was startled to see Jack Vance, looking very excited and dishevelled, and mopping his mouth with a blood-stained handkerchief.

"I say," exclaimed the latter, "have you seen Mugford?"

"No. What's the matter? what have you done to your mouth?"

"Why, I've had a beastly row with Noaks. I'll 'tell you after school."

"No, tell me now," cried Diggory, pulling his companion aside into a corner by the door. "Quick - what was it?"

"Why, he pounced down on Mugford, out there by the fives-court, and began twisting his arm and saying he'd pay him out for that paint-pot business. I went to the rescue, and the beast hit me with the back of his hand here on the mouth. I told him he was a cad, and said something about his father being only a man-servant, and having stolen our things. I'm sorry now, for it was rather a low thing to do, but I was in such a wax I didn't think what I was saying. Mouler was standing by, and he heard it, and laughed; and Noaks looked as if he'd have killed me. I believe he would have knocked me down, only Rowlands, the prefect, came up and stopped the row."

There was no time for any further details, and the two boys had to rush away to their seats in order to escape being marked as late.

One thing was certain - that the Triple Alliance were once more embroiled in a quarrel with their ancient foe the former leader of the Philistines, and they knew enough of their adversary's character to feel sure that he would not pass over an event of this kind without some attempt at revenge.

It is probable that, if this had happened at Horace House, Jack Vance would have received a good licking as soon as the classes were dismissed; but a few very plain and forcible words spoken by Rowlands on the subject of knocking small boys about caused Noaks to postpone his retaliation.

"Look here," he said, meeting Jack Vance in the quadrangle during the interval: "just you keep your mouth shut about me and my father. I've got two or three accounts to settle with you chaps already; just mind what you're up to." He clinched his fist as though about to strike, then, with an ugly scowl, turned on his heel and walked away.

It must have been about three days after this encounter with Noaks that our three friends were called upon to attend a mass meeting of the Third Form, to consider the advisability of starting a periodical in opposition to the school magazine. Important events connected with a later period of their life at Ronleigh render it necessary that we should not linger too long over the account of their first term; but some mention, however brief, should certainly be made of the memorable gathering to which we have referred. A notice pinned on to the black-board, and pulled down as soon as Mr. Watford entered the classroom, announced the project in the following words: -

"NOTICE."

"A meeting will be held in the 'old lab' directly after dinner to-day, to make plans for starting a magazine in opposition to *The Ronleian*. All members of the Third Form are specially requested to attend."

"FLETCHER II."
"J. A. BIBBS."

"You must come," said "Rats" to Diggory; "it'll be an awful lark."

"But what's it all about?"

"Oh, you'll hear when you get there. It's Fletcher's idea; he wants to start a new magazine. Eastfield, who edits *The Ronleian*, is Maxton's cousin; so Maxton's going to interrupt and get some other fellows to do the same. I'm going to be part of the opposition," added the youthful "Rats," beaming with delight, "and I have got a whole heap of paper bags I'm going to burst while Fletcher's speaking."

The "old lab," as it was called, was a small brick building which stood on one side of the asphalt playground. A new laboratory having recently been fitted up elsewhere, the former one was, for the time being, unused. It was not more than about fifteen feet long by seven or eight feet wide; and as "The Happy Family" mustered in force, the place was crowded to overflowing. The door having been closed, Fletcher Two mounted a low stone sink which ran along the end wall, and from this ready-made platform commenced to address the assembly : -

"Gentlemen, - We've met here, as you know, to talk over starting a fresh magazine. *The Ronleian* is a beastly swindle, and it's high time we had something different." (A voice, "No, 'tisn't," and the bursting of a paper bag.) "You shut up there! I say it is a swindle: they didn't give any account of that fourth eleven match against Robertson's second, and they made fun of us in the 'Quad Gossip,' and said that in 'The Happy Family' there was a preponderance of monkey." ("So there is, and you're it!" Laughter and another explosion.)

"What I propose is that we start a manuscript magazine for the Third Form, and that every fellow promise to take that, and never to buy a copy of the other. We might pass it round, and charge a penny each to look at it. Will you all subscribe?"

No one spoke, the silence only being broken by the sound of "Rats" blowing up another bag, which caused a fresh burst of laughter.

"Will you all subscribe?" once more demanded the speaker.

There were mingled cries of "Yes!" and "No!" and a stentorian yell of "No, you cuckoo! of course we won't," from Maxton, and another explosion.

"Look here, young 'Rats,' if you burst any more of those bags I'll come down and burst your head. - I forgot to say, gentlemen, that Mr. Bibbs has promised to assist in editing the paper; and I will now call upon him to give you an account of what it will contain."

Bibbs, the Third Form genius, was regarded by every one as a huge joke, and the very mention of his name caused a fresh burst of merriment. He was a sad-faced, untidy-looking boy, quick and clever enough in some things, and equally dull and stupid in others. The announcement that he would address the meeting had no sooner been made than half a dozen willing pairs of hands seized and hoisted him on to the platform; though no sooner had he attained this exalted position than two or three voices ordered him in a peremptory manner to "Come down!"

The greater part of the audience not caring the toss of a button whether Fletcher started his magazine or not, but thinking that it was rather good fun to interrupt the proceedings, now joined the opposition, and the unfortunate Bibbs was subjected to a brisk fire of chaff. One facetious class-mate, standing close to the sink, offered to sell him by auction; and hammering on the stones with the fragment of a bat handle, knocked him down for threepence to another joker, who said he'd do for a pen-wiper.

"Sing a song, Bibbs!" cried one voice; "Where's your neck-tie?" asked another; "What are you grinning at?" demanded a third; while the object of these pleasantries stood, with a vacant smile upon his face, nervously fumbling with his watch-chain.

"Go on!" cried Fletcher, who had descended from the platform to make room for his colleague; "say something, you fool!"

"The magazine is to be written on exercise-book paper," began Bibbs, and had only got thus far when he was interrupted by a perfect salvo of paper bags which little "Rats" discharged in quick succession.

With an exclamation of wrath Fletcher made a dive in the direction of the offender, and in a moment the whole gathering was in a state of confusion. The majority of those present siding with "Rats," began to hustle Fletcher, while two gentlemen having dragged Bibbs from his perch, jumped up in his stead, and began to execute a clog-dance.

In the midst of this commotion Maxton elbowed his way through the crush, and having pushed the two boys off the sink, mounted it himself, crying, -

"Look here, I'm going to speak; just you listen a minute. The reason why Bibbs wants to start a new magazine is because he wrote a novel once, and sent it to *The Ronleian* to come out so much each month, and they wouldn't have it."

"Shut up, Maxton!" cried Fletcher, rushing to the spot; "you've only come here on purpose to interrupt. Let's turn him out!"

"Yes, turn him out!" echoed the audience, who by this time were just in the spirit for "ragging," and would have ejected friend or foe alike for the sport of the thing - "turn him out!"

The two clog-dancers being quite ready to avenge the interruption of their performance, formed themselves into a storming-party, and carried the platform by assault. Maxton, struggling all the way, was dragged to the door, and cast out into the playground. Most of the restless spirits in the audience requiring a short breathing-space to recover their wind after the tussle, there followed a few moments' quiet, which Fletcher immediately took advantage of to mount the sink and resume the business of the meeting.

"The magazine," he began, "is going to be written on exercise-book paper. Any one who likes can contribute, and it's going to be more especially a paper for the Third Form."

The speaker went on to show that the periodical was destined to supply a long-felt want. *The Ronleian* ignored the doings of boys in the lower half of the school, and returned their contributions with insulting suggestions, pencilled on the margins, that the authors should devote some of their spare time and energy to the study of their English grammars and spelling-books. *The Third Form Chronicle*, as it was to be called, would recognize the fact that junior boys had as much right to be heard as seniors, and would afford them the opportunity of airing their views on any subject they chose to bring forward.

Fletcher had barely time to proceed thus far with his speech when an alarming interruption occurred, which put an immediate stop to his further utterance. Nearly at the top of the end wall there had formerly been a ventilator; this, for one reason or another, had been removed, and in the brickwork an open space about a foot square had been left. A hissing noise was suddenly heard outside, and the next moment a stream of water shot through the aperture, and descended in a perfect deluge on the heads of the company.

The fact was that Maxton, ever a reckless young villain, had discovered a hose fixed to one of the mains close to the building, and had immediately seized upon it as an instrument wherewith to wreak vengeance on his companions for having turned him out of the meeting.

Words cannot describe the uproar and confusion which followed. As one man the whole assembly made for the door, but only to find it fastened on the outside. The water flew all over the small building, drenching every one in turn. Some howled, some laughed, and only Bibbs had sufficient presence of mind to creep under the sink, which afforded a certain amount of shelter from the falling flood.

The deluge ceased as suddenly as it had begun, and an instant later the door was flung open, and the figure of a Sixth Form boy was seen barring the exit.

"Now, then," he demanded, "what are you youngsters making this awful row for? I've a jolly good mind to take all your names."

There was a moment's silence. Then Fletcher's voice was heard exclaiming, -

"Oh! it's only old 'Thirsty;' he's all right."

"Here, not so fast," answered the prefect, blocking up the doorway as some boys tried to escape; "what are you chaps doing in here? I thought you'd been told to keep out."

The originator of the meeting pushed his way through the crowd, and taking hold of the big fellow's arm in a familiar manner, said, -

"Oh, it's all right, 'Thirsty,' old chap. We just came inside, and some one squirted water all over us, and that's why we shouted. But we won't do it again."

"Oh, but it isn't all right," returned the other. "If I find any of you in here again, I'll help you out with the toe of my boot. Go on! I'll let you off this once."

The crowd rushed forth and quickly dispersed.

"That Thurston seems an awful decent chap," said Diggory; "I didn't think he'd let us off so easily."

"He's all right as long as you don't cross him," answered Carton. "He used to be pretty strict, but he doesn't seem to care now what fellows do. He's very thick with Fletcher's brother - that's one reason why he didn't do anything just now; but I can tell you he's a nasty chap to deal with when he's in a wax."

The prefect locked the empty building, and turning on his heel caught sight of our three friends, who were standing close by waiting for "Rats."

"Hullo, you new kids! what are you called?"

The usual answer was given, and Thurston passed on, little thinking what good cause he would have before the end of the year for remembering the names of the trio, and altogether unaware of the prominent part which the Triple Alliance was destined to play in his own private affairs as well as in the fortunes of Ronleigh College.

CHAPTER IX.

A HOLIDAY ADVENTURE.

The weeks slipped away, and the Triple Alliance soon got over their new-boy trials, and began to enjoy all the rights and privileges of Ronleigh College boys. They wrote letters to Miss Eleanor and to their former schoolfellows, and received in reply the latest news from The Birches.

"The Philistines are quite friendly now," wrote Acton. "We had a match against them last week on their ground, and they gave us tea after. It's awfully slow; I almost wish that chap Noaks was back."

"So do I," added Diggory, as he finished the sentence; "we could very well spare him."

"Oh, he's all right," answered Jack Vance; "that row's blown over now. As long as we leave him alone he won't interfere with us."

"Won't he!" returned the other; "you take my word for it, he hasn't forgotten what you said about his father, and he's only waiting for a chance to pay us out. Whenever I go near him he looks as black as ink."

It was customary at Ronleigh to have what was called

a half-term holiday. This was usually given on a Monday, to enable those boys who lived within a short distance of the school to spend the week end at home; while, in the winter or spring terms, the boarders who remained at the school usually devoted the greater portion of the day to a paper-chase.

"I shall go home," said Jack Vance to his two chums; "Todderton's only about half an hour's ride from here on the railway. And, I say, I've got a grand idea: I'm going to write and get my mater to invite you fellows to come too! It would be jolly to have a meeting there of the Triple Alliance, and I'm sure old Denson would let you go if we came back on Monday night."

Both Mugford and Diggory were charmed with the idea. "But d'you really think your mater would have us?" they asked.

"Of course she will, if I ask her," answered Jack, and straightway sat down to write the letter.

By Wednesday evening everything, including the formal invitation and the doctors permission to accept the same, had been obtained, and for the two following days the Triple Alliance could talk or think of little else besides their projected excursion. At length Saturday came, and as soon as morning school was over they rushed upstairs to change into their best clothes; and having crammed their night-shirts, brushes and combs, etc., into a hand-bag, hurried off to the railway station, in order that they might, as Jack put it, "be home in time for dinner."

Just as they were getting into the train, who should come out of the booking-office but young Noaks.

"Hullo!" said Jack. "He must be going home too; I hope he won't come in here."

The new-comer, however, had no intention of making another attempt to force his society on the Triple Alliance; he passed them with a surly nod, and entered a compartment at the other end of the train.

Jack Vance lived in the suburbs of Todderton, about twenty minutes' walk from the railway; but for all that he managed to carry out his intention of being home in time for dinner; and the three boys, after receiving a hearty welcome, were soon seated down to a repast which came very acceptable after seven weeks of school fare.

"Jack," said Mr. Vance, "you know that house that was to let just on the other side of The Hermitage? Who d'you think's taken it?"

"I don't know, father."

"Why, that man Simpson, the uncle of your friend what's-his-name."

"He isn't my friend," answered Jack. "You mean Noaks. Fancy his coming to live so near to us as that! We saw him in the train just now. He's here for the holiday."

"I ought to tell you," continued Mr. Vance, turning to Diggory, "that our next-door neighbour is called 'The Hermit.' He's a queer old fellow, who lives by himself, and never makes friends or speaks to any one. He's supposed to be very clever, and I've heard it said that he's got a very valuable collection of coins, and is quite an authority on the subject; it's one of his hobbies."

"I suppose," said Mugford thoughtfully, "that as he's a hermit that's why his place is called The Hermitage."

"Well done, Mug!" said Jack, speaking with his mouth pretty full; "you're getting quite sharp."

"Yes, that's it," continued Mr. Vance, laughing. "The old man's away from home just now; he was suffering from rheumatism very badly, and the doctor ordered him to a course of treatment at some baths."

The conversation turned on other topics, and when at length they rose from the table, Jack proposed a stroll round the garden.

There were many things to see - some pet rabbits, a swing, and an old summer-house, which Jack, being, we should say, of a decidedly nautical turn of mind, had turned into a sort of miniature shipbuilding yard for the construction of model vessels; though at present the chief use to which the place seemed to have been put was the production of a great amount of chips and shavings.

"I say," exclaimed the owner, after he and his friends had amused themselves for some time boring holes in the door with a brace, "I know what we'll do: let's go over and explore The Hermitage!"

Anything with a spice of excitement in it was meat and drink to Diggory. He immediately seconded the proposition, and Mugford, after a moment's hesitation, agreed to join his companions in the enterprise.

They strolled off down the path, and soon reached a long stretch of brick wall, the top of which was thickly covered with fragments of broken bottles.

"There's a place down at the other end where we can get over," said Jack. "I smashed the glass with a hammer, because I lost a ball and had to climb over and get it, one day last holidays."

The Hermitage was surrounded on all sides by a thick mass of shrubs and trees, through which a moment later the Triple Alliance were cautiously threading their way. Emerging from the bushes, they found themselves standing on a gravel path, green with moss and weeds, which ran round the house - a queer, dilapidated-looking building, which seemed sadly in want of repair: the plaster was cracked and discoloured, while the doors and windows had long stood in need of a fresh coating of paint.

"I say," whispered Mugford, "hadn't we better go back? what if the old chap's at home!"

"Oh, it's all right; there's nobody about," answered Jack. "Let's go on and see what the place is really like."

They tip-toed round the building. It was evidently unoccupied, though the delightful sense of uncertainty that at any moment some one might pounce out upon them or walk down the drive made the questionable adventure very charming.

"Have you ever been inside?" asked Diggory.

"No, rather not; I don't think any one has except the doctor, and an old woman who comes in to do the house-work."

"Well, then, I'm going in," answered Diggory, with a twinkle in his eye.

"Go on! Why, you might be had up for house-breaking!"

"Rubbish! I'm not going to steal anything. - Here, Mug, lend me your knife a minute."

"I don't believe this one's fastened," he continued, walking up to one of the windows. "No, it isn't. Bother! I'm awfully sorry, Mugford."

Using the big blade of the clasp-knife as a lever, Diggory had just succeeded in raising the sash the fraction of an inch, when the steel suddenly snapped off short at the handle.

"Oh, never mind," said the owner; "let's go back now. What if we're seen!"

"Oh, there's no fear of that," answered Jack, who was always infected with the adventurous spirit of his chum. - "Go on, Diggy; I'll come too."

By inserting their fingers in the aperture, the boys soon raised the sash, and a few seconds later Diggory mounted the ledge and scrambled through the window "Come on," he said; "the coast's all clear."

Jack Vance joined him immediately, and Mugford, not wishing to be left alone outside, was not long in making up his mind to follow his companions.

The room in which the three boys found themselves was evidently a library or study. Book-shelves, and cupboards with glass doors, containing geological and other specimens, occupied much of the wall space; while in the centre of the floor stood a large writing-table, covered with a miscellaneous collection of pens, ink-pots, bundles of papers, and a polished mahogany box which could easily be recognized as a microscope-case.

The intruders stood for a few moments gazing round in silence. The place did not look very interesting, and smelt rather damp and mouldy.

"I say," exclaimed Jack Vance, "look there: he don't seem very careful how he leaves his things when he goes away."

As he spoke he pointed across to the opposite side of the room, where, between two bookcases, an iron safe had been let into the wall. The heavy door was standing half open, while the floor beneath was strewn with a quantity of shallow wooden trays lined with green baize.

"Old bachelors are always untidy," remarked Diggory. "Let's see where this door leads to." He turned the handle as he spoke, and walked out into a gloomy little hall paved with cold, bare flagstones, which caused their footsteps to waken mournful echoes in the empty house.

"I say, you fellows, don't let's go any further," murmured Mugford;" we've seen enough now. Suppose the old chap came back and - " He never reached the end of the sentence, for Diggory suddenly raised his hand, exclaiming in a whisper, "Hark! what was that?"

The loud ticking of Mugford's old turnip of a watch was distinctly audible in the silence which followed.

"What is it, Diggy? what - "

"Hark! there it is again; listen."

The suspense became awful. At length Diggory dropped his hand. "Didn't you hear footsteps?" he asked. "I'm certain there's some one walking about on the gravel path."

"We shall be caught," whimpered Mugford; "I knew we should. What can we do?"

"Bolt!" answered Diggory, and began tip-toeing back towards the library door. "Stay here half a 'jiffy,'" he added; "I'll go and reconnoitre."

Ages seemed to pass while Jack Vance and Mugford stood in the dark passage awaiting their companion's return. At length the door was pushed softly open.

"It's all right; there's no one there. I must have been mistaken. Come along."

In a very short time the Triple Alliance were once more outside The Hermitage. Diggory lingered for a moment to close the window, and then followed his companions through the shrubs and over the wall.

"You are a great ass, Diggy, to go giving us a start like that," said Jack, as they paused for a moment to take breath before returning to the house.

"Well, I could have sworn I heard the gravel crunch as if some one was walking on it," returned the other. "I should think the place must be haunted."

A good tea, with all kinds of nice things on the table, soon revived the boys from the trifling shock which their nerves had sustained, and by the end of the evening their adventure was wellnigh forgotten. They were destined, however, to remember it for many a long day to come, and before many hours had passed they were heartily wishing that they had never set foot inside The Hermitage, but kept on their own side of the wall.

The party were seated at supper on Sunday evening, when a servant entered the room, and addressing her master said, "If you please, sir, there's a policeman called to see you."

Jack's father rose from his chair, remarking, in a jocular manner, "I expect it's one of you young gentlemen he's come after."

The meal was nearly over when Mr. Vance returned and reseated himself at the table.

"Did either of you hear the dog bark last night?" he asked.

"No; why?"

"Why, because old Fossberry's house has been broken into, and they think the thieves must have come through our garden; there were some footmarks in the shrubbery just on the other side of the wall."

The hearts of the Triple Alliance seemed to jump into their throats, and their mouths grew dry and parched. Jack stared at Mugford, and Mugford stared at Diggory, but none of them spoke.

"It seems," continued Mr. Vance, not noticing the effect which his first announcement had produced on at least three of his hearers, "that the old woman who looks after the house went there this morning, and found that the iron safe in which the old chap keeps his coins had been opened and the whole collection removed. The only trace of the thieves that the police have been able to discover is the broken blade of a clasp-knife, which was on a flower-bed near the window."

"What will they get if they are caught?" asked Jack faintly.

"Oh, penal servitude, I suppose; it's a serious business housebreaking."

"How quiet you boys are!" said Mrs. Vance a short time later. "I think you must be tired. Wouldn't you like to go to bed?"

The three friends were only too glad to avail themselves of this excuse for getting away into some place where they could indulge in a little private conversation. Diggory and Mugford slept together in the same room; Jack followed them in and closed the door.

"Well," he exclaimed, "we're in a nice mess."

"But we didn't steal the coins," said Mugford.

"Of course we didn't - the safe had been robbed before we went there - but it looks as if we'd done it; and if they find out we got into the house, I don't see how we're going to prove that we're innocent."

There was a short silence; then Diggory spoke.

"Look here, Jack: I was the one who proposed going inside the place; shall I tell your guv'nor?"

"Well, I was thinking of doing that myself, only I don't see what good it can do. If we tell him, he'll be bound to tell the police, to explain about those footmarks; and when it comes out that we got into the house, I should think we are pretty certain to be charged with having stolen the coins. I think the best thing will be to keep it dark: we didn't crib the things, and the thieves are sure to be caught in time."

Even after Jack had retired to his own room, Diggory and Mugford lay awake for hours discussing the situation; and when at length they did fall asleep, it was only to dream of being chased by "The Hermit" and a swarm of long-legged policemen, who forced their way into the Third Form classroom at Ronleigh, and handcuffed the unfortunate trio in the very bosom of "The Happy Family."

The following morning was spent in visiting such parts of the town of Todderton as were worth seeing.

"Upon my word," said Jack, "I feel funky to show my nose outside our gate, just as if I really had prigged those wretched coins. I shan't be at all sorry this evening to get back to Ronleigh. It's all in the paper this morning; it mentions the footmarks and the knife-blade, and says that as yet the police have not been able to discover any further traces of the robbers."

The conditions on which the half-term holiday was granted required every boy to return to school on the Monday evening, and accordingly, about seven o'clock, the Triple Alliance found themselves once more on their way to the railway station. They took their seats, and had hardly done so when young Noaks entered the compartment.

"Hullo, you fellows!" he exclaimed; "didn't you hear me whistle? I was standing over there by the book-stall."

Regarding this as an overture of friendship after their recent encounter, Jack Vance replied in an equally amicable manner, and after a few common-place remarks the party relapsed into silence. At Chatton, the station before Ronleigh, a man who had so far travelled with them got out, and the four boys were left alone. Hardly had the train started again when Noaks put down his paper, and turning to his companions said, -

"That's a rum business about that old chap's house being robbed, isn't it?"

Something in the speaker's look and in the tone of his voice caused the three listeners to experience an unpleasant quickening of their pulses.

"Yes," answered Diggory, with a well-assumed air of indifference. "I suppose they'll catch the thieves in time."

"I suppose so," returned the other, "especially if they find the chap who owns that knife with the broken blade."

The malignant look with which these words was accompanied showed at once that the speaker meant mischief. The three friends looked at one another in horrified amazement. Could it be possible that their visit to The Hermitage had already been discovered?

Noaks watched their faces for a moment, evidently well pleased with the effect which his remark had produced; then he burst out laughing.

"Look here," he continued, producing from his pocket a buck-handled clasp-knife: "I wonder if that's anything like it; I see the big blade's broken."

The Triple Alliance recognized it in a moment as one of the articles that had been rescued from Mugford's sale at The Birches; in fact, the owner's name appeared plainly engraved on the small brass plate.

Diggory was the first to find his tongue.

"What d'you mean? We didn't steal the coins!"

"My dear fellow, I never said you did. I only know that on Saturday I was looking over our wall, through an opening there happens to be in the shrubs, and saw you fellows climbing out of the old chap's window; and after you'd gone I noticed something lying in the path, and I hopped over, and picked up this knife."

"Give it here; it's mine," said Mugford, holding out his hand.

"No fear," answered the other, calmly returning the piece of lost property to his own pocket. "In this case finding's keeping; besides, I'm not sure if I couldn't get a reward for this if I sent it to the right place."

The train began to slacken speed as it approached Ronleigh station.

"Look here, Noaks," cried Jack Vance, in a fit of desperation, "what are you going to do? You know very well we are not thieves."

"I don't know anything of the sort," returned the tormentor, standing up to take his bag off the rack; "all I know is just what I've told you. See here, Mr. Vance," he continued, rounding on Jack with a sudden snarl, "you were good enough some little time ago to make some very caddish remarks about my father; in the future you'd better keep your mouth shut. I owe all three of you a dressing down for things that happened at Chatford, and now you'd better mind your P's and Q's if you don't want to be hauled up for housebreaking."

With this parting threat the ex-Philistine left the carriage. Mugford, Jack, and Diggory gazed at one another for a moment with anything but a happy look on their faces. One after another they slowly gathered up their things and stepped out on to the platform. Hardly had they done so when they heard their names called, and turning round beheld the small figure of "Rats" rushing forward to meet them.

"Hullo!" he exclaimed. "Old Ally sent me down to get a paper, and I thought you'd come by this train. I say, there's a fine row on up at the school - such a lark; I'll tell you about it as we go along."

Harold Avery

CHAPTER X.

A SCREW LOOSE IN THE SIXTH.

For the time being the three friends forgot their own troubles in their eagerness to hear "Rat's" description of certain events which had happened during their absence from Ronleigh.

"Look sharp; out with it!" they exclaimed. "What's happened?"

"Well," began Rathson, "it all came out through young Bayley acting the fool and spraining his ankle. You know we had the paper-chase this morning, and the hares ran out to Arrow Hill, and back again round by the canal and Birksam Church. Just after we'd rounded the hill, young Bayley jumped off the top of a high hedge, and twisted his foot so badly that he couldn't stand up. As it happened, there was a check just then, and Carton ran forward and told Allingford what had happened. He and Oaks came back, and said the only thing would be to get him to Chatton station, and so home by train. It was awfully decent of those chaps. They carried Bayley all the way, and then Oaks went home with him, and Allingford walked back, and so, of course, they missed half the run. Awfully brickish of them I call it, considering that it was only a kid like Bayley."

The Triple Alliance gave a murmur of assent.

"Was that what the row's about?" asked Diggory. "Oh, bless you, no; I haven't come to that yet. After he'd seen Oaks and Bayley into the train, old Ally started to walk home. There's a little 'pub' about half a mile out of Chatton called the Black Swan, and he thought he'd call and ask if they'd seen the fellows pass. You know Thurston the prefect, that chap who came to the door when we were having that meeting in the 'old lab.' Well, now, if he and Mouler, and two or three more of that sort, weren't sitting in the taproom, smoking, and drinking beer, and having a regular high old time. They'd lagged behind on purpose. Of course Allingford kicked them all out, and he and 'Thirsty' had a frightful row. They say the big chaps want to hush the matter up as far as they can, and not report it to old Denson, for fear he'd make it an excuse to put a stop to paper-chasing. Ally slanged Thurston right and left, and told him that if he chose to drink beer in a low 'pub' with the biggest blackguards in the school, he needn't expect that the fellows in the Sixth would have anything to do with him, and that he ought to send in his resignation as a prefect."

On entering the school buildings, our three friends were convinced of the truth of their comrade's story, and on their way to the schoolroom the question was repeated at least half a dozen times - "Have you heard about old 'Thirsty' being cobbed in the Black Swan?" Diggory thought of the conversation he had overheard in Acton's study, and mentioned it to Carton.

"Yes," answered the latter. "Big Fletcher's a beast. I know Thurston's very chummy with him, but I don't see that's got much to do with it. My brother, who left last term, said that 'Thirsty' used to be rather a jolly chap, only he's got a fearful temper when he's crossed. Most of the chaps like him as a prefect, because as long as you don't interfere with him he doesn't seem to care much what any one does. The real thing is he's going to the dogs, and, as Allingford says, he ought to resign."

Away in one of the Sixth Form studies the subject of their conversation was sitting with his hands in his pockets, frowning at the fire. He was roused from his reverie by some one putting his head round the corner of the door and exclaiming, -

"Hullo, 'Thirsty!'"

"Hullo, Fletcher! where on earth have you been all the evening?"

The new-comer was tall and lanky; he had a sharp, foxy-looking face, with thin, straight lips, and two deep lines which looked almost like scars between the eyebrows. He shut the door, and dragging forward a chair, sat down with his feet on the fender, and commenced warming his hands at the fire.

"Oh, I've been nowhere in particular," he answered, laughing. "But I say, young man, you seem to have raised a pretty good hornets' nest about your ears along this corridor."

"Yes, I know; they've had the cheek to send me that!"

He leaned back as he spoke, and taking a piece of paper from the table, tossed it across to his friend. It was a letter signed by most of the prefects, suggesting that he should send in his resignation.

"Humph!" said Fletcher; "that's a nice sort of a round robin, don't you call it? Well, what are you going to do?"

"Oh, I shall resign and have done with it. I'm sick of having to masquerade about as a good boy. I mean to do what I like."

"Pooh!" returned the other. "Now that you are a prefect, I wouldn't give up all the privileges and the right to go out and come in when you like just because a strait-laced chap like Allingford chooses to take offence at something you do. They can't force you to resign unless they go to the doctor, and they won't do that. I know what I'd do: I'd tell them pretty straight to go and be hanged, and keep their sermonizing to themselves."

Thurston turned on the speaker with a sudden burst of anger.

"Oh yes!" he exclaimed; "you're always saying you'd do this and do that, but when the time comes you turn tail and sneak away. Look here: you were the one who proposed going into the Black Swan this morning, and when young Mouler said Allingford was coming, you slipped out of the back door and left us to face the shindy."

"Well," returned the other, laughing, "I thought you chaps were going to bolt too. I hopped over the wall at the back into the field, and waited there for about a quarter of an hour, and then, as no one came, I made tracks home."

"That's all very fine. You took precious good care to save your own bacon; you always do."

"Oh, go on!" answered Fletcher, rising from his chair; "you're in a wax to-night. Well, ta, ta! Don't you resign."

This little passage of arms was not the first of the kind that had taken place between Fletcher and Thurston, and it did not prevent a renewal of their friendship on the morrow.

The latter, following either his own inclination or the advice of his chum, decided not to resign his position as a prefect, and in a few days' time the majority of the school had wellnigh forgotten the fracas at the Black Swan.

Among those in high places, however, the affair was not so easily overlooked. The big fellows kept their own counsel, but it soon became evident that Thurston was being "cut" and cold-shouldered by the other members of the Sixth; while he, for his part, as though by way of retaliation, began to hob-nob more freely than ever with boys lower down in the school and of decidedly questionable character.

"It's awfully bad form of a chap who's a prefect chumming up with a fellow like Mouler in the Upper Fourth," said Carton one afternoon. "I wonder old 'Thirsty' isn't ashamed to do it. And now he's hand and glove with those chaps Hawley and Gull in the Fifth; they've both got heaps of money, but they're frightful cads."

From the morning following their return to Ronleigh

the Triple Alliance had been kept in a continual state of uneasiness and suspense, wondering what action Noaks would take regarding his discovery of their visit to The Hermitage.

The days passed by, and still he made no further reference to the matter, and took no notice of any of the three friends when he happened to pass them in the passages. The fact was that for the time being his attention was turned in another direction. Like most fellows of his kind, Noaks was a regular toady, ready to do anything in return for the privilege of being able to rub shoulders occasionally with some one in a higher position than himself, and he eagerly seized the opportunity which his friendship with Mouler afforded him of becoming intimate with Thurston. It was rather a fine thing for a boy in the Upper Fourth to be accosted in a familiar manner by a prefect, and asked sometimes to visit the latter in his study; and when such things were possible, it was hardly worth while to spend time and attention in carrying on a feud with youngsters in the Third Form. But Noaks had never forgotten the double humiliation he had suffered at Chatford - first in being sent off the football field, and again in the disastrous ending to the attempted raid on the Birchites' fireworks; nor had he forgiven the Triple Alliance for the part which they had played, especially on the latter occasion, in bringing shame and confusion on the heads of the Philistines.

One morning, nearly a month after the half-term holiday, the three friends were strolling arm in arm through the archway leading from the quadrangle to the paved playground, when they came face to face with their old enemy. He was about to push past them without speaking; then, seeming suddenly to change his mind, he pulled up, took something from his pocket, and handing it to Jack Vance, said shortly, -

"There! I thought you'd like to see that; it seems a good chance to earn some pocket-money."

The packet turned out to be a copy of the Todderton weekly paper.

"I've marked the place," added Noaks, turning on his heel with a sneering laugh; "you needn't give it me back."

A cross of blue chalk had been placed against a short paragraph appearing under the heading "Local Notes." Jack read it out loud for the edification of his two companions.

"We notice that Mr. Fossberry has offered a reward of 50 pounds for any information which shall lead to the arrest of the thieves who entered his house some few weeks ago, and stole a valuable collection of coins. As yet the police have been unable to discover any further traces of the missing property, but it is to be hoped that before long the offenders will be discovered and brought to justice."

There was a moment's silence.

"I wish I'd told my guv'nor," muttered Jack Vance.

"Well, tell him now," said Diggory.

"Oh no, I can't now; he'd wonder why I hadn't done it sooner. Besides, I believe Noaks is only doing this to frighten us; he can't prove that we stole the coins, because we didn't. All the same, it would be very awkward if he sent the police that jack-knife, and told them he'd seen us climbing out of the old chap's window."

"Yes," answered Diggory; "I suppose it would look rather fishy. Bother him! why can't he leave us alone?"

CHAPTER XI.

SHADOWS OF COMING EVENTS.

The Easter holidays came and went as rapidly as Easter holidays always do, and before the Alliance had recovered from the excitement connected with their first experience of breaking up at Ronleigh, they were back again, greeting their friends, asking new boys their names, and, in short, commencing their second term as regular old stagers. Up to the present they had been content to "lie low," and had remained satisfied with making the acquaintance of their class-mates in "The Happy Family;" but now they began to take more interest in school matters in general, and to notice what was going on in other circles besides their own.

In answer to the eager inquiries of his two companions, Jack Vance said that he had seen nothing of Noaks during the holidays, except having passed him on one or two occasions in the street. The notice of the fifty pounds reward still appeared in the windows of the police station; but the robbery itself was beginning to be looked upon as a thing of the past, and was already wellnigh forgotten.

"I wonder if Noaks has still got my knife?" said Mugford.

"Oh, I don't know," answered Jack. "He's too much taken up with Mouler and Gull and all that lot to think about us. I shouldn't bother my head about it any further; he only showed us that paper out of spite, to put us in a funk."

It was pretty evident, to the most casual observer, that the quarrel which the Black Swan incident had occasioned between Thurston and his brother prefects had not yet been dismissed from the minds of either party. The former became more lax than ever in the discharge of his duties, and avoiding the society of his school equals, sought the companionship of such boys as Hawley, Gull, and Mouler, who at length came to be known throughout the College as "Thirsty's Lot." With the exception of Fletcher, the prefects left him severely alone. Allingford occasionally came down on him for allowing all kinds of misconduct to pass unchecked, but it was hardly to be expected that a fellow who was hand and glove with some of the principal offenders should have much influence or power in maintaining law and order; and these interviews with the captain usually ended in an exchange of black looks and angry words.

The consequences which resulted from this lack of harmony among those in authority may be easily imagined. "Old Thirsty never makes a row when he sees a chap doing so-and-so," was the cry. "Why should Oaks and Rowlands and those other fellows kick up bothers, and give lines for the same thing?" To all these murmurers the prefects turned a deaf ear. "I don't care what Thurston does," would be their answer; "you know the rule, and that's sufficient." Any further remonstrance on the part of the offender was met with a summary "Shut up, or you'll get your head punched," and so for a time the matter ended.

It was hardly to be expected that the light-hearted juveniles of the Third Form should trouble their heads to take much notice of this disagreement among the seniors. For one thing, they knew nothing of what was said and done in the Sixth Form studies, and even the prefects themselves never thought for a moment that this little bit of friction in the machinery of Ronleigh College would, figuratively speaking, lead to "hot bearings" and a narrow shave of a general breakdown.

So the members of "The Happy Family" pursued the even tenor of their way, getting into scrapes and scrambling out of them, feasting on pastry and ginger-beer, turning up in force on Saturday afternoon to witness the cricket matches, and coming to the conclusion that though Oaks and Rowlands might be a trifle strict, and rather freehanded with lines and "impots," yet all this could be overlooked and forgiven for the sake of the punishment which they inflicted on the enemy's bowling.

As it has been all along the intention of this story to follow the fortunes of the Triple Alliance, the record of their second term at Ronleigh would not be complete without some mention of their memorable adventure with the "coffee-mill."

Wednesday, the fourteenth of June, was Jack Vance's birthday, and just before morning school he expressed his intention of keeping it up in a novel manner.

"Look here!" he remarked to his two companions. "You know that little bootmaker's shop just down the road, before you come to the church. There's a notice in the window, 'Double Tricycle on Hire.' Well, the mater's sent me some money this year instead of a hamper, so I thought I'd hire the machine; and we'll go out for a ride, and take it in turns for one to walk or trot behind."

"Oh, I'd advise you not to!" cried "Rats," who was standing by and overheard the project.

"Why not?"

"Why, it's a rotten old *sociable*, one of the first, I should think, that was ever made. It's like working a tread-mill, and it rattles and bangs about until you think every minute it must all be coming to pieces. It's got a sort of box-seat instead of a saddle. Maxton hired it out one day the term before last, and he and I and Collis rode to Chatton. It isn't meant to carry three; but the seat's very wide, and they squeezed me in between them. There's something wrong with the steering-gear, and it makes a beastly grinding noise as it goes along, so Maxton christened it the 'coffee-mill.' Fellows are always chaffing old Jobling about it, when they go into his shop to buy bits of leather, and asking him how much he'll take for his coffee-mill, and the old chap gets into an awful wax."

"Oh, I don't care!" answered Jack. "It'll be a lark, and we needn't go far. - What d'you say, Diggy?"

Diggory and Mugford both expressed their willingness to join in the expedition, and arrangements were accordingly made for it to take place that afternoon.

"You'd better not let old Jobling see three of you get on at once," said "Rats." "I should send Mugford on in front and pick him up when you get round the corner."

Rathson's description of the "coffee-mill" was certainly not exaggerated. It was a rusty, rattle-bag concern - a relic of the dark ages of cycling - and .looked as if it had not been used for a twelvemonth. Jobling squirted some oil into the bearings, knocked the dust off the cushioned seat, and remarked that a shilling an hour was the proper charge; but that, as he always favoured the Ronleigh gentlemen, he would say two shillings, and they might keep it the whole afternoon.

Jack, as we have said before, was of rather a nautical turn of mind, and occasionally, when the fit was on him, loved to interlard his conversation with seafaring expressions.

"She isn't much of a craft to look at," he remarked, as they drew up and dismounted at the spot where Mugford stood waiting for them; "but we'll imagine this is my steam-yacht, and that we're going for a cruise. Now then, Diggy, you're the mate, and you shall sit on the starboard side and steer. Mugford's the passenger, so he'll go in the middle. I'm captain, and I'll work the port treadles. Now, then, all aboard!"

The boys scrambled on to the seat, and with some little amount of crushing and squeezing got settled in their places, and at the captain's word, "Half-speed ahead!" the voyage commenced. They went lumbering and clattering through the outskirts of the town, and at length, after having roused the dormant wit of one shop-boy, who shouted "Knives to grind!" after them, they gained the highroad. For half a mile the voyage was prosperous enough; then the adventures began.

They were going at a good pace down a gentle slope, and on turning a corner saw immediately in front of them a narrow piece of road with a duck-pond on one side and a high bank on the other. Some one had carelessly left a wheelbarrow standing very nearly in the centre of the highway, and there was only just room to pass it on the water side.

"Starboard a little!"

The steering gear worked rather stiffly. Diggory gave the handle a hard twist, and it went round further than he intended.

"Port!" cried the captain, "hard a-port!" But it was too late, and the next moment the "coffee-mill" ran down the sloping bank and plunged into the duck-pond. It gave a violent lurch, but fortunately its breadth of beam kept it from overturning, and the water, being not more than a few inches deep, only wet the boots of the mariners.

"You great ass, Diggy! why didn't you *port?*" demanded the captain.

The mate, who as a matter of fact could not have told the difference between the nautical "port" and home-made ginger-beer, answered promptly, "So I did;" and the two officers commenced to punch each other with their disengaged hands. This combat, which was conducted with the utmost good feeling on both sides, had been continued for nearly a minute, when the passenger, on whose unoffending back a large proportion of the blows were falling, remarked, -

"Well, if we aren't going to stop here all day, when

you've quite done we'd better think about getting out."

They were at least four yards from the shore, and it was impossible to reach it dry-shod.

"Some one must take off his boots and socks and haul her out," said Diggory.

"Well, I can't," answered Jack; "the captain never ought to leave the ship."

"Oh, I'll go," answered Mugford, laughing; and accordingly, after performing some complicated gymnastic feats in getting off his boots, he slid from the seat into the water, and so hauled the "coffee-mill" back to *terra firma*.

It would be impossible to describe in detail all the alarming incidents which happened during the outward passage.

They had not gone a quarter of a mile further when something went wrong with the brake. They flew down a long hill, holding on for dear life, nothing but the grand way in which the mate managed this time to steer a straight course down the middle of the road saving them from destruction. Nevertheless, mounting the last slope was such hard labour that Mugford had to turn to and "work his passage," by every now and again taking a spell at the treadles.

"Look here!" said Diggory at length: "don't you think we've gone far enough? we shan't be back in time for tea."

"Oh, I forgot," answered the captain. "We'll see. Stand

by your anchor! Let go-o-o!"

The "coffee-mill" stopped, and Jack Vance pulled out his watch.

"By me it's half-past twelve, and I'm four hours slow: twelve to one, one to two, two to three, three to four - half-past four. Yes, it's time we turned round. Now, then, 'bout ship!"

The tricycle clanked and rattled away merrily enough on the return journey until it came to the long hill, which this time had to be climbed instead of descended.

"Don't let's get off," said Jack; "we ought to rush her up this if we set our minds to it."

With a great deal of panting and struggling they succeeded in getting about half-way; then suddenly there was a crack, and the machine, instead of going forward, began to run back. Faster and faster it went, the pedals remaining motionless under their feet.

"The chain's gone," gasped the captain. "There's a cart behind! Quick, run her aground!"

Of course the mate turned the handle the wrong way. On one side of the road was an ordinary hedge, while on the other lay a deep ditch, and into this a moment later the "coffee-mill" disappeared with every soul on board!

There was an awful moment, when earth, sky, arms, legs, wheels, and bushes seemed all mixed together, and then Jack Vance found himself resting on his hands and knees in a puddle of dirty water. Diggory and Mugford had been driven with considerable violence into the thickest part of a thorn hedge, and proceeded to extricate themselves therefrom with many groans and lamentations.

"Well," said the mate, as they proceeded to drag the machine out of the ditch, "I should think, Jack, you've celebrated your birthday about enough; now you'd better give over, or we shall all be sent home in a sack."

"Me!" cried the captain, with great indignation. "It was *your* fault, you dummy! you put the helm over wrong again, you - "

"Hullo, you kids!" interrupted a voice behind them, and turning round the three friends saw the burly form of John Acton pushing a bicycle up the hill. "Hullo!" he continued; "it's young Trevanock. What's up? Have you had a spill?"

"Yes; the chain broke, and we ran into the ditch."

"Umph! bad business. Now you'll have to foot it, I suppose."

"Yes," answered Jack ruefully; "and we're bound to be back late pushing this old thing all the way. I wish old Jobling would try a ride on it himself."

"Oh! is that the 'coffee-mill'?" exclaimed the prefect, laughing. "Well, look here! If you're late, I'll see whoever's on duty, and tell him about the breakdown, and see if I can get you off."

"Oh, thanks awfully!" chorused the small boys.

"I've half a mind to say I wouldn't," continued Acton, looking round as he put his foot on the step of his machine, and nodding his head at Diggory. "I owe you a grudge for not telling me what I wanted to know about my young brother's love-letter."

The football captain was as good as his word: he got the Triple Alliance excused the "impot" which would otherwise have been awarded them for arriving at the school half an hour late, and the only misfortune which resulted from their eventful excursion was that Jack Vance had to expend a further portion of his postal order in paying Jobling for repairing the broken chain. The day, however, did not close without another incident happening to one of the voyagers, which, though trifling in itself, proved, as it were, the shadow of coming events which were destined to seriously affect the well-being and happiness of all the Ronleigh boys.

Crossing the quadrangle soon after tea, Diggory saw something bright lying on the gravel; it proved to be a silver match-box with the letters C. T. engraved on the front. He took it with him into the school-room, and holding it up as the boys were assembling at their desks for preparation, asked if any one knew who was the owner.

"Yes, I do," answered young Fletcher: "it's Thirsty's; I've seen it often."

Preparation of the next day's work having ended, Diggory's attention was occupied for a time in discussing with Carton the merits of some foreign stamps. Just before supper, however, he remembered the match-box, and hurried away to restore it to its rightful owner.

Thurston was evidently at home, for a prolonged shout of laughter and the clamour of several voices reached Diggory's ears as he approached the study. As he knocked at the door the noise suddenly ceased, there was a moment's silence, and then a murmur in a low tone, followed by a scuffling of feet and the overturning of a chair.

"Who's there? you can't come in!" shouted the owner of the den.

"I don't want to," answered Diggory, through the keyhole. "I've brought your match-box that I picked up in the 'quad.'"

"Oh, it's only a kid," said the voice of Fletcher senior; and the next instant the door was unlocked by Thurston, who opened it about six inches, and immediately thrust his body into the aperture, as though to prevent the possibility of the visitor getting any sight of the interior of the room.

"Oh, thanks; you're a brick," he said, taking the box, and immediately closed the door and turned the key.

Diggory was retracing his steps along the passage, wondering what could be the object of all this secrecy, when he nearly ran into the school captain.

"Hullo, young man!" said the latter, "where have you been?"

"To Thurston's study."

"What have you been there for?" demanded Allingford sharply, with a sudden change in his tone and manner.

"Only to give him his match-box that I picked up in the 'quad.'"

The captain eyed the speaker narrowly, as though half inclined to doubt the truth of this explanation; then, apparently satisfied with the honest expression of the small boy's face, told him to get down to supper.

The latter wandered off, wondering more than ever what could have been the object of the private gathering in Thurston's study which he had just interrupted.

"It's what I told you before," remarked Carton, when Diggory chanced to mention what had happened. "Thirsty's going to the dogs, and I believe big Fletcher's got a lot to do with it. Allingford can't interfere with them as long as they keep to themselves. I don't know what they do, but I shouldn't be surprised if there is a rare old kick-up one of these fine days."

Mischief certainly was brewing, and the "kick-up" came sooner than even Carton himself expected.

CHAPTER XII.

THE WRAXBY MATCH.

Wednesday, the twenty-fourth of July, saw the whole of Ronleigh College in a state of bustle and excitement. The near approach of the holidays was sufficient in itself to put every one in high spirits, while, in addition to this, the afternoon was to witness the chief cricket contest of the season - the annual match against Wraxby Grammar School. During the hour before dinner the ground itself was a scene of brisk activity: the school colours flew at the summit of the flagstaff; the boundary flags fluttered in the breeze; a number of willing hands, under the direction of Allingford, put a finishing touch to the pitch with the big roller, while others assisted in rigging up the two screens of white canvas in line with the wickets.

"I do hope we lick them," said little "Rats" to Jack Vance as they stood by the pavilion, watching Oaks mixing some whiting for the creases; "we *must* somehow or other."

"Why?"

"Why? because they've beaten us now three times running; and the last time when our chaps went over to Wraxby and got licked at footer their captain asked

Ally if in future we should like to play a master! Such rot!" continued the youthful "Rats," boiling with wrath; "as if we couldn't smash them without! Look here, I'd give - I'd give sixpence if we could win!" and with this burst of patriotic enthusiasm the speaker hurried away to join Maxton, who, with an old sprung racquet in one hand and the inside of an exploded cricket-ball in the other, was calling to him from the adjoining playing field to "Come and play tip and run, and bring something that'll do for a wicket."

The feelings expressed by "Rats" as regards the result of the match were shared by the whole school, and by none more so than the members of the Third Form.

"The Happy Family" turned up to a man, and encamped *en masse* upon the turf within twenty yards of the pavilion. Bibbs was the last to arrive on the scene of action, and did so with a bag of sweets in one hand, a book in the other, and a piece of paper, pinned by some joker to the tail of his coat, bearing the legend, "Please to kick me" - a request which was immediately responded to in a most hearty and generous fashion by all present.

Kicking the unfortunate Bibbs afforded every one such exquisite enjoyment that an effort was made to prolong the pastime by forcible attempts to fasten the placard on to other members of the company, and a general *melee*, would have followed if the attention of the combatants had not been attracted in another direction. Ronleigh having won the toss and elected to go in first, the Wraxby men strolled out of the pavilion to take the field.

They were a likely-looking lot of fellows - the faded

flannel caps and careless way in which they sauntered towards the pitch proclaiming the fact that each one was a veteran player.

"That chap with the wicket-keeping gloves in his hand is Partridge, their captain," said Carton; "and that fellow who's putting out the single stump to bowl at is Austin. He does put them in to some tune; you can hardly see the ball, it's so swift."

There was a faint *clang* from the pitch.

"See that!" cried Fletcher junior: "that chap Austin's knocked that single stump out of the ground first ball. My eye, he'll make our fellows sit up, I'll bet."

"No, he won't," cried "Rats" excitedly. "Old Ally'll knock him into a cocked hat. He'll soon break his back," added the speaker complaisantly. "Hullo! men in - Parkes and Rowland."

There is something in the short space of time preceding the first *clack* of the bat at a cricket match which rivals in interest even that exciting moment at football when the centre forward stands hovering over the ball waiting for the whistle to give the signal for the contest to commence.

The noisy clatter of "The Happy Family" ceases as the crowd of boys, ranged all down the sides of the field, turn to watch the opening of the game.

It is an ideal day for cricket, with a fresh breeze blowing, just sufficient to temper the hot afternoon sunshine and cause a flutter of cricket-shirts and boundary flags. Rowland takes centre, twists the handle of his bat round and round in his hands, and is heard amid the general hush to say, "No, no trial." Austin glances round at the motionless figures of his comrades, signals to *long-on* to stand a little deeper, and then delivers the ball. With an easy and graceful forward stroke, the batsman returns it sharply in the direction of the opposite wicket, and an almost imperceptible movement, like the releasing of a spring, takes place among the fielders. So begins the battle.

"Twenty up!" had just been called from the pavilion when a sharp catch in the slips disposed of Parkes.

"Never mind!" cried "Rats." "Here comes old Ally; he'll make them trot round a bit!"

The captain commenced his innings with a heart-warming leg hit, which sent the ball to the boundary, a wave of legs and arms marking its track as the spectators, with a joyous yell, rolled over one another to escape being hit.

For some time cheer followed cheer, and "The Happy Family" clapped until their hands smarted; then suddenly there arose a prolonged "*Oh, oh!*" from all the field.

"Hullo! what's the matter?" asked Bibbs, looking up from the book he was reading.

"What's the matter?" shouted Maxton wrathfully, snatching away the volume and banging Bibbs on the head with it. "Why don't you watch the game? Old Ally's bowled off his pads!"

It was only too true: the captain's wicket was down,

and "The Happy Family," after a simultaneous ejaculation of "*Blow it!*" tore up stalks of grass, and began to chew them with a stern expression on their faces.

This disaster seemed but the forerunner of others. Redfern, the next man, had hardly taken his place at the wicket when a sharp *click*, the glitter of bails twirling in the air, and a Wraxby shout of "Well bowled!" announced his fate; while ten minutes later Rowland, one of the mainstays of the home team, was caught in a most provoking manner at *cover-point*.

"Oh, bother it all!" sighed "Rats;" "this is nothing but a procession."

"Now, Oaks, old chap, do your best for us!" cried Allingford.

"All right," returned the other, laughing, as he paused for a moment outside the pavilion to fasten the strap of his batting-glove; "I'm going to make runs this journey, or die in the attempt."

Oaks was undoubtedly a regular Briton, just the sort of fellow to turn the fortunes of a losing game. He walked up to the wicket as coolly as though it were enclosed within a practice net, patted down the ground with the flat of his bat in a manner which seemed to imply that he had "come to stay," and then proceeded to hit three twos in his first "over."

This dashing commencement was but the prelude to a brilliant bit of rapid scoring: twos and threes followed each other in quick succession. Allingford shouted, the crowd roared, while "The Happy Family" gambolled about on one another's chests and stomachs, and squealed with delight. Like the poet's brook, Oaks might have exclaimed, "Men may come, and men may go, but I go on for ever." When Wraxby changed the bowling, he welcomed the new-comer by sending the first ball into the next field, and continued to cut and drive in such a gallant manner that even Bibbs, standing up to get the full use of his lungs, shouted, "Go 'long!" and "Well hit!" until his face was the colour of a poppy.

"I say!" exclaimed Carton, as the eighth wicket fell, "I wish one of these next two chaps would hang on a bit, and give Oaks a chance of getting a few more; it must be nearly eighty up."

"Thurston, you're in!" came from the scorer.

The boy named was sitting by himself, on the end of a form close to the telegraph, moodily scraping up the ground with the spikes of his cricket-shoes. He knew that most of his comrades in the eleven would give him the cold shoulder, and so did not mingle with them inside the pavilion. He rose, and prepared to obey the summons.

"Let's give him a cheer," said "Rats;" "he may do something. - Go it, Thurston! Sit tight, and keep the pot boiling!"

The big fellow turned his head in the direction of "The Happy Family," and with something of the old good-humoured smile, which had seldom of late been seen upon his face, answered: "All right, my boy, you see if I don't."

"Jolly fellow old Thirsty," remarked "Rats," swelling

Harold Avery

with pride at this friendly recognition. "He can play when he likes, but he hasn't troubled to practise much of late. He used always - Phew! my eye, what an awful crack!"

A terrifically swift ball from Austin had risen suddenly from the hard ground. Thurston had no time to avoid it, but turning away his face, received the blow on the back of his head. He dropped his bat, staggered away from the wicket, and fell forward on his knees.

To suffer for the cause of the school in a cricket or football match was a thing which, like charity, "covered a multitude of sins." Allingford hurried out of the pavilion and ran towards the pitch, while Partridge and a few more of the "Wraxby men gathered round their wounded opponent and helped him to his feet.

"You'd better come out, Thurston," said the Ronleigh captain; "I'll send the next man in."

"No, I'll go on," replied the other, in rather a shaky voice; "I shall be all right in a minute."

It requires something more than ordinary pluck for a batsman to stand up to fast bowling and show good form after having been badly hit. For a time a great deal of determination, and the exercise of a considerable amount of will power, are necessary to conquer the natural inclination to shrink from a possible repetition of the injury; and those who watched the dogged manner in which Thurston continued to defend his wicket, being themselves practical cricketers, rewarded him with loud shouts of encouragement and praise.

Oaks piled on the score with unflagging energy, while the careful play of his companion defied all attempts of the Wraxby bowlers to dissolve the partnership.

"Bravo, 'Thirsty!'" shouted the spectators. "Go 'long' - and another!"

At length, just as the telegraph operator had received the welcome order, "A hundred up!" the ball shot, and crashed into Thurston's wicket. He came slowly back from the pitch, still holding his hand to the back of his head; and though his individual score had barely run into double figures, he was greeted on all sides with hearty cheers.

Payne, the last man, just succeeded in cracking his *duck's-egg*, and the innings closed for 104.

As the fielders came trooping in, a small boy ran past the Third Form encampment exclaiming, "I say, you chaps, old Punch is in the lower road, over by that tree!" Which announcement had no sooner been made than the greater part of "The Happy Family" sprang to their feet, and went scampering across the field in the direction of the opposite hedge.

The cause of this stampede, it must be explained, was the arrival of an itinerant vendor of ice-cream, whose real name, Samuel Jones, had been changed to Punch on account of the prominence of his nasal organ. His presence within the grounds of Ronleigh College was not approved of by the authorities, and his trade with the small boys, who were his particular patrons, was carried on through a gap in the hedge. Punch's establishment ran on four wheels, and was ornamented with a number of daubs representing Union Jacks and

Royal Standards, which formed the framework of an alarming portrait of the Prince of Wales, from which adornment one might be led to suppose that on some previous occasion His Royal Highness had patronized the stall. The ice-cream was shovelled out of a tin receptacle, and pasted in lumps on to the top of very shallow glasses, the standard price for which was one penny; and there being a scarcity of spoons, the customers usually devoured the delicacy in the same manner as a dog does a saucer of milk. Cynical members of the upper classes at Ronleigh, who had ceased to patronize the stall, charged Punch with not being over-particular in washing the glasses, and of making the "stuff," as they called it, with cornflour instead of cream. But the small boys were not fastidious; and as each one had two helpings, which they ate as slowly as possible to prolong the enjoyment, they were still refreshing themselves when the home team moved out to field.

"Look sharp!" cried "Rats," giving Bibbs's elbow a sudden jerk which caused that worthy to plaster the end of his nose with the remains of his third ice. "Come on! let's see the beginning."

The second half of the game proved, if anything, more exciting than the first. Two wickets fell before 10 appeared on the telegraph.

"Oh, we shall lick them easily!" cried "Rats" jubilantly; while Fletcher junior gave vent to his feelings by handing Bibbs's bag of sweets round to the company.

But there were still some hard nuts to be cracked in the Wraxby team, and one soon appeared in Partridge, the captain. Over after over went by, and the score rapidly increased: "Thirty up!" - "Forty up!" - "Fifty up!" Two more wickets were taken; but Partridge seemed to have fairly got his eye in, and gave the home team as much leather-hunting as Oaks had provided for the visitors. To make matters worse, Austin, arriving on the scene sixth man in, appeared to be also possessed with a determination to carry his bat; and though he was eventually run out by a sharp throw-in from square-leg, it was not until eighty runs had been registered for the Grammar School.

The closing scene of the game caused an amount of excitement unparalleled in the history of Ronleigh cricket.

As the last man of the Wraxby team went in to bat, the telegraph was changed from 90 to 100. "Over" had just been called, and the invincible Partridge stepped forward to play, evidently making up his mind for another boundary hit. Thurston had been put on to bowl at the top end, and stood ready to recommence the attack.

"Four to equal, five to beat," sighed "Rats." "Bother it all, they're sure to win."

A cricket match needs to be very narrowly watched, or the spectator whose eye has strayed for a moment from the game misses some fine piece of play. The incident which finished the contest between Ronleigh College and Wraxby Grammar School occupied barely three seconds of time; yet it was remembered and spoken about many years after those concerned in it had passed on to swell the ranks of the "old boys."

Partridge commenced the over with a hard, straight drive, and at the same instant Thurston gave a little jump into the air with his right arm stretched above his head. The ball had passed like lightning between the wickets, and the spectators looked for a moment to see where it had gone; then a wild shriek of joy from "The Happy Family" rent the air, -

"Caught!"

It was true enough. With a splendid one-handed catch Thurston had brought the well-fought contest to a close, and secured a victory for Ronleigh College.

This brilliant feat, coupled with the gallant manner in which he had continued his innings when hurt, and so enabled Oaks to run up the score, caused the black sheep of the Sixth Form to be regarded as the hero of the day. Allingford shook him by the hand, and a noisy crowd hoisted him shoulder high and carried him three times round the quadrangle.

Thurston certainly had good reason to feel proud of the part he had played in the chief match of the season, and might in years to come have always looked back with pleasure on this twenty-fourth of July. Unfortunately another event of a sadly different character was destined to make it a red-letter day in his career at Ronleigh. The feeling of respect and good-will which his prowess in the field had awakened in the minds of his former friends afforded him a splendid opportunity for reassociating himself with all that was worthy and honourable in school life. The chance no sooner presented itself, however, than it was flung away, and was lost for ever.

Evening preparation was over, and supper, an informal meal, attendance at which was not compulsory, was in progress. The door of Thurston's study was once more locked on the inside, as it had been when Diggory went to return the match-box to its rightful owner.

Fletcher senior, Hawley, and Gull sat on three sides of the small table, while Thurston himself occupied the fourth.

"Hang it all!" exclaimed the latter, throwing down a handful of playing cards upon the table, and pushing back his chair. "I shan't play any more to-night; I've got no more tin."

"Oh, go on; I'll lend you some," answered Fletcher. "I don't care whether I win or lose; it's only the game I play for."

As a matter of fact, Fletcher nearly always *did* win, and was mightily displeased on the rare occasions when he lost.

"No; I've borrowed enough already," returned the other. "I shan't be able to square up as it is till next term. It's all very well for fellows like you three, who have rich people, and can write home any time for a fiver; but I'm not so flush of cash. - Look here, Gull, have you got that banjo? Sing us a song."

"All right," answered Gull, reaching down and picking a small five-stringed instrument off the floor; "what'll you have?"

"Oh, something with a good swing to it. I feel like kicking up a row."

Gull tuned up, struck a few chords, and then launched out into a rattling nigger song with an amount of "go" and clatter sufficient to inspire the hearer with an almost irresistible desire to get up and dance. The three listeners shouted the chorus at the top of their voices, pounding the table with their fists by way of a sort of drum accompaniment. Gull was just preparing to commence the fourth verse when there was a knock at the study door.

"Wait a jiff," said Thurston. - "Who's there? What d'you want?"

"Why," came the answer, uttered in rather a drawling tone, "I wish you fellows wouldn't make so much row. I can't possibly work. Do be quiet."

"Oh, go to Bath!" shouted Thurston. - "It's only that old stew-pot Browse," he added. "The beggar's got the next study, and he's cramming up for some 'exam.' - Go on, Gull."

The entertainment continued, and waxed more noisy than ever, the performers hammering the table with a ruler and two walking-sticks to add zest to the choruses.

Soon there came another interruption, very different in tone from the mild expostulation of the studious Browse. The door was violently shaken, and from without came the sharp, peremptory order of the school captain, -

"Look here, Thurston, just shut up; we've had enough of this horrible row for one night. Stop it, d'you hear?"

"All right," growled the owner of the study; "keep your hair on, old fellow!"

"Sh! steady on, Thirsty," said Fletcher, in a low tone. "Don't go too far, or he'll put a stop to our next merry meeting. I know Allingford, and he's rather a hard wall to run your head against."

"That confounded old Browse has gone and sneaked!" cried the other, with a flush of passion on his face. "Let's wait till Ally's gone, and then make a raid on the old stew-pot."

Hawley and Gull sprang to their feet with a murmur of assent; Fletcher shrugged his shoulders and remained silent.

"What we'll do is this," continued Thurston. "He sits with his back to the door. I'll pop in first and throw this tablecloth over his head; then, while I hold him down, you chaps upset the things and put out the light. Then we'll rush out all together, and he won't know for certain who did it."

Five minutes later the conspirators crept out into the passage, and tip-toed towards the door of the adjoining study. Fletcher lingered behind, and, instead of following the expedition, stole softly away in the opposite direction. Another moment, and the unfortunate Browse was struggling to rise from his chair, with his head enveloped in the tablecloth. Hawley and Gull, following immediately in rear of their leader, sent the table, with its load of books and writing materials, over with a crash, threw the chairs into different corners of the room, and were about to scatter the contents of the bookcase over the floor, when Allingford suddenly burst into the room, and stood glaring round like an angry lion.

With one swing of his right arm he sent Thurston staggering against the wall, and then, stepping forward without an instant's hesitation, he dealt each of the other marauders a swinging box on the ear.

The two Fifth Form boys were big, strong fellows, and for a moment it seemed as though a stand-up fight would ensue. The captain, however, followed up his attack with amazing promptness, and before his antagonists had time to think of resistance he had taken them both by the shoulders and sent them flying into the passage.

"There!" he exclaimed. "I'll teach you gentlemen to come playing pranks on Sixth Form studies. What business have you got here, I should like to know? - As for you," continued the speaker, casting a scornful glance at the originator of the outrage, "I should have thought a fellow who's a prefect ought to know better than to go rioting with every scamp in the school."

Thurston's conduct on the cricket field had clearly proved him to be no coward. He stood his ground, and returned Allingford's angry glances with a look of fierce defiance. He attempted to make some reply, but somehow the words failed him, and turning on his heel he walked away to his own study.

"Confound that fellow Fletcher!" he muttered between his teeth. "He always takes precious good care to sneak away when there's any row on. If it wasn't for that money I owe him, I'd punch his head."

Half an hour later there was a sharp rap at the door, and Allingford, Oaks, and Acton entered the room.

"Well," said Thurston, looking up with a frown from the book he was reading, "what d'you want now? I don't remember asking you fellows to come and see me. A chap can't call his study his own nowadays."

"No," answered Acton grimly. "If a chap wants to work, a lot of blackguards come and wreck his furniture."

"Look here, Thurston," said the captain coldly, "we've no wish to stay here longer than we can help. We've come simply to tell you this - that after what's happened to-night the prefects are determined that to-morrow morning you send in your resignation to the doctor."

"And supposing I don't choose to send in my resignation?" returned the other.

"Then," answered the captain calmly, "we shall send it in for you."

There was a moment's silence; then Thurston rose from his chair, and closing his book flung it down with a bang upon the table.

"All right," he said; "I'll do it. You fellows have been set against me from the first. I know all about it, and before I leave this place I'll pay you out."

"I almost wish we'd left it till after the holidays," said Oaks, as the three prefects walked down the passage.

"No," said Allingford firmly; "if we hesitate, and the fellows see it, we're lost. It must be done at once."

"Well, perhaps so," answered Oaks; "but I'll tell you this - Thurston means mischief. I wish he was going to leave. He won't forget this ina hurry, and my belief is we shall hear more about it next term."

CHAPTER XIII.

THE ELECTIONS.

Thurston's resignation, as might have been expected, gave rise to a considerable amount of excitement and conflicting opinion. Nearly every boy in the school saw clearly that he was both unworthy and unfitted to fulfil the duties of a prefect, but the peculiar circumstances under which he had, as "Rats" put it, been given "notice to quit," caused a large number of his schoolfellows to side with him, and condemn the action of the captain. Only a few of the general public knew exactly what the row had been. The Sixth Form authorities, refusing to be catechized, would answer no questions; while the other side took good care to spread abroad a very one-sided account of the affair.

The Wraxby match was fresh in everybody's mind. "Awfully hard lines I call it," said the cricketers. "He won that game for us; why didn't they let him go on a few days more till the end of the term?" While those young gentlemen, of whom a few are to be found in every school, who cherish a strong dislike to anything in the shape of law and order, were, of course, loud in their expressions of dissatisfaction at the removal of one who always winked at their transgressions.

At the commencement of the winter session it soon

became evident that seven weeks of summer holiday had not dispelled the cloud which had overshadowed the close of the previous term. No sooner had the first excitement of meeting and settling down subsided a little than the question of Thurston's deposal cropped up again, and caused an unusual amount of interest to be felt by all Ronleigh in the forthcoming elections.

Every school has its own methods of choosing those who are to fill the posts and offices in connection with its various institutions, and it will be well to describe, in a few words, how this was done at Ronleigh, in order that the reader may follow with greater interest the working out of an important event in the history of the college.

The elections took place twice a year - at the commencement of the summer and winter terms - their chief object being to appoint what was known as the Sports Committee (who had the management of athletics and of the forthcoming cricket or football season), two librarians, and a keeper of the reading-room. In addition to this, when any of the prefects left, fresh ones were chosen in their places. Only members of the Sixth Form were eligible for this office, which was not conferred before the choice of the boys had been confirmed by the sanction of the head-master, and was understood to last for the remainder of the recipient's school life.

On the second or third morning of the term a paper was posted up on the notice-board in the big schoolroom, announcing the fact that the elections would take place two days later, and mentioning exactly what each voter was required to do. Every boy who had been two terms at the school received a voting paper, which he filled up at his leisure and handed over to the returning officers at a special assembly called for the purpose.

At the commencement of this particular winter term the school reassembled on a Tuesday, and on Thursday notice was given that the elections would take place on the following Saturday afternoon.

According to the usual custom, when fresh prefects were to be chosen, the names of all the Sixth Form boys who were not already holding that office were mentioned on the notice, to show who were eligible for the position. Thurston's name did not appear on the list; some one added it in pencil, another hand crossed it out, and an hour or two later it was added again, this time in red ink.

This simple action seemed the signal for a general agitation on Thurston's behalf. His friends throughout the school openly proclaimed their intention of voting for him, and exhorted others to do the same. Almost to a man the Sixth and Remove sided with the captain, but Hawley and Gull in the Fifth, Noaks and Mouler in the Upper Fourth, and other fellows in the lower forms made up their minds to secure Thurston's return, and set to work to carry out their project with a zeal worthy of a better cause.

Two fresh prefects were required, and the friends of law and order were unanimous in naming Fielding and Parkes as the most suitable candidates to fill the vacancies. Rival posters appeared on the double doors leading to the playground: -

REMEMBER THE WRAXBY MATCH,

AND

VOTE FOR THURSTON.

PLUMP FOR PARKES,

AND HAVE A

PROPER PREFECT.

But this method of carrying on the campaign was soon brought into disrepute, owing to the fact that certain juveniles, seeing in this new idea of bill-posting a fresh field for practical joking, began to adorn the walls of the "grub-room," and other spaces which did not often come under the eye of a master, with placards exhibiting inscriptions which had no bearing on the elections - such irrelevant remarks as, "nooks Two wants kicking !" or, "*Lost*-my wits. (Signed) B. BIBBS," being calculated to occasion a considerable amount of strife and bad blood without serving any useful purpose.

The Lower School was in a fever heat of excitement, and it is quite possible that the little pleasantries which have just been alluded to were occasioned by difference of opinion on the one absorbing topic of the day. The close of the previous holidays had witnessed a general parliamentary election, and with the details of contests which had taken place in their native towns vividly impressed upon their minds, the younger boys, from the Lower Fourth downwards, threw themselves into the present conflict with an amount of energy and spirit which was not to be found in the more sober and deliberate action of their seniors.

The greater number of the old "Happy Family" had now been removed into the Lower Fourth, and this form in particular was rent with opposing views, and shaken with continued outbursts of hostility between the rival factions. The Triple Alliance were loyal to the old *regime*, and were supported by "Rats," Carton, and several of their old friends.

"Acton saved us from getting into a row after that 'coffee-mill' business," remarked Diggory.

"Rowland gave Noaks a dressing down when he hit me in the mouth," said Jack Vance.

"And old Ally boxed Mouler's ears when they made me upset that paint," added Mugford.

"Rats" declared that he meant to conduct what he called a "house-to-house visitation," and accordingly, beginning at the bottom of the form, the first person he called upon was Grundy, a great lout of sixteen, who had been at the tail end of the Lower Fourth for the last twelve months. As it happened, Grundy was a strong partisan of the opposite side, and not only refused to vote for Parkes, but, seizing hold of the unfortunate canvasser, proceeded to twist his arms and pinch his ears for daring to oppose the election of Thurston.

Fletcher Two, whose sympathies, as might have been expected, were with his brother's chum, organized open-air meetings in one corner of the field where the big cricket-roller could be used as a platform. But here, again, the love of larking which is so characteristic of the lawless small boy came into evidence, and with that touch of nature which makes the whole world kin, friend and foe alike joined in the spree of interrupting the proceedings. Just when the orator had reached the most important point in his harangue, and was pouring forth a torrent of impassioned eloquence, the platform would begin to move, or the audience would insist on turning the gathering into an imaginary "scrum," and almost crushing the life out of those who happened to be in the middle of the crowd.

Poor Bibbs especially became a target for the humour of the electors. According to Fletcher's instructions, he had written out a speech and learned it by heart; but though he was being continually called upon to deliver it, he never got beyond the opening "Ahem! Gentlemen," before a sudden movement of the platform precipitated him into the arms of his irreverent hearers, or a shout of "Play up at the cocoanuts!" followed by a shower of acorns, bits of stick, and pieces of turf, caused him to jump down and hastily seek shelter behind the roller.

For two days, especially in the Lower School, the excitement continued steadily to increase, and small boys being seized in out-of-the-way corners were made to assert at one time that they would vote for Thurston, and at another that they would vote for Parkes or Fielding, and so, in order to escape with a whole skin, were forced to commit perjury at least a dozen times between the hours of breakfast and tea.

One incident, which as far as the Lower Fourth was concerned tended considerably to embitter the contest, is worthy of record as a notable feature of this memorable campaign.

The occupants of dormitory No. 13 were rabid Thurstonians; dormitory No. 14, on the other hand, in which slept the Triple Alliance, Maxton, "Rats," and Carton, were to a man supporters of Parkes and Fielding. On Friday evening the two doors, which were exactly opposite to each other, being left open, the process of undressing was enlivened by a continual fire of abuse and insulting remarks, which might have led to a regular scrimmage between the two parties if the presence of the prefect, patrolling the passage, had not prevented either side from advancing beyond the threshold of their own doorway.

"I wouldn't vote for a chap like Thurston, who goes boozing in a common 'pub' like the Black Swan," cried "Rats;" "but that's just the sort of man for you. You're a cheap lot, the whole crew of you!"

"Look here, young 'Rats,'" retorted Fletcher junior from the opposite room, wandering rather wide of the subject in hand. "Why don't you write home and ask your people to buy you a new pair of braces, instead of mending those old ones up with string? You look just like a young street arab, and that's about what you are!"

"Don't you fellows talk about broken braces, and looking like street arabs," cried Diggory, "when only yesterday old Greyling sent Stokes out of class and told him to go down to the lavatory and wash his face. That's a sample of you Thurstonians!"

"Look here!" shouted the boy alluded to, springing out of bed, and appearing in his night-shirt at the opposite end of the dormitory. "You know very well that Grundy flipped a pen full of ink over me, and that was why I had to go out and wash my face."

"I know you looked altogether a different fellow when you came back," returned Jack Vance: "I hardly knew you!"

There was a momentary pause in the discussion, and Bibbs, thinking this a suitable opportunity for the delivery of his speech, stepped forward, and took up his stand in the doorway. Hardly, however, had he pronounced the opening "Ahem! Gentlemen," when a cake of soap, flung by Maxton, struck him a violent blow in the pit of the stomach, and he was still rolling and groaning on his bed in the throes of recovering his lost wind when the prefect arrived to turn out the light.

The occupants of the two dormitories lay down, but not to sleep.

"You mark my word," said Diggory, "as soon as the prefects have gone down to supper those chaps from over the way'll come across and pay us out for throwing that soap. We'd better put a chair against the door."

"Look here!" remarked Fletcher junior to his room-mates. "I shouldn't be at all surprised if Maxton and those other fellows in No. 14 come over and try to rag us; let's lie awake a bit and listen."

For half an hour all was quiet and still, and the watchers in No. 14 were turning over and preparing to go to sleep, when "Rats" started up, exclaiming in a whisper, "They're coming! I heard some one in the passage. There 'tis again! Jump up, you chaps, and let's make a sortie."

Now, strange to say, an exactly similar alarm had just been given by Fletcher junior in No. 13, and the reason was simply as follows: - Mr. Greyling, the master of the Lower Fourth, in walking towards his bedroom in slippered feet, was seized with a sneezing fit, and halting just outside the two dormitories, gave vent to his feelings with a loud "Et-chow!" After a moment's pause he sneezed again, and had hardly done so before both doors were suddenly flung open, and with a cry of "Ah, you sneaks!" and another of "Come on, you blackguards!" a crowd of white-robed figures rushed out, brandishing pillows and startling Mr. Greyling to such a degree that he exclaimed "Great Scott!" and dropped his candle.

What followed is too sad to be related in detail. Mr. Greyling scattered largess in the shape of lines among the crowd, and the next day the occupants of the two dormitories went about thirsting for each other's blood.

On Saturday, just before morning school, the voting papers were collected, and directly after dinner the boys assembled to hear the result of the poll. According to the usual custom, no masters were present. Allingford presided, and the excitement was intense.

A hush of expectation fell on the crowded room as the captain mounted the platform on which stood the head-master's desk. Up to the present time elections at Ronleigh had been little more than a matter of form, but on this occasion every one felt that something more was at stake than the mere distribution of the school offices.

"Gentlemen, the business of this meeting, as you are

very well aware, is to announce the result of the elections.

"The following," continued Allingford, referring to the paper which he held in his hand, "have been chosen to act as the Sports Committee: Myself chairman, Oaks, Acton, Rowland, Parkes, Redfern, and Hoyle.

"The two former librarians, Clarkson and Lang, have been re-elected.

"Dale, who for some time past held the position of keeper of the reading-room, having left, the choice of a successor has fallen between Lucas and Ferris, who, singularly enough, both received the same number of votes. Each of these gentlemen being equally ready to withdraw in the other's favour, I exercised my prerogative as captain of the school, and gave the casting vote in favour of Lucas."

At this there was a slight murmur among the audience, though whether of dissent or approval it was impossible to tell. The interruption was only momentary, for every one was too much interested in the next announcement to care much what became of the post of keeper of the reading-room.

"As you all know, two vacancies have occurred among the prefects, to fill which the following gentlemen have been chosen, and their election duly sanctioned by the head-master: Parkes and Fielding."

The words had hardly passed the speaker's lips when the whole room was in an uproar. Cheers, howls, whistling, and the stamping of feet filled the air with an indescribable din; members of the Lower Fourth fought one another across the desks; and it was some minutes before Allingford could obtain sufficient silence to enable him to finish his speech.

"This," he said, in conclusion, "is the result of the present election. I believe there has been some little difference of opinion among you, especially in regard to the selection of the two fresh prefects; there are so many worthy fellows in the Sixth that one can hardly wonder at your finding some difficulty in making your choice. One thing is certain - namely, that the two gentlemen who have been elected to what is and always has been a very honourable position at Ronleigh are eminently fitted for the work. The duties of a prefect are often difficult, and the reverse of pleasant; but I think you will agree with me when I say that in any large school it is eminently satisfactory to find that a certain amount of the government and discipline can be entrusted to the boys themselves, and I feel sure that you will give Parkes and Fielding the same willing support as you have always accorded to myself and the other prefects."

As the captain finished speaking, Hawley, Gull, Noaks, and several other boys sprang to their feet, their appearance being the signal for a fresh outburst of cheers and groans. Young "Rats" commenced to hiss like a small steam-engine, while Grundy made frantic but futile attempts to reach over from the desk behind and smite him on the head with a French dictionary.

"If any one wishes to speak," said the chairman, "he is at liberty to do so; but, of course, we can't have more than one at a time."

With the exception of Hawley, those who had risen sat

down again.

"I want to ask," said the former, "what were the numbers in the voting for the prefects?"

"Parkes received fifty-six votes, and Fielding forty-eight."

"Did Thurston receive any votes?"

"Yes."

"How many?"

"That," returned the captain, "is a question which, for certain reasons, I think it would be best not to answer."

"I think," interrupted Gull, rising to his feet, amid a murmur of excitement, "that we have a perfect right to insist on the figures being made public; everything in connection with these elections ought to be fair and open."

"I don't think," answered Allingford quietly, "that any one has ever had reason to accuse me of being unfair in any of my dealings; it is exactly because I think it would be hardly fair to Thurston himself that I propose not to publish the number of votes awarded to unsuccessful candidates."

The subject of this remark sat in the front row but one, lolling back against the desk behind, with his hands in his pockets and a sneering smile on his lips.

"I don't care what you do," he exclaimed, with a short laugh. "I can guess pretty well what's coming."

"There!" cried Gull; "you hear what Thurston says. Now let's have the figures."

"Very well," answered the captain. "If you insist, you shall have them. The number of votes for Thurston was sixty-one."

"Then, if he got more votes than either Parkes or Fielding, why isn't he elected?"

"Because the doctor would not sanction it. The names have to be submitted to him for approval, and he appointed Parkes and Fielding."

"Did you try to influence him to overlook Thurston?" demanded Gull angrily. But an immediate outburst of such cries as "Shame!" "Shut up!" and "Sit down!" showed the speaker he had gone too far, and rendered it unnecessary for Allingford to reply to the question.

"I think," said Fletcher senior, rising to his feet when this interruption had ceased, and looking round with a foxy smile on his face, "that, with all due respect to the gentlemen who have been elected as prefects, it is a great pity that the doctor should not have consented to confirm the choice of the school, and reappoint Thurston. I think if the matter were laid before him in a proper light he might be induced to reconsider his decision."

"Well, will you go and see him about it yourself?" asked Allingford, with a slight sneer.

"No; of course I shouldn't go alone," returned Fletcher. "I think it's a matter that should be taken up by the whole school."

Harold Avery

There was a moment's lull in the proceedings, broken only by a confused murmur of voices; then Acton jumped to his feet. The football captain was popular with everybody, and the sight of his jovial face and sturdy figure was greeted with a burst of cheers.

"Look here, you fellows," he began. "I'm no speaker, but I can say enough to serve the purpose. I think we are very much indebted to our captain, not only for presiding over this meeting, but for what he has done and is always doing for the good of the school. I remember Ronleigh when it wasn't such a decent place as it is to-day. A lot of things went on here when I was a kid that wouldn't be put up with now, and I don't think the school ever played such good games of cricket and football as we see at the present time. A lot of this, you may take my word for it, is due to our captain, and I think we can't show our appreciation of his work in a better way than by giving him three cheers. Now, then, take the time from me. Three cheers for Allingford. HIP, HIP, HURRAH!"

The big assembly shouted till the roof rang and the windows rattled; then the meeting slowly dispersed, a feeble attempt to raise three cheers for Thurston being met with as many groans as plaudits.

CHAPTER XIV.

A PASSAGE OF ARMS.

The Triple Alliance, in common with the rest of their schoolfellows, little thought, on returning from their summer holidays, what a memorable epoch the coming term would prove in the history of Ronleigh College; still less did any one imagine what important results would arise from the action of the three friends, and how much would depend on the loyalty of these youngsters for their *Alma Mater*.

They settled down to enjoy a peaceful thirteen weeks of work and play. Jack Vance reported that the robbery of "the Hermit's" coins was regarded at Todderton as quite a piece of ancient history; and as Noaks appeared to have forgotten the existence of the clasp-knife, and, growing every day more intimate with Thurston and Co., seemed more than ever inclined to go his way and leave his former foes alone, the latter made up their minds to banish dull care, and consider their unfortunate misadventure as a storm which they had safely weathered.

The wave of excitement caused by the elections soon passed over. The new prefects entered upon their duties, and in the performance of the same apparently met with no ill-will or opposition; yet to every keen observer it was evident that the recent contest had left behind it a distinct under-current of dissatisfaction, and for the first time in the memory of all concerned Ronleigh was a house divided against itself - no longer united in a common cause, but split into two factions, one pulling against the other, thinking more of party interests than of the honour and welfare of the whole community.

The first occasion on which this spirit clearly manifested itself was some ten days after the elections, when the college played their first football match of the season against Ronleigh town. Thurston's name had, as usual, been included in the list of the eleven which was posted up on Wednesday morning, but before school was over it was noised abroad that he had refused to play.

"I say, you fellows, have you heard about 'Thirsty'?" said Fletcher junior, as the Lower Fourth straggled into their classroom after interval. "I wonder if it's true."

"Oh, it's true enough," answered Grundy from the back desk; "and I'm jolly glad he's done it. I heard him say this morning that if Allingford and those other fellows wouldn't put up with him as a prefect, they shouldn't have him in the team."

"Well, I call that rot," cried Jack Vance: "the team doesn't belong to Allingford or to anybody else - "

"Oh, shut your mouth, you young prig!" interrupted Grundy, and the entrance of Mr. Greyling put a stop to any further conversation.

I am inclined to think that a much nobler spirit would

pervade such field-sports as cricket and football if the fact could be more firmly impressed upon the minds of both players and spectators that, providing the conduct of each side is fair and generous, and that every one does his "big best," it is equally creditable to lose as to win. Certainly both sides should strive their hardest to gain the day; but let boys especially remember, in an uphill game, when scoring goes against them, that it is to the honour of the slaughtered Spartans and not of the victorious Persians that the pass of Thermopylae has become a household word.

In addition to the loss of Thurston, who, to do him justice, was a very good forward, the school team was weakened still further by an unfortunate accident which befell Rowlands, who twisted his ankle, and was forced to leave the ground at the very commencement of the game. The Town were unusually strong, and the bulk of the back work fell on Allingford. The captain played a magnificent game, and covered himself with glory; but in spite of all that he and his men could do, after a gallant fight the visitors claimed the victory with a score of four goals to two.

On the morning after the match, just before school, the members of the Triple Alliance were strolling across the entrance-hall, when they noticed a crowd of boys surrounding the notice-board. The gathering seemed to consist mainly of members of the lower classes, and the manner in which they were elbowing each other aside, laughing, talking, and gesticulating, showed that some announcement of rather uncommon interest and importance must be exposed to view.

Our three friends hurried forward to join the group. Pinned to the board with an old pen-nib was a half-sheet of scribbling-paper, and inscribed thereon, in what was evidently a disguised handwriting, were some verses, which were seen at once to refer to the previous afternoon's defeat. They were as follows: -

COLLEGE V. TOWN.
Air, "Bonnie Dundee."

To the boys of the college 'twas Allingford spoke:
"When we play the Town team there are heads to be broke;
So let ten veteran players come now follow me,
And fight for the honour of ancient Ronleigh."

Chorus.

"Then put up your goal-posts, and mark your touch-line;
We'll grind them to powder, and put them in brine.
Let boarders and day boys all come out to see
Us fight for the honour of ancient Ronleigh."

The ten merry men mustered quick at his call -
There were forwards, and half-backs, and goal-keeper tall;
But one who was wont in the forefront to be
No longer was seen in the ranks of Ronleigh.

Chorus: "Then put up your goal-posts, and mark," etc.

Too soon their rejoicings and empty their boast,
For the Town fellows very soon had them on toast;
And the bystanders sighed as they saw frequently
The ball pass the "back" of our ancient Ronleigh.

Chorus: "Then put up your goal-posts, and mark,"
etc.

From this draw a moral, you fellows who rule:
Sink personal spite when you act for the school;
And whatever your notions of prefects may be,
Let's have the right men in the team at Ronleigh.

Chorus: "Then put up your goal-posts, and mark,"
etc.

Something in these doggerel lines excited Jack Vance's wrath above measure, the last verse especially raising his anger to boiling-point, so that it fairly bubbled over. Jack was a loyal-hearted youngster; he was nothing to Allingford, but Allingford was something to him, as head and leader of the community of which he himself was a member. The sight of the captain toiling manfully through the long, unequal contest of the previous afternoon, doing practically double work to make up for the loss of his fellow-back, and to prevent a losing game degenerating into a rout, rose up once more before the small boy's mind, and, as has been said before, his wrath boiled over.

"Well, I call that a beastly shame. The chap who wrote it ought to be kicked round the field."

"My eye," cried Grundy, "listen to what's talking! Kicked round the field, indeed! Why, I think it's jolly good: it serves Allingford and those other fellows just right for turning Thurston out of the team."

"What a lie!" retorted Jack. "You know very well they didn't turn him out; he went out of his own accord."

"Here, don't give me any of your cheek," said Grundy, sidling up to his antagonist in a threatening manner; "you mean to say I'm a liar, eh?"

The advent of three Fifth Form boys - one of whom took Grundy by the shoulders and pushed him away, with the command to "Get out and lie on the mat" - put an end, for the time being, to the altercation. The crowd increased: boys of all ages stopped to read the verses; some few laughed, and pronounced them jolly good; but to do them justice, the greater number of Ronleians were too jealous of the honour of their school to see much fun in this attempt to lampoon their football representatives. Just as the bell was ringing for assembly, the paper was torn down by Trail, the head of the Remove, who ripped it up into fifty pieces, and in answer to Gull's inquiry what he did that for, replied, "I'll jolly soon show you!" in such a menacing tone that the questioner saw fit to turn on his heel and walk away with an alacrity of movement not altogether due to any particular eagerness to commence work.

The Lower Fourth were straggling down the passage on the way to their classroom, when they heard a scuffle and the clatter of falling books. Grundy had seized Jack Vance by the collar from behind, and was screwing his knuckle into his victim's neck.

"Yes; you called me a liar, didn't you?"

"So you are! Let go my coat!"

"Oh, so you stick to it, do you? I'll - "

The sentence was interrupted by Jack giving a sudden twist and striking his antagonist a heavy blow in the chest, which sent him staggering against the opposite wall. Grundy was nearly a head taller than Vance; but the latter's blood was up, and in another moment the dogs of war would have assuredly broken loose had not the flutter of a gown at the end of the passage announced the advent of Mr. Greyling.

The class had finished translating from their Latin author, and had just commenced writing an exercise, when a note was passed over to Jack Vance from the desk behind; it was short and to the point: -

"Will you fight me after twelve at the back of the pavilion? - H. GRUNDY."

Jack read the challenge, turned round and nodded, and then went calmly on with his work as though nothing had happened.

This cool way of treating the matter did not altogether please Grundy, who had rather expected that his adversary would elect to "take a licking." He had, however, every reason to count upon an easy victory, and so promptly despatched another note, which contained the words: "Very well. I'll smash you."

Later on a third epistle was handed over: "Don't tell any one, or there'll be too much of a crowd."

It was not until the interval that the two other members of the Triple Alliance were informed of the coming conflict.

"You don't really mean you're going to fight him?" said Mugford.

"Of course I am."

"You'll get licked!" added Diggory, with a sigh.

"I don't care if I am. If I land him one or two, he won't be in a hurry to lick me again. Don't you remember what you said ages ago at The Birches, Diggy, when you went down that slide on skates? Well, it's the same thing with me now. I'm going to show him, once and for all, that he's not going to ride rough-shod over me for nothing."

During the last hour of school, which happened to be devoted to algebra, the only member of the Triple Alliance who seemed able to work was Jack Vance. Diggory made a hash of nearly every sum, while Mugford simply collapsed, and could not even remember that like signs made *plus*, and unlike *minus*.

"I say, Diggy," whispered the latter, "don't you think Grundy'll lick him?"

"I don't know," returned the other, with a desperate attempt to be cheerful; "you never know what may happen. He may - "

"Trevanock, stop talking," interrupted Mr. Greyling. "If I have to speak to you again for inattention, you'll stay in and work out these examples after twelve."

At length the faint jangle of the bell announced the fact that the eventful hour had arrived: the Lower Fourth passed on into the big schoolroom, and were dismissed with the other classes.

Jack betrayed not the least sign of excitement, and

insisted on going down into the grub-room to feed two white mice before setting out for the "front." His two friends, however, weighed down with anxiety, and with dismal forebodings as to the result of the coming conflict, were obliged to seek support by informing "Rats" of what was about to take place, and begging him to give them the benefit of his cheering company.

Young "Rats," who was always ready to take part in anything from a garden party to a game of marbles, immediately accepted the invitation.

"Jolly glad you told me," he cried; "wouldn't have missed seeing it for anything. Jack Vance and Grundy - whew-w-w!"

The long whistle with which he concluded the sentence had certainly an ominous sound, but the appearance of their principal was the signal for the seconds to hide their fears under an assumed air of jovial confidence.

"You'll be certain to lick him, Jack," said Diggory, with a face as long as a fiddle; - "won't he, 'Rats'?"

"Lick him!" answered "Rats;" "I should think so! Lick him into fits; I could do it myself."

"He's a beastly bully," added Mugford solemnly; "and bullies always get licked - in books."

"I don't care," answered Jack jauntily, "if I lick him or not, but I know he'll find me a pretty hard nut to crack."

Ronleigh had no recognized duelling-ground, but when a premeditated encounter did take place, the combatants usually resorted to a little patch of grass situated between the back of the pavilion and the edge of the adjoining field. Here it was possible to conduct an affair of honour without much fear of interruption.

Grundy was already at the trysting-place, accompanied by Andson, a chum from the Upper Fourth, and Fletcher junior. It was quite an informal little gathering, and the business was conducted in a free-and-easy manner, and with an entire absence of the cut-and-dried ceremony which characterized similar undertakings in the palmy days of the prize ring.

"Look here, young Vance," said Grundy, "if you like to apologize for calling me a liar, I'll let you off; if not, I'm going to punch your head."

"Punch away!" answered Jack stolidly, and all further attempt at pacification was abandoned.

The principals took off their coats and collars, while their companions drew aside to give them room, and the signal was given to commence the action.

Grundy made no attempt at any display of science; he simply relied on his superior strength and size, and charged down upon his adversary with the intention of thumping and pounding him till he gave in. Jack Vance knew very little about the "noble art," except that it was the proper thing to hit straight from the shoulder; and following out this fundamental principle, he succeeded in landing his opponent a good hard drive between the eyes, which made him see more stars than are to be witnessed at the explosion of a sixpenny rocket. Grundy drew back, and after blinking and rubbing his nose for a moment, came on again, this time with greater caution. Jack, on the other hand, emboldened by his previous success, made an unwise attempt to rush the fighting, and was rewarded with a sounding smack on the cheek-bone which broke the skin and sent him staggering back into the arms of Diggory.

Once more the combatants approached each other, this time with a little more feinting and dodging, which showed a certain amount of respect for the weight of each other's fists. At length, urged on to further feats of arms by impatient ejaculations of "Now, then, go into it!" and "Keep the game alive!" from Fletcher and Andson, they closed again, and after a sharp interchange of rather random pounding, Jack smote his opponent on the nose, and received in return a heavy blow on the chest which very nearly sent him to the ground.

After this there was another short breathing-space; a thin stream of blood was trickling from Grundy's nasal organ, while Diggory and Mugford noticed with aching hearts that their comrade was beginning to look rather limp, and was getting short of breath.

What would have been the ultimate result of the contest had it been resumed I am sure I cannot say, but I fear that, taking Grundy's superior weight and height into consideration, the story of the fight would have been recorded among the trials and not the triumphs of the Triple Alliance. As it was, a sudden interruption brought the encounter to a premature close.

"Hullo, you young beggars! what are you up to?"

The voice was that of Allingford, who, attracted by

cries of "Go it!" - "Give him another!" - "Bravo, Vance!" and other warlike shouts, had hurried round to the rear of the pavilion to find out what was happening.

"Hullo!" he continued, stepping forward and grasping Grundy by the shoulder; "what's up? what's the joke?"

"It's only a bit of a fight," said Andson; "they had a row this morning."

"What, d'you mean to say you're fighting that youngster? Why don't you choose some one a bit smaller?" demanded the captain, rather bitterly.

"Well, it's his own doing," growled Grundy. "I offered to let him off, but he wanted to have it out."

"Pshaw!" returned the other. "Look here, I've half a mind to give you two a jolly good 'impot' to keep you out of mischief. Now stop it, d'you hear, or I'll send both your names in to Denson."

Fletcher and Andson had already beaten a retreat, and Grundy was preparing to follow, when Allingford called him back.

"Come," he said, in a kinder tone. "I don't know what your quarrel's about, but finish it up like men, and shake hands."

The boys did as they were told, and though the salutation was not a very hearty one, it helped to extinguish the smouldering sparks of anger which might at some future meeting have been once more fanned into a flame.

Grundy disappeared round the corner of the building; but Allingford remained for a moment or two, watching Jack Vance as he fastened on his collar and resumed his coat.

"Well, what was the row about?"

"Oh, nothing."

"Nonsense; fellows don't fight for nothing. What was it? Any great secret?"

"Oh no," answered Jack, laughing: "it began about that lot of verses that was pinned upon the notice-board this morning. Grundy said Thurston was turned out of the team, and I said he wasn't."

The captain smiled thoughtfully, and going down on one knee examined the wounded cheek. "Put some cold water to it," he said, and then walked away.

That look was worth fifty bruises, and for it Jack would have continued the fight with Grundy to the bitter end. Diggory and Mugford fell upon his neck, and were loud in their declarations that in another round their champion would have "knocked the stuffing out" of his opponent. That this would really have been the case is, as I remarked before, rather doubtful; but one fact is certain - that the conflict caused the three friends to be more firmly established than ever in their loyalty to the side of law and order.

For a couple of days fellows continued to talk about the skit on the eleven, and to hazard guesses as to who was the writer. As the majority, however, pronounced it "a dirty shame," and spoke of the author as "some mean skunk," the poet wisely concluded to conceal his identity, and by the end of the week the matter was, for the time being, practically forgotten.

CHAPTER XV.

THE READING-ROOM RIOT.

Thurston followed up his withdrawal from the football team by a number of other actions which clearly showed a determination to spend what was known to be his last term at Ronleigh in living at open enmity with those who had once been his friends and associates. He never played unless it was in one of the rough-and-ready practice games, composed chiefly of stragglers, who, from being kept in and various other causes, were too late for the regular pick-ups, and came drifting on to the field later in the afternoon. He severed his connection with the debating society, and shunning the society of his comrades in the Sixth, was seen more frequently than ever hobnobbing with Gull and Hawley, or lounging about in conversation with Noaks and Mouler.

Fletcher senior, a mean, double-faced fellow, continued, as the saying goes, "to run with the hare and hunt with the hounds."

"It's an awful pity about old 'Thirsty,'" he would say to his brother prefects. "I try to keep him a bit straight; but upon my word, if he will go on being so friendly with such cads as Gull and Noaks, I shall chuck him altogether."

The speaker's methods of endeavouring to keep his chum straight were, to say the least of it, not very effective, and, if anything, rather more calculated to encourage him still further in his descent along the downward road.

"Look here!" said Fletcher, as they sat one evening talking in Thurston's study: "don't you think you'd better make peace with Allingford and the rest, and be a nice white sheep again, instead of a giddy old black one? I can tell you at present they don't look upon you as being a particular credit to the Sixth."

"I don't care what they think; they're a beastly set of prigs, and I'll have nothing more to do with them - with Allingford especially."

"Well, of course," answered Fletcher, with an air of resignation, "the quarrel's yours and not mine. I must own that I think Allingford made a great deal of unnecessary fuss over that Black Swan business, and acted very shabbily in making you send in your resignation just before the holidays. There's something, too, that I can't understand about the doctor's not confirming your re-election; and I think there ought to have been some further attempt made to get you to remain in the team - you did a lot of good service last season. However, my advice is, Put your pride in your pocket, and return to the fold."

Young Carton had shown that he possessed a certain amount of insight into character when he told Diggory that Thurston was a dangerous fellow to cross. The ex-prefect's brow darkened as Fletcher enumerated this list of real or imaginary grievances, and at the conclusion of the latter's speech there was a short silence.

"Yes," said Thurston, suddenly making the fender jump and rattle with a vicious kick. "Allingford's got his knife in me; he's bent on spoiling my life here. But that's a game two can play at. I've got a plan or two in my head, and I'll take the change out of him and those other prigs before the term's finished."

Grundy still continued to brag and swagger in the Lower Fourth, but his attitude towards Jack Vance suddenly underwent a change. Towards the latter he assumed quite a friendly bearing, and though still remaining a stanch Thurstonian, refrained from making himself aggressively obnoxious to the Triple Alliance. The hatchet had been buried for nearly a fortnight when an event happened which caused Ronleigh College to be once more convulsed with excitement and party feeling - a certain air of mystery which pervaded the whole affair tending to considerably increase the interest which the occurrence itself awakened.

Allingford had not, perhaps, been altogether wise in his choice of Lucas as keeper of the reading-room. The latter was a studious, hard-working boy in the Fifth, whose parents were known to be in comparatively poor circumstances, and the captain had named him in preference to Ferris, thinking that the guinea which was given as remuneration to the holder of this post, as well as to the two librarians, would be specially acceptable to one who seldom had the means to purchase the books which he longed to possess.

The duties of the keeper of the reading-room were to receive and take charge of the papers and magazines, to keep the accounts, and to be nominally responsible for the order of the room. I say nominally, as the law relating to absolute silence was never actually enforced; and as long as the members amused themselves in a reasonably quiet manner, and without turning the place into a bear-garden, they were allowed to converse over their games of chess or draughts, and exchange their opinions on the news of the day.

Lucas was, if one may say it, a little too conscientious in the execution of his duties, and rather apt to be fussy and a trifle overbearing in his manner. He posted copies of the rules on each of the four walls of the room, and insisted on decorous behaviour and perfect silence. The consequence was that he soon became the butt of innumerable jokes: fellows said they weren't in school, and meant to enjoy themselves.

"Rats" hit on the idea of carrying in an old newspaper under his coat. This he surreptitiously produced, and pretended to read as though it belonged to the room. At a favourable moment, with an exclamation of, "Well, this is a rotten paper!" he suddenly crunched the sheet up in his hands and tore it into fifty pieces. Lucas, naturally imagining that the property of the room was being destroyed, rushed up exploding with wrath. An explanation followed, and the whole assembly went off into fits of merriment, at the latter's expense.

By the time this trick was worn out, other waggish gentlemen had introduced the practice of dropping wax matches on the floor and treading on them, and of hunting an imaginary moth - an irresistibly humorous proceeding, in which the participators rushed about brandishing books and magazines, ever and anon crying, "There he is!" and smiting on the head some quiet, unoffending reader. Some evil-minded young miscreant went so far as to put bits of india-rubber on the top of the stove, the consequence being that in a short time a mysterious smell arose of such a fearful and distressing nature that every one was obliged to bolt out into the passage.

Those boys who at the time of the elections had formed the rank and file of the Thurstonian party, saw here an opportunity for showing their resentment of what they still chose to consider unfair conduct on Allingford's part. As a result, so they said, of the captain's favouritism, Lucas had been forced into a position for which he was entirely un-fitted; and with the expressed determination "not to stand him at any price," they proved themselves ever ready to assist in keeping up a constant repetition of the disturbances which have just been described.

These games, it need hardly be said, were not carried on when any of the prefects or members of the Sixth happened to be present; but during the half-hour between the end of tea and the commencement of preparation, when it rarely happened that any of the seniors put in an appearance, the conduct of the place went steadily from bad to worse. Lucas lost his head and lost his temper, and in doing so lost all control of his charge; and at last things were brought to a climax in the manner we are about to describe.

At the back of the room was one of those short desks which can be changed at will into a seat, the top part falling over and making a back-rest, while the form remains stationary. In connection with this article of furniture Gull one evening introduced a new pastime, which he called putting fellows in the stocks, and which consisted in decoying innocent small boys into taking a seat, then suddenly pushing them backwards on to the floor, and imprisoning their feet between the form and the reversible desk - a position from which they only extricated themselves with considerable difficulty.

Lucas made a couple of attempts to interfere and stop the proceedings, and when at length, for the third time, a thud and a shout of laughter announced that still another victim had fallen into the trap, he rose in wrath, and ordered Gull to leave the room.

"I shan't," returned the other. "Keep to yourself, and mind your own business."

"That's just what I'm doing; you know the rules as well as I do. It's my business to keep order in this room."

"Rubbish! Who do you think cares for your rules, you jack-in-office?"

"Will you leave the room?"

"No, of course I won't. If you want to act 'chucker-out,' you'd better try it on."

In desperation Lucas resolved to play his last card. "Look here, Gull," he said, rising from his seat. "You know I'm not your match in size or strength, or you wouldn't challenge me to fight; but this I will do: unless you leave the room, I shall go at once and report you to Dr. Denson."

The offender, seeing perhaps that this was no empty threat, evidently considered it the wiser plan not to risk an interview with the head-master.

"Oh, keep your wig on!" he answered, with a scornful laugh. "I shouldn't like to make you prove yourself a sneak as well as a coward. I'm going in a minute."

The assembly, who for the most part considered the stocks joke very good fun, and were possessed with all the traditional schoolboy hatred for anything in the shape of telling tales, showed their disapproval with a good deal of booing and hissing as Gull sauntered out of the room, and Lucas bent over his accounts with the despairing sense of having lost instead of gained by the encounter.

It soon became evident that the matter was not to be allowed to drop without some show of feeling, for on the following morning the unfortunate official was greeted with jeers and uncomplimentary remarks wherever he went.

Just before tea Diggory and Jack Vance were crossing the quadrangle on their way from the gymnasium to the schoolroom, when they were accosted by Fletcher junior.

"I say," remarked the latter, in rather a knowing manner, "if you want to see a lark, come to the reading-room before 'prep.'"

"Why, what's up?"

"Oh, never mind; don't tell any one I told you," and the speaker passed on.

"Shall we go?" said Diggory.

"We might as well," answered his companion,

laughing. "I wonder what the joke is! Another moth-hunt, or some more of that 'stocks' business, I suppose."

When the two friends entered the reading-room, it presented an unusually quiet and orderly appearance. About twenty boys were seated at the various desks and tables, all occupied with games of chess or draughts, or in the perusal of magazines and papers. Even Grundy, who never read anything but an occasional novel, was poring over the advertisement columns of *The Daily News*, with apparently great interest, while young Fletcher was equally engrossed in the broad pages of *The Times*. An attempt to put "Rats" in the stocks utterly failed, from the fact that those who were usually foremost in acts of disorder refused to render any assistance, and even went so far as to nip the disturbance in the bud with angry ejaculations of "Here, dry up!" - "Stop it, can't you?"

"I say," murmured Diggory, after sitting for a quarter of an hour listlessly turning over the pages of a magazine, "Fletcher's sold us about that lark; I don't see the use of staying here any longer."

Hardly had the words been uttered when some one in the passage outside crowed like a cock. There was a rustling of newspapers, and the next instant all four gas-jets were turned out simultaneously, and the room was plunged in total darkness. What followed it would be difficult to describe. The door was flung open, there was an inrush of boys from the passage, and the place became a perfect pandemonium. Tables were overturned, books and magazines went whizzing about in the darkness, a grand "scrum" seemed in progress round Lucas's desk, while amid the chorus of whoops, whistles, and cat-calls the latter's voice was distinctly audible, crying in angry tones, -

"Leave me alone, you blackguards; let go, I say!"

Jack and Diggory listened in amazement to the uproar with which they suddenly found themselves surrounded, and not wishing to risk the chance of having a form or a table upset on their toes, remained seated in their corner, wondering how the affair would end.

At length, piercing the general uproar, came the distant *clang, clang* of the bell for preparation. The tumult suddenly subsided, and there was a rush for the passage. Hardly had this stampede been accomplished when some one struck a match and lit the gas-jet nearest the door: it was Gull.

He stood for a moment looking round the room with a sardonic smile upon his face, evidently very well pleased with the sight which met his gaze. The place certainly presented the appearance of a town which had been bombarded, carried by storm, and pillaged for a week by some foreign foe. Most of the furniture was upset or pulled out of place, magazines and papers lay strewn about in every direction, ink was trickling in black rivulets about the floor, and draughts and chess men seemed to have been scattered broadcast all over the place. In addition to our two friends, three other boys, who had evidently taken no active part in the proceedings, still remained at some seats next to the wall; while Lucas, with hair dishevelled, waistcoat torn open, and collar flying loose, stood flushed and panting amid the *debris* of his overturned desk.

"Well, I'm sure!" said Gull, with a short laugh; "you

fellows seem to have been having rather a bit of fun here this evening. I thought I heard a row, and I was coming to see what it was; only just when I got to the door, about fifty chaps bounced out and nearly knocked me down. - What have they been up to, eh, Lucas?"

"Never you mind," answered the unfortunate official, choking with rage; "the bell's gone, so all of you clear out."

"Well, you can't blame me this journey," retorted Gull, calmly striking another match and lighting the next gas-jet. "It seems to me this is a little too much of a good thing. You'll have to lick a few of them, Lucas, my boy; and if you can't manage it yourself, you'd better get some one else to do it for you - your friend Allingford, for instance."

The master on duty in the big schoolroom had to call several times for silence before the subdued hum of muttered conversation entirely ceased. Every one had heard of the reading-room riot, and was anxious to discuss the matter with his companions.

"Who did it? who did it?" was the question asked on all sides.

"I don't know," would be the answer. "They say it wasn't the fellows who were in the room - some of them put the gas out; but it was a lot of other chaps, who rushed in after, who did all the damage and caused such 'ructions.'"

"It seems to me," remarked Diggory to his two chums, "that it was a put-up job, all arranged beforehand."

"Then who d'you think planned it?" asked Mugford.

"I don't know, but I believe Gull had a hand in it."

"Oh, I don't think that," answered Jack Vance. "He came in and lit the gas; if he'd been in it, he'd have skedaddled with the rest."

"Um - would he?" returned Diggory, nodding his head in a sagacious manner; "I'm rather inclined to think he came in on purpose."

By the end of supper a fresh rumour spread which caused the affair to assume a still graver and more important aspect. Lucas had reported the whole thing to the head-master, and the latter had expressed his intention of inquiring into it on the following day. The truth of these tidings was proved beyond all possibility of doubt when, next morning at breakfast, an announcement was made that the school would assemble immediately after the boys left the hall, instead of gathering, as usual, at nine o'clock.

Every one knew what this meant. The subject had been discussed for hours in most of the dormitories on the previous evening, and when Dr. Denson ascended his throne there was no necessity for him to strike the small hand-bell - the usual signal for silence; an expectant hush pervaded the whole of the big room, showing clearly the interest which every one felt in the business on hand.

"I need hardly say," began the doctor, in his clear, decisive manner, "that my object in calling you together is to inquire into a disgraceful piece of disorder which took place in the reading-room last night. I am astonished that such outrageous behaviour should be possible in what, up to the present time, I have always been proud to regard as a community of gentlemen. Such an offence against law and order cannot be allowed to pass unpunished. I feel certain that the greater number of those here present had no share in it, and I shall give the culprits a chance of proving themselves at all events sufficiently honourable to prevent their schoolfellows suffering the consequences which have arisen from the folly of individuals. Let those boys who are responsible for what occurred last evening stand up!"

With one exception nobody stirred; a solitary small boy rose to his feet, and in spite of the gravity of the situation a subdued titter ran through the assembly. Apparently the whole of the row and disturbance of the previous evening was the handiwork of one single boy, and that boy the youthful "Rats."

"Well, Rathson," said the head-master grimly, "am I to understand that you single-handed overturned forms and tables, scattered books and papers to the four winds, and nearly tore the clothes off another boy's back?"

"N - no, sir," answered "Rats" plaintively.

"Then will you explain exactly what you did do?"

"I was reading - and the gas went out - and some one emptied a box of chess-men over my head - and I - I hit him - and then there was a lot of pushing, and I pushed, and - " concluded "Rats" apologetically - "and I think I shouted."

"H'm!" said the doctor; "so that's all you did. Sit down, sir. - Lucas!"

"Yes, sir."

"Do you remember what boys were in the reading-room last night?"

"Yes, sir, but I don't think they were responsible for what happened; it was done by others who came in from outside."

There was a silence.

"I ask once more," said the head-master, "what boys took part in this disturbance? let them stand up!"

Once more young "Rats" alone pleaded guilty.

"Very well, then," continued the doctor sternly; "the whole school will be punished: there will be no half-holiday on Wednesday afternoon, and the reading-room will be closed for a fortnight. - Sit down, Rathson; you are the only boy among the many who must have been connected with this affair - the only one, I say, who has any sense of manliness or honour. Write me a hundred lines, and bring them to me to-morrow morning."

The prospect of having to work on Wednesday afternoon caused, the boys themselves to take up the doctor's inquiry, and the query, "Who did it?" became the burning question of the hour.

The riot had evidently been carefully planned beforehand, and the plot arranged in such a manner that those who took part in it might do so without being recognized.

It was impossible to discover who really were the culprits, though the majority of the boys put it down as having been done by "some of 'Thirsty's' lot," and as being a further proof of the latter's well-known animosity towards Allingford, who had, of course, appointed Lucas as keeper of the room.

"Look here!" said Diggory, accosting Fletcher Two in the playground: "what made you tell us to come to the reading-room last night? How did you know there was going to be a row?"

"I didn't," murmured the other warily. "All I knew was that they were going to put 'Rats' in the 'stocks;' I hadn't the faintest idea there was going to be such a fine old rumpus."

"Umph! hadn't you?" muttered Diggory, turning on his heel; "I know better."

CHAPTER XVI.

THE CIPHER LETTER.

The reading-room row, as it was called, had pretty well blown over, when one morning Diggory accosted Jack Vance and Mugford, who were both seated at the latter's desk, sharpening their knives on an oil-stone.

"I say, you fellows, look what I've found." As he spoke, he laid on the desk a slip of paper; it was evidently a scrap torn out of some exercise-book, and inscribed upon it were several lines of capital letters, all jumbled together without any apparent object in their arrangement, and, to be more exact, placed as follows: -

NVVGRMGSVTBNDSVMGSVUVOOLD
HKZHHLMGLHFKKVIGSVGDLXZM
HLUDZGVIZIGHGZMWRMTRMHRW
VGSVXFKYLZIWFMWVIGSVHGZRIH.

"Well, what is there funny about that?" asked Jack; "it looks to me as if some one had been practising making capitals."

"Is it a puzzle?" inquired Mugford.

"No, but I'll tell you what I think it is," answered

Diggory, sitting down, and speaking in a low, mysterious tone: "it's a letter written in cipher."

"A letter?" repeated Mugford, glancing at the paper. "Why, how could any one read that rubbish - NVVG?"

"Of course they can, if they know the key. Didn't I say it was written in cipher, you duffer? Every letter you see there stands for something different."

"Then why didn't they write the proper letters at once, and have done with it?" grumbled Mugford.

"Because, you prize ass," retorted Diggory, with pardonable asperity, "they didn't want it read."

"Then if they didn't want it read, why did they write it at all?" exclaimed Mugford triumphantly.

"Oh, shut up! you're cracked, you - "

"Look here," interrupted Jack Vance, "where did you find the thing?"

"Why, you know the window in the box-room that looks out on the 'quad;' well, there's a little crack under the ledge between the wooden frame and the wall, and this note was stuck in there. I should never have seen it, only I was watching a spider crawling up the wall, and it ran into the hole close to the end of the paper. Some fellows must be using the place as a sort of post-office; don't you remember Fred Acton made one in the wainscotting at The Birches? only these fellows have invented a cipher. Well, I'm going to find it out, and read this note, just for the lark."

"How are you going to do it, though? I don't see it's possible to read a thing like this; you can't tell where one word ends and a fresh one begins."

"There is a way of finding out a cipher," answered Diggory; "it tells you how to do it in that book that we bought when Mug had his things sold by auction at Chatford."

"What, in Poe's tales?" asked Mugford. "Yes; in one of the stories called 'The Gold Bug.' Where is the book?"

"I lent it to Maxton, but I should think he's finished it by this time. I'll go and see."

"All right," said Diggory, pocketing the slip of paper; "you get it, and then I can show you what I mean. Come on, Jack; let's go out."

The two friends were just rising from the form on which they had been sitting, when they were accosted by Browse, who, strolling up with a pair of dilapidated slippers on his feet, which caused him to walk as though he were skating, inquired in drawling tones, "I say, have either of you kids got a watch-key?"

Jack Vance handed him the required article, which happened to be of the kind which fit all watches.

The Sixth Form "sap" was very short-sighted, and proceeded to wind up his timepiece, holding it close to his spectacles throughout the operation.

"I can't think how it is," he continued, in his sing-song tone, "I'm always losing my key. I've had two new ones already this term. I always stick them in a place where I think they're sure not to get lost, and then I forget where I put them. Thanks awfully."

"What a queer old codger Browse is!" remarked Diggory, as the big fellow moved away; "no one would ever think he was so clever."

"No," answered Jack Vance. "By-the-bye, did you hear that he had another row with 'Thirsty' last night?"

"No; what about?"

"Oh, the same thing as before. Some fellows were making a beastly row in Thurston's study, and Browse couldn't work, so he threatened if they weren't quiet he'd report them to the doctor. 'Thirsty' came out in an awful wax, and said for two pins he'd knock Browse down; and young Collis, who was standing at the top of the stairs, says he believes he'd have done it if some of the other fellows in the Sixth hadn't come out and interfered."

In the course of the afternoon Diggory secured Mugford's copy of Poe's tales, and (sad to relate) spent a good part of that evening's preparation in trying to unravel the secret of the mysterious missive which he had found in the box-room. So intent was he on solving the problem that, instead of going down to supper with the majority of his companions, he remained seated at his desk, poring over the experiments which he was making according to directions given in the famous story of "The Gold Bug."

"Well, how are you getting on ?" inquired Jack Vance, as the crowd came straggling back from the dining-hall.

"Oh, pretty well," answered the other. "The first thing you have to do is to find E; it's the letter which occurs most frequently. Well, in this case V is the letter which comes oftenest - there are fourteen of them - so V is E. Then, when you know what E is, you search for the word 'the.' There are certain to be several 'the's' in the piece; so you look for instances in which the same two letters come before E, or, in this case, before V. Well, here it is, G S V, five times; so you are pretty certain that G S V is 'the,' or, in other words, that G is T, S is H, and V is E. That's as far as I've got at present; but I mean to worry out the rest of it to-morrow."

While Diggory was holding forth in the big schoolroom on his methods of reading a cipher, a conversation of a very different character, and on a matter of grave importance, was taking place in the study of the school captain.

Allingford and John Acton were seated in front of the former's little fireplace talking over matters connected with the football club. Suddenly there was a sound of hurrying feet in the passage; the next instant the door burst open, and in bounced Browse. The two prefects gazed at him for a moment in open-mouthed astonishment; then Acton broke the silence, exclaiming, "Why, Browse, what's the matter?"

The "sap" certainly presented an extraordinary appearance. His spectacles were gone; his hair was pasted all over his face, as though he had just come up from a long dive; his clothes were torn, and in a state of the wildest disorder; while the strangest part of all was that from head to foot he seemed soaking wet, drenched through and through with water, which dripped from his garments as he stood.

"Why, man alive!" cried Allingford, "what have you been up to?"

"It's those blackguards!" gasped Browse, choking with rage, and shaken for once in a way out of his usual drawl; "it's that Thurston and his crew - I know it was!"

"But what was? what's the matter?"

With some little difficulty the two prefects at length succeeded in extracting from their excited comrade an account of his wrongs; even then such an amount of cross-questioning was necessary that it will be best to make no attempt at a verbatim report, but rather to give the reader a more concise version of the story.

From Browse's statement it appeared that just before supper some one had come to his study, saying: "Smeaton wants you in the 'lab;' look sharp!" The door had only been opened about a couple of inches, and then closed again. From the few words thus spoken Browse did not recognize the voice; but thinking that his particular friend Smeaton (another tremendous worker) was engaged in some important experiments, and needed his assistance, he hurried away, never dreaming but that the message he had received was genuine.

In order to reach the laboratory, it was necessary to traverse the box-room and the gymnasium, both of which were in darkness, the lights being turned out by the prefect on duty when the boys assembled for preparation.

Across the first of these chambers Browse groped his

way in safety. Hardly, however, had he crossed the threshold of the second, when he was suddenly seized and held fast by several strong pairs of hands. His indignant expostulations were met with a titter of suppressed laughter; he was roughly forced down upon his knees, and while in this position what seemed like two buckets of cold water were emptied over his devoted head. This having been done, he was dragged to his feet, thrust back into the box-room, and the door leading into the gymnasium was slammed to and locked on the inside. From first to last not a word had been spoken, and at the very commencement of the struggle Browse's spectacles had been knocked off. These two circumstances had entirely prevented him from recognizing the shadowy figures of his assailants. He made one attempt to force the door open, but finding it securely fastened, had come straight away to the captain's study.

"It's that Thurston and some of his gang," he repeated in conclusion; "they did it to pay me out for interfering with their noisy meetings."

Allingford and John Acton sprang to their feet. The idea that the rowdy element should be so powerful in Ronleigh that a Sixth Form boy could with impunity be seized and drenched with cold water, was not very pleasing to one who was largely responsible for the order of the school, and the captain's face was as black as thunder.

"All right!" he exclaimed; "leave this to me. Go and change your clothes."

The two prefects hurried down the passage.

"Wait a minute," said Allingford. "Which is Thurston's study?"

Acton knocked at the door; and receiving no answer, pushed it open and looked in. The room was empty.

"Come on," cried Allingford; "the 'gym!' They may be there still."

They rushed down the stairs, scattering a group of small boys who were roasting chestnuts at the gas-jet in the passage, and on through the box-room, but only to find the door on the other side standing wide open, and the gymnasium itself silent and deserted - two empty water-cans, lying in a big pool of wet on the cement floor, being the only remaining traces of the recent outrage.

"They're gone," said Acton. "What shall we do?"

"We'll find one of them, at all events," replied his companion; and returning once more to the neighbourhood of the studies, he shouted, -

"*Thurston!*"

There was a faint "Hullo!" and a moment later a door opened half-way down the passage.

"Well, what d'you want?"

Allingford walked quickly forward. "Look here," he demanded sternly, "where have you been? What have you been doing?"

"Doing!" echoed Thurston; "why, I've been sitting here

for the last two hours with old Smeaton. I asked him to let me come and work in his study to-night. There's some of this Ovid I can't get on with, and he promised he'd help me out with it if I'd tell him what it was I didn't understand."

The captain hesitated a moment, rather nonplussed by this unexpected reply. "I believe you know something about this affair with Browse," he continued. "Who did it?"

"Who did what?" demanded Thurston snappishly. "If you mean when he came banging at my study door last night - "

"No, I don't mean that," interrupted Allingford. "I mean this blackguard's trick that was played on him to-night."

"I don't know what you're talking about," retorted Thurston angrily. "Look here, Allingford, I'll thank you not to call me a blackguard for nothing, for I suppose that's what you're driving at. If you don't think I'm speaking the truth, ask Smeaton. I suppose you'll take his word, if you won't take mine."

Smeaton, whose veracity it was impossible to doubt, confirmed the last speaker's assertions, and Allingford and Acton were forced to beat a retreat, feeling that they had certainly been worsted in the encounter.

"What's to be done?" asked Acton, as they re-entered the captain's study.

"I don't know," answered the other, flinging himself into a chair. "The only thing I can see is to report it to the doctor."

"Oh, I shouldn't do that; it's more a piece of personal spite than any disorder and breach of rule, like that reading-room affair. I think it's a thing which ought to be put down by the fellows themselves. Who was in Thurston's study last night?"

"I don't know. It may have been those fellows Gull and Hawley, but you can't accuse them without some evidence; you see what I got just now for tackling Thurston. Ever since the elections there seem to be a lot of fellows bent on bringing the place to the dogs. Thurston's hand and glove with the whole lot of them, and it's hard to say who did this thing to Browse."

A report of what had happened was rapidly spreading all over the school. One by one the other prefects dropped in to the captain's study to talk the matter over. Most of them were inclined to agree with Acton in considering it a thing to be taken up by the boys themselves, and the discussion was continued till bedtime.

"Well, I'll tell you what I think I'd better do," said Allingford, preparing to wish his companions good-night. "I'll report it to the doctor, and ask him not to take any steps in the matter until we've had a chance of inquiring into it ourselves."

The story of Browse's mishap, as we have just said, soon passed from mouth to mouth, until it was common property throughout the college. The remarks which the news elicited were often of an entirely opposite nature, according to the character of the boys who made them. Noaks and Mouler laughed aloud, declaring it a rare good joke; but to the credit of the Ronleians of that generation be it said, the majority shook their heads, and muttered, "Beastly shame!" "What'll be done?" was the question asked on all sides. "Will it be reported to the doctor?"

"If it is," said "Rats," "we shall lose another half-holiday. Confound those fellows, whoever they are! I should like to see them all jolly well kicked."

On the following day the first assembly for morning school passed without anything happening, though every one looked rather anxiously towards the head-master's throne as Dr. Denson took his seat.

The brazen voice of the bell had just proclaimed the eleven o'clock interval, when the Triple Alliance, hurrying with their companions of the Lower Fourth along the main corridor leading to the schoolroom, found that the passage was nearly blocked by a large crowd of boys standing round the notice-board.

"Hullo!" said Diggory, "another rhyme?"

This time, however, the placard was in good plain prose, and ran as follows: -

"NOTICE.

"A meeting of the whole school will take place directly after dinner in the gymnasium. A full attendance is urgently requested, as the matter for consideration is of great importance.

A. R. ALLINGFORD."

"Humph," muttered Fletcher senior to himself, as he turned on his heel after reading the notice, "the fat's in the fire now, and no mistake."

CHAPTER XVII.

DIGGORY READS THE CIPHER.

The gymnasium was filled with a dense crowd of boys; "Rats," Maxton, and some other members of the Lower Fourth were fighting for seats on the parallel bars, and throughout tho whole assembly there was a subdued murmur of interest and expectation. The last gathering of the kind had been a court-martial held some two years previously on a boy suspected of stealing. Old stagers, in a patronizing manner, related what had happened to their younger comrades, adding, "What, weren't you here *then?* Well, you are a kid!" and forgetting to mention that at the time they themselves were wearing knickerbockers, and doing simple arithmetic in the lowest form.

At one end of the room was a big chest containing dumb-bells and single-sticks, and Allingford, mounting on the top of this as the last stragglers from the dining-hall joined the assembly, called for silence.

There was no attempt at eloquence or self-assertion in Allingford's remarks; brief they were almost to bluntness, but well suited to the audience to whom they were addressed. It was the old, well-tried captain of Ronleigh who spoke, and the boys of Ronleigh who listened, and the manner in which the words were

Harold Avery

given and received might have reminded one of a speech of Sir Colin Campbell's in the Indian Mutiny, and the answer of the Highlanders he addressed: -

"Ninety-third, you are my own lads; I rely on you to do yourselves and me credit."

"Ay, ay, Sir Colin; ye ken us, and we ken you."

"I think you all know," began the captain, "the reason of this meeting being called together. Last night Browse was set on in this room - in the dark, mind you - knocked down, and drenched with cold water. Some fellows may think it a good joke. I don't; I think the fellows who did it were cads and cowards. I reported the matter to the doctor, and he consented to act in accordance with the wishes of the prefects, and leave the matter in the hands of the boys themselves rather than inquire into it himself, which would probably only have meant another punishment for the whole school." ("Hear, hear!")

"Now, what I want to say is this. I've been here a good many years - longer than any one, except Oaks and Rowlands and two or three more. I love the place, and I'm proud of it. I'd sooner be captain of Ronleigh than of any other public school you could mention" (cheers); "but I tell you plainly, the place is going down. There's been a good deal too much of this rowdy element showing lately, and it's high time it was put a stop to.

"Some of you, I know, have lately taken a dislike to me, and think I don't act rightly." ("No, no!") "If I'm to blame, I'm sorry for it, for I've always tried to do my best. I ask you not to look upon this matter as a personal affair, either of mine or of any of the other prefects, but to consider only the welfare of the school. I say again that if Ronleigh is to retain its reputation, and be kept from going to the dogs, it's high time these underhanded bits of foul play like the reading-room row and this attack on Browse were put a stop to; and I beg you all to join in taking measures to prevent anything of the kind occurring again in the future."

The speaker concluded his remarks amid a general outburst of applause.

"So we will," cried several voices; "three cheers for old Ally!"

"In my opinion," began Oaks, as soon as order was restored, "the first thing is to try to find out who did it; surely a fellow can't be set on by three or four others without somebody knowing something about it. - Haven't you yourself any idea who it was, Browse?"

"Well, I can't swear," answered Browse readily. "I couldn't see, because it was dark, and my spectacles were knocked off; but I'm pretty certain it was some of Thurston's lot - Gull, or Hawley, or some of those fellows. They did it because I complained when they kicked up a row and interfered with my work."

This reply created a great sensation, and the air was rent with a storm of groans, cheers, and hisses.

Oaks, who seemed to have taken upon himself the duties of counsel for the prosecution, held up his hand to procure silence.

"Shut up!" he exclaimed; "every one will be heard in

time. Browse thinks it might have been Gull, Thurston, or Hawley. - Now, Gull, what have you got to say? Where were you last night?"

"In bed, asleep," answered Gull promptly.

There was a laugh.

"I don't mean that. What we want to know is, what were you doing after 'prep'?"

"Well, I was about some private business of my own."

"What was it?"

"I don't see why I should tell you all my private affairs."

"Well, in this instance we mean to know; so out with it. What were you doing directly after 'prep' last night?"

There was a hush of expectation. Every one thought an important disclosure was about to be made.

"All right," answered Gull calmly; "if you must know, I'll tell you. I was in the matron's room, getting her to sew two buttons on my waistcoat."

A roar of laughter interrupted the proceedings; the defence had scored heavily. Oaks was for the moment completely nonplussed, and Thurston seized the opportunity of making a counter-attack. He strode forward, and mounting the chest addressed the assembly as follows: -

"Gentlemen, however low Ronleigh may have sunk, there is still, I believe, left among us a certain amount of love of fair play, and therefore I ask you to give me a hearing. The saying goes, 'Give a dog a bad name and then hang him.' I'm a dog on which certain people have been good enough to bestow a bad name. I know I've got it, and to tell you the truth I don't much care. All the same, I don't see why I should be hung for a thing which is no fault of mine. You've just heard what Gull's had to say. I can prove that I was in Smeaton's study when this thing happened; and I daresay, if Hawley is to be cross-examined, he'll be able to show that he was somewhere else at the time. What I say, however, is this - that it's very unfair and unjust to practically accuse fellows of a thing without having some grounds for so doing. I don't want to brag, but there have been times, as, for instance, at the last Wraxby match" (cheers), "when the school thought well of me" (loud cheers). "Now I'm a black sheep; but there ought to be fair play for black sheep as well as for white ones." ("Hear, hear!") "Allingford said something about underhanded bits of foul play. Well, I, for one, am not afraid to be open and speak my mind. If the place is going to the dogs because of it's being continually in a state of disorder, then the fault lies with the prefects." (Sensation.) "They're the ones who ought to check it, and if they are incompetent, and can't do their duty, it's no excuse for their trying to shift the blame on to fellows who are innocent, but who happen to stand in their bad books."

The speech had just the effect which Thurston intended it should have. The English schoolboy has always been a zealous champion of "fair play," though sometimes misled in his ideas as to what the term really implies. A vague sense that the prefects were at fault, and that

Harold Avery

this inquiry was a blind to cover their shortcomings, spread through the meeting. Oaks was interrupted and prevented from questioning Hawley, and it seemed as though the good influence of Allingford's opening speech would be entirely lost, and that the meeting would bring about a still more hostile attitude on the part of the rank and file towards those in authority.

The Thurstonians, however, attempting to make the most of this temporary triumph, met with an unexpected disaster, which quickly turned the changing tide of public opinion.

During a momentary pause in the hubbub which followed Thurston's address, Fletcher senior, with the usual smile upon his face, began to speak.

"Thurston has just said that as regards these rows the fault lies with the prefects, and that they are culpable in trying to shift the blame on to other fellows without first getting sufficient evidence to warrant their so doing. As one of the prefects, I think it only fair to myself to mention that I was not in favour of this meeting being called. I suggested to my friend Allingford that this matter should be allowed to rest until some inquiries had been made - "

"Stop!" cried the captain sternly. The two lines were deepening between his eyebrows, and the corners of his mouth were drawn down. The boys had seen that look before, as he stood at the wicket when runs were few and the bowling dangerous. "Stop! Speak the truth: you're not my friend."

"Allingford says we are not friends," continued the speaker, with the same eternal smile upon his lips. "I'm sorry to hear it. I know I've always tried to be his friend, ever - "

"You're lying!" interrupted the other sharply. "Take care, or I'll prove it!"

There was a dead silence all over the room. Fletcher did not know what was coming, and though he felt uneasy, he had gone too far to go back.

"I can't understand," he began, "why you should have this unkind feeling towards me. I can only repeat, in spite of what you say, that I *am* your friend."

"Very well," returned the other, with an angry flash in his eyes, "as it was partly an attack on myself, I had meant to have said nothing about it; but since you persist in your miserable hypocrisy, I'll expose you. - You remember," he continued, turning to the audience, and speaking with a ring of bitter scorn in his voice, "that paltry rhyme that was fastened on the notice-board after the Town match? Well, allow me to introduce you to the author of it. He was too modest to sign his name to it, but here he is, all the same - a fellow who tries to bring ridicule and contempt on his own side; who stabs a man in the dark, and in the daylight professes to be his friend."

A derisive groan rose from the crowd.

"You can't prove it!" retorted Fletcher, turning first white and then red.

"I can prove it up to the hilt. You had the confounded cheek to borrow from me the very book of songs you used when you wrote the parody, and you were fool enough to leave the rough copy in it when you brought it back. It's there now, in your writing. Shall I send for it? it's on my study table at this moment."

The culprit muttered something about it's being "only a joke," but his reply was lost amid a storm of hoots and hisses.

"Sneak!" cried one voice; "Turn him out!" yelled another; while the object of this outburst of animosity, recovering himself sufficiently to glance round with a contemptuous sneer on his face, fell back, and endeavoured to hide his confusion by entering into conversation with Gull and Thurston.

Fletcher had come a nasty cropper, and reaped what, sooner or later, is the inevitable reward of double-dealing.

Once more the sympathy of the meeting was enlisted on the side of Allingford and the prefects, and the crowd dispersed, resolved to discover, if possible, who had made the attack on Browse, and determined that such acts of disorder were not to be tolerated in the future.

"Hullo, old chap!" said Thurston, entering his friend's study a few moments later; "you made rather a mess of that speech of yours. I'm inclined to think you've damaged your reputation."

"I don't care," returned the other; "we're both leaving at the end of this term. As for Allingford, just let him look out: it'll be my turn to move next, and there's plenty of time to finish the game between now and Christmas."

It was a bright, crisp afternoon. Almost everybody hurried away to change for football.

"Where's Diggy?" asked Jack Vance, as he and Mugford strolled out to the junior playing field."

"Oh, he said he wasn't coming; he's stewing away at that stupid cipher. He can't find any word except 'the;' he'll never be able to read the thing."

It being a half-holiday, the games lasted a little longer than usual. At length, however, the signal was given to "cease fire," and a general cry of "Hold the ball!" put an end to the several contests.

The crowd of players were tramping across the paved playground, and surging through the archway into the quadrangle, when Jack Vance and Mugford were suddenly confronted by Diggory. He held some scraps of paper in his hand, and appeared to be greatly agitated.

"Come here," he cried, seizing each of them by the arm; "I've got something to show you."

"Well, what is it?" asked the other two. Their friend, however, would vouchsafe no further reply than, "Come here out of the way, and I'll tell you."

He dragged them along until they reached the deserted entrance to some of the classrooms; then, stopping and turning to them with an extraordinary look of mingled triumph, mystery, and excitement, exclaimed, -

"I've read the cipher!"

"Pooh! what of that?" answered Jack, rather annoyed at being taken so far out of his way for nothing. "I expect it isn't anything particular after all."

"It is, though," returned the other confidently; "and you'll say so too when you read it."

"Well, tell us first how you managed to find it out."

"That's just what I was going to do. You know I found that G was T, S was H, and V was E; well, I tried and tried, and I couldn't get any further. I wrote down the alphabet, and put V opposite E, and T opposite G, and S opposite H. I stared at it and stared at it, and all of a sudden - I don't know how I came to think of it - I noticed that E is the fifth letter from the *beginning* of the alphabet, and V is the fifth letter from the *end*. The same thing held good with the next letter: G was seventh from the beginning, and T was seventh from the end."

Diggory paused as though to see what effect this announcement would have on the faces of his friends.

"Well!" they exclaimed; "go on!"

"Why, then, I saw in a moment what they'd done: *they'd simply transposed the whole alphabet* - A. was Z, and Z was A!"

"Oh!" cried Jack Vance; "I see it now."

"Of course, it was as plain as print. I put the two alphabets side by side, one the right way and the other upside down, and I read the cipher in two minutes, and here's what you might call the translation."

As he spoke he held out a scrap of scribbling-paper. Jack Vance took it, and read as follows: -

"Meet in the 'gym' when the fellows pass on to supper. The two cans of water are standing inside the cupboard under the stairs."

Mugford stared at Jack Vance, and Jack stared at Diggory. "D'you see?" cried the latter eagerly.

"Yes."

"Well, what then?"

"Why, it must have something to do with this row about Browse."

"Of course: the fellows who did it didn't want, I suppose, to be seen talking together too much just before it happened, and so they invented this way of making their plans."

"But who can it be?" asked Mugford. "It seems to me it's just like one of those secret society things in Russia."

"So it is, and we must find out who they are," answered Diggory, smacking his lips with great relish. "We'll see once more what can be done by the Triple Alliance."

The more the three friends thought over the matter of the cipher letter, the more their curiosity and interest were excited.

"I believe it's either Noaks or Mouler," said Mugford;

"they were both of them siding with Thurston, and trying to kick up a row at the meeting."

"Oh, they'd neither of them have the sense to invent a thing like this," answered Jack. "They may be in it, but there's some one else besides."

Diggory scouted the idea of letting any other boys share their secret. The honour of having discovered and exposed the plot must belong to the Triple Alliance alone, and it must be said that they had accomplished their task unaided by any outsiders.

That evening and the following day the greater portion of their free time was spent in discussing the great question as to what should be done. The cipher note evidently had direct connection with the attack on Browse, but the translation of the letter was in itself like finding a key without knowing the whereabouts of the lock which it fitted. The question was, by whom and for whom it had been written.

Afternoon school was just over, and the three friends were standing warming their feet on a hot-water pipe, discussing the likelihood of making any other discoveries which might tend to throw more light on the subject, when suddenly a happy thought entered the head of Jack Vance.

"Look here, Diggory. You said you found this note in a crack in the wall under one of the grub-room windows, and that you thought some fellows were using it as a sort of post-office. Well, have you been there to see if anything's been put there since?"

"No!" cried Diggory. "Good idea! I'll go now at once."

He walked quickly out of the room, and came back a few moments later at a run.

"I've got one!" he exclaimed, in a low, eager tone. "Don't let any one see; come to my desk."

The note this time was very brief: -

ZUGVIGVZFMWVIGSVKZE.

Diggory hastily fished out his double alphabet, wrote down the proper letters as Jack read out those on the paper, and in a few seconds the translation was complete, and read as follows: -

"*After tea under the pav.*"

The three boys stared at it in silence.

"What does it mean?" asked Mugford.

"Why," cried Diggory excitedly, "I see. Something's going to happen after tea this evening in that place under the pavilion - you know where I mean?"

The other two nodded their heads. The pavilion at Ronleigh being raised some distance above the level of the field, there was a space between the floor and the ground used for storing whiting-buckets, goal-posts, and a number of forms, which were brought out on match-days to afford seats for visitors. The door of this den had no lock, and opened on the piece of waste turf at the back of the building. Small boys used it as a cave when playing brigands, and for so doing had their ears boxed by irate members of the Sports Committee. It was too low to admit of any one's moving about except in a stooping posture, and pitch dark unless the door was left wide open.

"What do you think it is?" said Mugford.

"I don't know," answered Diggory; "but I mean to go and see."

"If they catch you prying about, and find out that you've been watching them, you'll get an awful licking."

"I don't care if I do; I mean to go."

"Well, we'll go with you," said Jack Vance. "Remember it's the Triple Alliance, and we vowed always to stand by each other whatever happened."

"Yes," answered Diggory, "and so we will; but there's less chance of one being seen than three. No; I'll go alone."

CHAPTER XVIII.

A SECRET SOCIETY.

It was a clear, starlight night. Diggory was one of the first to leave the dining-hall, and, passing swiftly out of the quadrangle, was soon hurrying across the junior playing field. On reaching the pavilion, all was quiet and deserted, and he stood for a moment considering what should be his next step.

The thin hedge dividing the two playgrounds was by this time bare of leaves, and afforded no hiding-place; the only chance of concealment was to take shelter inside the den itself - a place which has already been described. This, however, seemed rather like venturing into the lion's mouth. What was going to happen? Would anything take place, or was it only a wild-goose chase after all?

"Here goes!" muttered Diggory to himself. He opened the door, pulling it to again after him as he crept inside; then taking a step forward in the pitchy darkness, promptly fell over a bucket with an appalling crash. Scrambling once more to his feet, he felt in his waistcoat pocket, and finding there a fusee which he remembered to have taken from a box owned by "Rats," he struck it, and by the aid of its feeble glare crept behind the heap of benches which lay piled up close to the opposite wall.

Hardly had he done so when there were a sound of footsteps and a murmur of conversation; the door was opened, and some one crept into the den. No sooner had the new-comer crossed the threshold than he stopped, sniffed audibly, and exclaimed, -

"Hullo! what a stink of fusees! Who's been here, I wonder?"

Diggory instantly recognized the voice as belonging to Noaks, and the sound of it brought a momentary recollection of the time when he and Jack Vance had lain concealed behind the hedge opposite to Horace House. His heart beat fast, and he vainly wished that he had had sufficient forethought to come provided with some ordinary matches. Several more boys entered, and one of them struck a light. Diggory, peering through an aperture in the pile of forms, saw at a glance who they were - Fletcher senior, Thurston, Noaks, and Hawley.

"There don't seem to be any one about," continued Noaks, peering into the corners; "yet it's rum there should be such a smell of fusees."

"I expect it was the man," said Thurston, producing a candle-end, and sticking it in an empty ginger-beer bottle which lay on the ground. "He was in here this afternoon after some of those old boxes, and I expect he lit his pipe. The smell is sure to hang about when the door's shut."

The four boys sat down on two upturned buckets and a couple of old hampers, with the candle in their midst, and Diggory gave vent to an inward sigh of relief.

"Well," began Thurston, "one reason we meet here to-night is because I wanted to explain to you fellows that we can't have any more of those pleasant little parties in my study - at all events, for the present. Until this row about Browse has blown over, every one'll be watching us like cats watching a mouse. We ought not to be seen speaking together, and that's where that cipher business that old Fletcher invented will come in jolly useful. We can say anything we want to without appearing to meet."

"By-the-bye," interrupted Noaks, "what became of that last note? Mouler told me about it, or I shouldn't have come. Some one had taken it away before I went to look."

"Perhaps it was Gull," answered Thurston. "Where is he?"

"He's got some turned work to do," answered Hawley.

"Mouler's outside keeping *cave*" added Noaks. "We thought it would be well for some one to keep a look-out in case anybody came."

"Well, what I was going to say," continued Thurston, "is, that for the present we'd better lie low, and not be seen going about together. It was a good thing Gull and I managed to turn the tables on Oaks at that inquiry; it would have been jolly awkward for the rest of you to have proved an *alibi*. Of course it was agreed that I should keep out of it, as it was a dead certainty they'd pounce down on me first; so I went and sat all the evening with old Smeaton. Ha, ha! the fool quite thought I meant it when I asked him to help me about my work. But I say, how did it come off? I haven't heard the particulars."

"Oh, simply enough," answered Hawley. "Noaks and Mouler and Gull and I did the trick; young Grundy's was the voice that told Browse to go down to the 'lab.' Grundy hung about at the top of the stairs, and as soon as he saw Browse come back and make for Allingford's study, he let us know the coast was clear, so we unlocked the door and skedaddled. Gull went straight away to the matron's room, and asked her to sew the two buttons on his waistcoat; he'd pulled them off on purpose. He is a cunning beggar, that Gull. Fancy his staying behind to light the reading-room gas, and telling Lucas he'd only just come! Why, he did more of the wrecking than any two of us put together."

"D'you think young Grundy's to be trusted?" asked Noaks.

"Oh yes," answered Hawley; "he's been on our side all along. He had a fight with young what's-his-name not long ago, about that skit on the Town match. Besides, I've told him that if it gets out that he had a hand in that Browse business, he'll be expelled. So he'll keep his mouth shut right enough."

"Oh, by-the-bye," cried Thurston, turning to his particular chum, "have you heard anything more about that poem of yours?"

Fletcher senior, who had been sitting all this time scowling in silence at the candle, answered shortly, "No."

"Hullo!" returned his friend, "what's the matter? You seem precious glum to-night. What's up? Are you going to chuck this business and turn good?"

"You asked me whether I'd heard anything more about that rhyme I wrote," answered the other, rousing himself, and speaking with a thrill of anger in his voice. "I say no, but I've *seen* a jolly lot."

"How d'you mean?"

"Why, there's not a fellow in the Sixth but gives me the cold shoulder. Allingford sets the example, and there's hardly one of them will give me a civil word. They'd like to oust me from the prefects like they did you, but they shan't, and, what's more, I'll get even chalks with some of them before I leave."

"Hear, hear!" exclaimed Thurston; "that's just what I say. And now the question is, what shall we do?"

"Nothing at present," answered the other. "We must wait until this affair's blown over. There's no need to run the risk of getting expelled; and, besides, we want some time to think of a plan."

The faint *clang, ter-ang* of a bell sounded across the playing field. Noaks and Hawley rose to their feet.

"'Prep!'" exclaimed the latter. "We must be off." A new cause for anxiety now presented itself to Diggory's mind in the thought that he would be late in taking his place in the big schoolroom. He knew that Noaks and Hawley would have to be in time for the assembly; but the two Sixth Form boys were not amenable to the same rule, and might linger behind.

Thurston, however, rose to his feet, blew out the candle, and the four conspirators groped their way in a body out through the low doorway.

Diggory waited until he thought they must have reached the school buildings, and then prepared to follow. The bell had stopped ringing some minutes, and without looking very carefully where he was going, he ran as fast as he could out of the match-ground, and across the junior field. Suddenly, right in front of him, and within fifty yards of the paved playground, a dark figure seemed all at once to rise out of the ground. It was Noaks! The latter had dropped a pencil-case, and had been left by his companions searching for it on his hands and knees.

"Hullo!" he exclaimed, catching the small boy by the arm. "Who are you? and where have you been?"

"What's that to you?" answered Diggory boldly; "let me go."

The remembrance of that mysterious smell of a fusee flashed across Noaks's mind.

"Look here!" he cried sharply. "You tell me this moment where you've been."

"In the other field."

"What were you doing there?"

"Running."

There was a moment's silence. Noaks had a strong suspicion that the other knew something about the secret meeting; it was equally possible, however, that he did not. Young madcaps were often known to let off steam by careering wildly round the field after dark, and if this had really been the case in the present instance, it would be folly to say anything that should awaken suspicion. The big fellow hesitated; then a happy thought occurred to him: he dragged his captive across the paved playground, and stopping under the gas-lamp which lit up the archway leading into the quadrangle, began a hasty examination of the contents of the latter's pockets. There was no time to lose, and failing to find what he sought, Noaks gave the youngster a final shake, saying as he did so: "Look here, have you forgotten that coin robbery? Because, if you have, I haven't. I've got that knife still. Don't you fall foul of me, or you'll have reason to be sorry for it, d'you hear?"

The two boys ran quickly across to the big school-room, and entered just in time to take their seats before the master on duty called, "Silence!"

As might have been expected, none of the Triple Alliance put in an appearance at supper that evening; as a matter of fact, they were congregated in a quiet corner of the box-room, listening to a graphic account of Diggory's adventures. Noaks's threat about the pocket-knife revived all their former feelings of dread and uneasiness respecting their unfortunate expedition to The Hermitage, and there was a grave look upon their faces as the narrative concluded.

"You see," said Diggory, as he brought his story to a close, "the thing was this: he wasn't quite sure whether I knew anything or not, but he said that to frighten me in case I did."

"I don't see that we can do anything," began Mugford uneasily. "You say they aren't going to kick up any other row just yet, and it would be an awful thing if Noaks found it out, and sent my knife to the police."

"No, I don't see very well what I can do," answered Diggory. "Somehow it seems rather mean to hide away and then go and tell what you've overheard. I think it's best to leave it, and keep a sharp look-out and see what happens next."

"Fancy Fletcher inventing that cipher," said Jack Vance, "and being mixed up with that lot. He is a double-faced beast; it was just like him making that underhanded attack on the football team."

"Yes," added Mugford; "and fancy Gull being in both those rows, and making every one believe he wasn't! They must be a deep lot."

"So they are," answered Diggory complacently; "but they aren't a match for the Triple Alliance."

"I say, what made Noaks search your pockets?" asked Jack, as the three friends prepared to break up their "confab."

"Oh, for a long time I couldn't imagine, and then all of a sudden I thought why it was. Don't you see, he wanted to find if I had any more fusees. My stars, I was glad 'Rats' had only given me one instead of the box!"

CHAPTER XIX.

A CHAPTER OF ACCIDENTS.

The firmest friendships, we are told, have been formed in mutual adversity; and among the many trials which served to strengthen and confirm the loyalty and unity of the Triple Alliance, a string of minor disasters which overtook them one unlucky day early in December must certainly not be overlooked.

The after results of this chapter of accidents cause it to assume an additional importance as being the "beginning of the end," alike of this narrative and of an eventful period in the history of Ronleigh College. The reader will understand, therefore, that in turning our attention for a short time to an account of the afore-mentioned misfortune of the three friends, we are not wandering from what might be called the main line of our story.

"It all came about," so said Jack Vance, "through Carton's having the cheek to go home some ten days before proper time." The latter certainly did, for one reason or another, leave Ronleigh on Wednesday, the eleventh of December; and by his own special request, our three friends came down to the station to see him off.

Harold Avery

"Have you got anything to read going along?" asked Diggory, as they stood lingering round the carriage door.

"Yes," answered Carton. "Look here, you fellows, you might get in and sit round the window till the train starts; it'll keep other people from getting in, and I shall have the place to myself."

The Triple Alliance did as they were requested.

"Aha, my boys!" continued Carton, rubbing his hands together, "when you're stewing away in 'prep' this evening, think of me at home eating a rattling good tea, and no more work to prepare after it for old Greyling."

"Oh, rubbish!" cried Jack. "I wouldn't go now even if I had the chance. Why, you'll miss all the fun of breaking up; and young 'Rats' is making up a party to fill a carriage, and we're going to have a fine spree. Then by the time we get home for Christmas it'll be all stale to you. Pshaw! I wouldn't - hullo! - here, stop a minute! - why, she's off!"

Off she certainly was. There had been a sharp chirrup of the whistle, and at almost the same moment the train began to move. Diggory tried to let down the window to get at the handle of the door; but the sash worked stiffly, and before he succeeded in making it drop, the train had run the length of the platform, and the station was left behind.

The four boys gazed at one another for a moment in blank astonishment, and then burst into a simultaneous roar of laughter.

"You'll have to go as far as Chatton now," said Carton. "Never mind; you can get back by the next train."

"Yes; but the question is if we've got any money," answered Jack Vance ruefully. "It's fourpence the single journey, so the fare there and back for three of us'll be two bob. Here's threepence; that's all the tin I'm worth. - what have you got, Diggy?"

"Four halfpenny stamps, and half a frank on my watch-chain," was the reply. "But I don't think these railway Johnnies 'ud take either of those."

On examination, the only articles of value Mugford's pockets were found to contain were an aluminium pencil-case which wouldn't work, and a dirty scrap of indiarubber.

"Look here," cried Carton, "I'll give you two shillings. It's my fault; and I've got something over from my journey-money."

The offer was gladly accepted, and at length, when the train reached Chatton, the three chums wished their companion good-bye, laughing heartily over their unexpected journey.

"What time's the next train back to Ronleigh?" asked Jack, as he paid the money for their fare to the ticket-collector.

"Let's see," answered the official: "next train to Ronleigh - 5.47."

Jack's face fell. "Isn't there any train before that?" he asked. "We've got to be back at the school by half-past five."

"Can't help that," returned the man; "next train from here to Ronleigh's 5.47. And," he added, encouragingly, "she's nearly always a bit late."

The boys wandered disconsolately through the booking-office of the little country station, and halted outside to consider what was to be done.

"It's five-and-twenty past four," said Jack Vance, looking at his watch, "and it's a good six miles by road; we shall never walk it in the time."

"It's a good bit shorter by rail," mused Diggory, "if we could walk along the line. That tunnel under Arrow Hill cuts off a long round."

"We couldn't do that," said Mugford; "there are notice-boards all over the shop saying that trespassers on the railway will be prosecuted."

"Oh, bother that," cried Jack Vance, suddenly smitten with Diggory's idea. "Who cares for notice-boards? We'll go home along the line. If we trot every now and then, we shall get back in time."

"Well, we'd better walk along the road as far as that curve," said Diggory, "and then they won't see us from the station."

The trio started off in the direction indicated, hurrying along the permanent way, hopping over the sleepers, and seeing how far they could run on one of the metals without falling off. At length they entered a cutting, the steep banks of which rose gradually until they towered high above their heads on either hand. Before long the mouth of the tunnel was reached, and, as if by mutual consent, the three friends came to a halt.

There was something forbidding about the dark, gloomy entrance - the stale, smoky smell, and the damp dripping from the roof, all tending to give it a very uninviting aspect.

"It's awfully long," said Mugford; "don't you think we'd better turn back?"

In their secret hearts his two companions were more than half inclined to follow this suggestion; but there is a form of cowardice to which even the bravest are subject - namely, the fear of being thought afraid - and it was this, perhaps, which decided them to advance instead of retreat.

"Oh no, we won't go back," cried Diggory. "Come along; I'll go first." And so saying, he plunged forward into the deep shadow of the archway.

The ground seemed to be plentifully strewn with ashes, which scrunched under their feet as they plodded along, and their voices sounded hollow and strange.

"My eye," said Jack, "it's precious dark. I can hardly see where I'm going."

"It'll be darker still before we see the end," answered Diggory. "Some one was telling me the other day that there's a curve in the middle."

"Hadn't we better go back?" faltered Mugford.

"No, you fathead; shut up."

The darkness seemed to increase, and the silence grew oppressive.

The boys were walking in single file, Diggory leading, and Jack Vance bringing up the rear.

"I say," exclaimed the latter, as he stumbled over a sleeper, "I shouldn't like to be caught here by a train."

"That can't happen," retorted Diggory; "didn't you hear the man say there wasn't another till 5.47?"

"Yes," added Mugford; "but there might be a luggage, or one coming the other way."

"Well, all you'd have to do would be to cross over on to the other line."

Imperceptibly the boys quickened their pace until it became almost a trot.

"Hurrah!" cried Diggory, a few moments later, as a far-distant semicircle of daylight came into view. "There's the other end."

"Stop a minute," cried Jack, emboldened by the prospect of soon being once more in the fresh air; "let's see if we can make an echo."

The little party halted for a moment, but instead of hearing the shrill yell for the production of which Jack had just filled his lungs, their ears were greeted with a far more terrible sound, which caused their hearts to stop beating. There was, it seemed, a sudden boom, followed by a long, continuous roar. Diggory turned his head, to find the far-off patch of light replaced by a spark of fiery red, and the terrible truth flashed across his mind that in the excitement of the moment he could not remember for certain which was the down line.

It was well for the Triple Alliance that at least one of their number was blessed with the faculty of quick decision and prompt action, or the history of their friendship might have had a tragic ending.

Diggory wheeled round, and catching hold of Mugford, cried in a voice loud enough to be heard above the ever-increasing din, "Quick! get into the six-foot way, and lie down!"

What followed even those who underwent the experience could never clearly describe. They flung themselves upon the ground: there were the thundering roar of an earthquake, coupled with a deafening clatter, as though the whole place were falling about their ears, and a whirling hurricane of hot air and steam.

In ten seconds, which seemed like ten minutes, the whole thing had come and gone, and Diggory, scrambling to his feet in the dense darkness of the choking atmosphere, inquired in a shaky voice, "Are you all right, you chaps?"

There was a reply in the affirmative, and the three boys proceeded to grope their way along in silence, until the broad archway of the tunnel's mouth appeared through a fog of steam and smoke.

"I say, you fellows," cried Diggory, as they emerged into the fresh air, "I wouldn't go through there again for something."

"It was a good thing you gave me that shove," said Mugford; "I felt as though I couldn't move. And we were standing on the very line it went over."

"Yes: I couldn't remember for the moment which was 'up' and which was 'down.' I thought, too, we should be safer lying flat on the ground when it passed; had we stood up in the six-foot way, we might have got giddy and fallen under the wheels."

The conversation was suddenly interrupted by a strange voice shouting, -

"Hullo, you young beggars! what are you a-doing there?"

The boys turned to see from whence this inquiry proceeded. Half-way up the cutting on their left was a little hut, and beside it stood the man who had spoken. The same glance showed them another thing - namely, that just beside this little shanty was one of the notice-boards Mugford had mentioned, warning the public that persons found trespassing on the railway would be prosecuted.

"Come along," cried Jack Vance; "let's bolt."

Unless they doubled back into the tunnel, their only way of escape lay in scaling the right side of the cutting, as a short distance down the line a gang of platelayers were at work, who would have intercepted them before they reached the open country.

"Come along," repeated Jack Vance, and the next

moment he and his two companions were clambering as fast as they could up the steep side of the embankment, clutching at bushes and tufts of grass, and causing miniature landslips of sand and gravel with every step they took.

The man shouted after them to stop, and seeing that they paid no attention to his commands, promptly gave chase, rushing down the narrow pathway from the hut, and scrambling after them up the opposite slope.

Jack Vance and Diggory, whose powers of wind and limb had benefited by constant exercise in the football field, were soon at the top; but Mugford, who was not inclined to be athletic, and who had already been pretty nearly pumped in hurrying out of the tunnel; was still slowly dragging himself up the ascent, panting and puffing like a steam-engine, when his comrades reached the summit.

His pursuer was gaining on him rapidly, and it was in vain that his two friends (too loyal to make good their escape alone) stood, and with frantic gestures urged him to quicker movement. Just, however, as the capture seemed certain, a great piece of loose earth giving way beneath the man's weight caused the latter to fall forward on his face. In this posture he tobogganed down the slope, with more force than elegance; and with a yell of triumph Jack and Diggory stretched out their hands, and dragged Mugford up to the level grassy plateau on which they stood.

Close behind them was a wood, and without a moment's hesitation they plunged through the hedge, and dashed on through the bushes. The dry twigs cracked, and the dead leaves rustled beneath their feet.

Harold Avery

Suddenly, not more than fifty yards away to their right, there was the loud explosion of a gun, and almost at the same instant a harsh-voice shouted: "Hi there - stop! Where are you going?"

"Oh," panted Jack, "it's one of the keepers! Run for all you're worth!"

The opposite edge of the wood was not far distant. The three youngsters rushed wildly on, and stumbling blindly over the boundary hedge, continued their mad gallop across a narrow field. Over another hedge, and they were in a sunken roadway. Then came the end. Mugford staggered over to the opposite bank, and falling down upon it with his hand pressed to his side, gasped out, "Awful stitch - can't go any further!"

Years afterwards, when the Triple Alliance met at an Old Boys' dinner, they laughed heartily in talking over this adventure; but there were no signs of mirth on any of their faces at the time it was happening. Then as Jack Vance and Diggory stood staring blankly at each other in the deepening winter twilight, they suddenly blossomed out into heroes - heroes, it is true, in flannel cricket-caps and turned-down collars, but heroes, at all events to my mind, as genuine in the spirit which prompted their action as those whose deeds are known in song and story. The barking of a dog in the field above showed that the keeper was following up their trail.

"Bun for it!" panted Mugford; "don't wait for me!"

"Shan't!" said Jack and Diggory in one voice; and the latter, sticking his hands in his trouser pockets, began to whistle.

"Go on!" cried Mugford.

"Shan't!" repeated his companions.

It was evident that the Triple Alliance would sink or swim together, and it so happened that by a piece of unexpected good fortune they were destined to realize the latter alternative. There was a clatter of wheels, the quick stamp of a fast-trotting horse, and a baker's cart came swinging round the corner. Diggory, whose wits never seemed to desert him at a critical moment, recognized it at once as belonging to the man who supplied the school, and springing forward he beckoned to the driver to stop, crying, -

"I say, give us a lift into Ronleigh, and we'll pay you a shilling. We belong to the college."

The man peered round the canvas covering, and at once recognized the boys' cap and crest.

"All right," he said. "Hop up; I'll find room for you somewhere."

The danger was past; with an audible sigh of relief the three youngsters clambered into the vehicle, and the next moment were bowling rapidly along in the direction of the town.

"I say," cried Jack, "this is a stroke of good luck. Why, we shall be back in time after all."

The remainder of their conversation was lost to the ears of the driver, but seemed to consist mainly of a series of attempts on the part of Mugford to say something, which were always interrupted by a chorus

Harold Avery

of groans, and shouts of "Shut up!" from his two companions.

At length the cart arrived at Ronleigh, and set down the three passengers at the corner of Broad Street, the principal thoroughfare; and here their adventures seemed to have terminated.

I say *seemed*, because, as a matter of fact, something still remains to be told in the history of this eventful day; but before proceeding to the close of the chapter, it will be well to say a word or two with regard to a certain person connected with it who is as yet unknown to the reader.

Ronleigh was fortunate in having a staff of masters who won the respect and confidence of the boys. Some poor-spirited fellows there are who will always abuse those set in authority over them; but at Ronleigh there was happily, on the whole, a mutual good understanding, such as might exist in a well and wisely disciplined regiment between officers and men.

Exceptions, however, prove the rule; and when at the commencement of the present winter term a new junior master had come to take charge of the Third Form, it was evident from the first that before long there would be trouble. Mr. Grice was a very short man, with a pompous, hectoring manner, which was, somehow, especially exasperating to fellows who stood a good head and shoulders taller than the master. His rule was founded on the fear of punishment, and the sceptre which he wielded was a small black note-book, in which he entered the names of all offenders with an accompanying "Hundred lines, Brown!" or "Write the lesson out after school, Smith." Lastly, Mr. Grice was not a gentleman. Boys, I know, pay little attention to the conventionalities, and are seldom found consulting books on etiquette; but those who have been well brought up, and accustomed at home to an air of refinement, are quick to detect ill-breeding and bad manners in those older than themselves, and who "ought to know better." So it came about that Mr. Grice was unpopular, and the boys in his class bemoaned their fate, and called him uncomplimentary nicknames.

We left the three friends standing at the corner of Broad Street. The church clock had just struck the quarter-past five, and by this time it was dark, though the street was lit up by the gas-lamps and the long rows of shop windows.

"I hope no one sees us," said Jack Vance. "I'm mud all over. We must look sharp, or we shall be late."

"Hullo!" exclaimed Diggory, "look out! Here's that wretched little Grice coming; there, he's stopped to look into the ironmonger's shop. We must dodge past him somehow, or he'll want to know where we've been."

The trio crossed quickly over to the opposite side of the street, and hurried off at full speed in the direction of the school.

All boys were supposed to be on the school premises by half-past five, and at that time the door leading to the outer world was locked by the prefect for the day.

Oaks, who happened to be on duty, was standing in the passage talking to Allingford when the three juveniles arrived, out of breath and flushed with running.

"Hullo, you kids! where have you been?" inquired the captain.

Diggory launched out into a brief description of their many adventures; Oaks laughed heartily. "Well," he said, pulling out his watch, "you've just got back in time; half a minute more, and you'd have been outside, my boys."

The prefect locked the door, and continuing his conversation with Allingford, started off down the passage. On reaching what was the main corridor on the ground floor, they paused for a moment, and stood warming their hands at the hot-water pipe, and it was while thus engaged that they were suddenly accosted by Mr. Grice, who bustled up to them in a great state of excitement.

"Are you on duty, Oaks?"

"Yes, sir."

"Have any boys come in late?"

"No, sir."

"Well, three boys passed me in the town; I think one of them was young Trevanock. I called to them to stop, but they took no notice. When they come in, you send than to me."

"They weren't late, sir," answered Oaks; "they came in about a minute ago."

"Oh, nonsense. I looked at my watch when I saw them in the town, and then it was five-and-twenty past; they couldn't have come up in five minutes. You must either have let them in, or not closed the door at the proper time."

Prefects at Ronleigh were not in the habit of being lectured as though they were lower-school boys. Oaks bit his lip.

"I closed the door on the stroke of half-past," he answered.

"Well, you say those boys came in about two minutes ago. By me it's now twenty to six, so they must have been late."

"They were in before half-past, sir; your watch must be wrong."

"Don't keep contradicting me, sir," said the master.

"We are supposed to work by the school clock, sir," interposed the captain.

"I'm not aware that I addressed any remark to you, Allingford," retorted Mr. Grice, rapidly losing all control of his temper. "You need make no further attempt to teach me the rules of the school; I flatter myself that I am sufficiently well versed in them already."

A crowd of idlers, attracted by the angry tones of the master's voice, had begun to collect in the passage, and the captain flushed to the roots of his hair at being thus taken to task in public.

"I merely said, sir, that we work by the school clock."

"And I say, hold your tongue, sir. - Oaks, remember you report those three boys for being late."

"I can't do that, sir," answered Oaks stolidly, "for they were in time."

Mr. Grice boiled over. "You are a very impertinent fellow," he cried. "I shall report you both to the doctor." And so saying, he turned on his heel and walked away.

There was a buzz of astonishment among the bystanders. The idea of a captain of Ronleigh being reported to the doctor was something novel indeed, and by the time the first bell rang for tea, a report of the collision between Mr. Grice and the prefects had spread all over the school.

CHAPTER XX.

SOWING THE WIND.

The passage of arms between Mr. Grice and the two prefects was eagerly discussed by boys of all ages. Exaggerated reports spread from mouth to mouth, each teller of the story adding to it some details drawn from his own imagination, until, away down in the Second Form, it was confidently asserted that Oaks had called Mr. Grice a "little tin monkey," and that Allingford had boxed the master's ears; which enormities would most certainly result in the expulsion of the two offenders.

As a matter of fact, the expected storm never burst. The first thing the doctor did on receiving Mr. Grice's complaint was to compare that gentleman's watch with his own. "Hum'" he said shortly, "I suppose you're aware that you *are* ten minutes fast?"

A few moments later Mr. Grice withdrew, looking rather crestfallen. As may be imagined, the result of his interview with the head-master was never made public, and in the meantime Ronleians old and young were expressing their high approval of the conduct of their captain and his lieutenant. The gilt was beginning to wear off the Thurstonian gingerbread, and sensible fellows, who could tell the difference between jewel and paste, were less inclined than ever to be led by the nose by such fellows as Gull and Hawley. Here was an instance in which the prefects had taken a stand against palpable injustice, and the action had caused the whole body to rise several pegs in everybody's estimation.

The near approach of the Wraxby football match caused a revival of good, honest public spirit. If only Ronleigh could beat the Grammar School this year at footer as well as at cricket, every one felt that their cup of joy would run over, and the champions who were to strive for the wished-for victory were naturally regarded, for the time being, as standing on more exalted ground than their fellows. Ever since the exposure of Fletcher senior as the author of "College *v.* Town," the poem had become a weapon turned against the writer and his party. Boys had gone to the bottom of the matter, and discovering the real reason of Thurston's absence from the team, had declared that a fellow who out of spite would refuse to give his services to uphold the honour of the school had forfeited all claim on their consideration or sympathy. Such was the state of popular feeling when, with the clang of the getting-up bell on Thursday morning, the twelfth of December, a day commenced fraught with unexpected episodes and situations closely affecting the interests of the Triple Alliance.

One might have thought that their adventures on the previous afternoon had afforded them sufficient excitement for at least one week; but these were destined to prove but the prelude to an event of still greater importance. The three friends went into school at nine o'clock, looking forlorn and miserable. Some-thing, indeed, had happened to mar their happiness, and the cause of their depression was as follows: -

Soon after breakfast, when the contents of the post-bag had been distributed as usual, Mugford accosted his two chums, who were strolling up and down the quadrangle. A look of abject misery was on his face, and in his hand he held an open letter.

"Hullo!" cried Jack Vance; "what's up? You look as if you had lost a sovereign and found sixpence!"

"Matter enough," murmured Mugford, whose heart was evidently in his mouth: "I'm going to leave."

"Going to leave!" exclaimed Diggory; "what ever d'you mean?"

"Well, I don't mind telling you fellows," answered the other. "You know my guv'nor isn't well off, and he says he's lost money, and can't afford to keep me at Ronleigh. I know I'm no good, and you fellows'll get on all right without me, and - "

The sentence not being completed, the two other boys glanced at the speaker's face, and from previous indications in the tone of his voice were not surprised to find that he was crying. Two years appear a long time when one is on the bright side of twenty, and the friendship seemed to have lasted for ages. At the near prospect of separation all Mugford's little failings were forgotten, and both Diggory and Jack Vance felt that life without him would be a blank.

"Oh, dash it all!" said the latter; "you mustn't go? Isn't there anything we can do? Shall I write to your guv'nor?"

The idea of Jack Vance addressing a remonstrance to

Harold Avery

his respected parent caused the ghost of a smile to appear on Mugford's doleful face.

"No, it's no good," he answered. "There's nothing for it; I shall have to leave."

During the interval which divided morning school and the free time before dinner the three friends mooned about together, trying in vain to regard the future in a more cheerful light, and to make plans for keeping touch of each other by an interchange of letters and a possible meeting in the holidays.

"It's all very well," said Jack Vance to Diggory, when late on in the afternoon he happened to come across the latter flattening his nose against the glass of the box-room window - "it's all very well talking about writing and all that; but this is the end of the Triple Alliance."

"Yes," answered Diggory, after a moment's thought, "I suppose it is. I wish we could do something more before it's broken up."

As he spoke, he passed his hand mechanically along the lower surface of the window ledge; then with a sudden exclamation he went down on his knees, and picked something out of the wall.

It was another note written in cipher!

The missive was certainly very brief, consisting of only seven letters: -

"GLMRTSG."

"Hullo!" said Jack Vance; "they're at it again!"

His companion made no reply, but taking out a pencil, copied the cipher on the back of an envelope, and then replaced the mysterious document in the crack between the window-frame and the bricks.

"What are you doing that for?"

"Why, because they may miss it, and smell a rat. Come on; let's get the key and see what it means."

In this instance the translation of the cryptograph did not occupy much time; Diggory produced his double alphabet, and soon spelt out the word: -

"*To-night.*"

The two chums gazed at each other for a few moments in silence.

"What does it mean?" queried Jack.

"I don't know, unless it is that they are going to have another meeting after tea under the pavilion."

"Let's find Mug, and hear what he thinks."

In discussing their new find and attempting to solve its meaning, the three friends forgot for the time being the melancholy tidings they had received that morning, and gave themselves up to a full enjoyment of the mystery.

"I can't see," said Mugford, "that it means anything else than that they are going to have another meeting."

"Yes, that's it. I shall go down to the pavilion again after tea, and see what's up. I shouldn't wonder if there is going to be another row. Fletcher said he meant to do something before he left, and there isn't much time now before the end of the term."

"Shan't Mug or I go this time?" asked Jack Vance; "it's rather a risky business."

"No, I'll go; I know now just where to hide."

During the half-hour between tea and evening prepa- ration Jack Vance and Mugford lingered about in the dark and deserted quadrangle, anxiously awaiting their comrade's return. Once only was the silence broken, by Maxton chasing young "Rats" from the gymnasium into the big school, shouting, "I'll lick you, you little villain!" but with this exception, our two friends had the place to themselves.

It was a raw, cold night; every one seemed, very naturally, to be keeping indoors, and there were no signs of any members of the secret society being abroad. Jack Vance and his companion trotted softly up and down, endeavouring to keep themselves warm. At length, when their patience was wellnigh exhausted, there was a sound of footsteps, and Diggory was descried coming through the archway leading to the playing fields.

"Well," cried his two chums, in low, eager tones, "what have you heard?"

The answer was certainly one they had least expected,

"Nothing."

"Nothing! what d'you mean?"

"Why, they didn't come; there wasn't any meeting. I waited and waited, until I saw it was no use staying any longer; so then I gave it up as a bad job."

"Did the note really say to-night?"

"Yes: I went down just before tea to see if it was still there, and I brought it away with me. Here, look for yourself."

As he spoke, Diggory produced the slip of paper from his waistcoat pocket. By the light of the archway lamp it was compared with a hastily-constructed key, and the former translation was found to be correct.

The Triple Alliance had certainly for once in a way "drawn blank," and the preparation bell putting an end to their further deliberations, they directed their steps toward the schoolroom, wondering more than ever what could be the meaning of that significant word, "To-night."

Now, the real reason of the three friends being thus at fault in their investigations was simply this: they were exactly twenty-four hours behindhand in their attempt to unravel the mystery. The conclusion they had come to with regard to the meaning of the note was correct: a tacit understanding had existed for some time among the inner circle of the Thurstonian party that this should be the signal for a gathering of the clan; but the note, when Diggory had found it, had been lying in the impromptu post office for a day and a half, and the meeting to which it was a summons had already taken place on the previous evening.

For the reader, who is a privileged person, we intend to put back the clock, and leaving the Triple Alliance dividing their attention between attempts to discover the meaning, first of their Latin author, and secondly of the enigma formed by this perplexing single-worded epistle, we will give a short account of the gathering to which it referred.

It was while the greater number of their school-fellows were gathered in numerous little groups, whiling away the free time before preparation discussing the various rumours that were current respecting Mr. Grice's encounters with Oaks and Allingford, that the same five conspirators assembled for another secret "confab" in the den beneath the pavilion.

In one way it was a fortunate thing for Diggory that he did not discover the note sooner, for hardly had Thurston set the lighted candle in the empty bottle than Noaks picked it up, and peered carefully into each of the four corners, and behind the heaps of benches and other lumber.

"What are you doing that for?" asked Gull.

"Oh, only to see that no one's come who wasn't invited. D'you remember last time what a stink there was of a burnt fusee? Well, after you'd gone I found young Trevanock knocking about the field, and I wouldn't swear but what he knew something about our meeting. I searched the young beggar's pockets; but he hadn't got any more lights, so I let him go."

The party grouped themselves round the candle, as they had done on the previous occasion, when Diggory had watched their movements from behind the pile of forms, and Thurston, with an inquiring look at Fletcher, asked, "Well, what's the object of this pleasant little reunion?"

"I suppose you can pretty well guess," answered the other. "The last time we were here we all agreed that before the end of the term was up we'd get even chalks with Allingford and Co. Well, seeing there's only eight days left, I thought it was about time we had another meeting, and decided what we were going to do. - By-the-bye," added the speaker, turning with something like a sneer on his lips, and addressing his chum, "it's the Wraxby match on Saturday; I suppose they haven't asked you to play in the team?"

The shaft went home, and Thurston's face darkened with anger.

"No," he answered indignantly, "and I wouldn't play, not if they all went down on their knees and begged me to. What do I care about the Wraxby match? If I could, I'd put a stopper on it, and bring the whole thing to the ground."

"Well," continued Fletcher calmly, "that's just what we're going to do. If you'd asked me this morning how we could put a spoke in Allingford's wheel, and pay out him and a lot of those other prigs like Oaks and Rowlands, I couldn't have told you; but now the thing's as easy as pat. They'll find out they haven't cold-shouldered me at every turn and corner for nothing. I'll give them tit for tat, and after Christmas, when I've left this beastly place, I'll write and tell them who did it."

"You seem to have got your back up, old chap," said Thurston, referring to the bitter tones in which the last

Harold Avery

few sentences had been spoken; "but out with it - what's your plan?"

"Why, this: I'd no idea what a chance we should have when I stuck that note in our pillar-box, but here it is all ready made. Allingford and Oaks have had a row with little Grice; he's reported them, and it's quite natural they should want to pay him out for doing it. As they're such good boys, I don't suppose they'll try anything of the kind; but we might undertake the job, and do it for them."

The speaker paused to see if he had been understood.

"What!" exclaimed Thurston bluntly, "you mean, play Grice a trick and make it appear they'd done it because of this rumpus about locking the door?"

"That's about it," returned the other, laughing. "What could we do better?"

Noaks murmured his approval of the scheme, but Gull and Hawley were silent. To tell the truth, since the big row following their attack on Browse had put a stop to any further chance of card-parties and other amusements in Thurston's study, their attachment to the ex-prefect had considerably lessened. Like many others of their kind, they were thoroughly selfish at heart, and saw no good in running any personal risk to settle the quarrels of a third person. The party feeling which had characterized the last school elections, and caused for the time being a spirit of ill-will and opposition towards the school leaders, had just about died a natural death; and if another public meeting had been called in the gymnasium, not half a dozen fellows would have shouted for Thurston, or allied themselves against the side of law and order. All this had tended to make Hawley and Gull lukewarm in their adherence to the cause. Noaks, however, who would have paid any price for the privilege of being able to hobnob with those who were in any higher position than himself, was ready to follow his two Sixth Form cronies to any extreme they might suggest.

"Well," he inquired, "and what's to be the trick?"

"I only just thought of one on the spur of the moment," answered Fletcher; "but if no one else has a better to suggest, I daresay it'll do. We might screw up little Grice's bedroom door so as to get him down late in the morning; his room's right away at the end of the passage. There is a screw-driver belonging to Oaks lying in one of the empty lockers - it has his name on the handle; and if we happened to drop it as we came away, I think that in the face of this row it would look uncommonly like his doing. D'you twig?"

There was something so mean and cowardly in this scheme, and in the manner in which the proposal was made, that even Thurston gave vent to an exclamation of contempt.

"So that's your little game, is it?" he inquired.

"Yes, that's it; that's my little project for putting a stop to the Wraxby match. There'll be an awful row, and the doctor'll keep the team from going. Now, then, who'll do the trick? - Will you, Hawley?"

"No fear," answered Hawley. "Gull and I did most of the last two blow-ups; it's some one else's turn now. Suppose you do it yourself, as it's your idea."

Fletcher frowned: in matters of this sort he liked to make the plans and get others to execute them. "Well, I was thinking one of you might," he began.

"Oh, bother!" interrupted Thurston, whose revengeful spirit had been once more aroused by the mention of the Wraxby match - "it's nothing; you and I'll do it."

"And I'll help if you like," added Noaks, who thought the present occasion a good opportunity to distinguish himself.

"All right," continued Thurston: "you go down town and get some screws, Noaks - two or three good long ones."

"Well, we'll fix to-morrow night," said Fletcher. "Keep awake, and meet at the top of B staircase, say at one o'clock; then there's no fear but what every one'll be asleep."

The Triple Alliance had for some hours ceased to puzzle their brains over either Virgil or cipher notes, and the whole of Ronleigh College was apparently wrapped in slumber, when three shadowy figures assembled on the landing at the top of staircase B, and proceeded noiselessly along the corridor, and down the side passage at the end of which Mr. Grice's room was situated.

"Have you got the screws?"

"Yes," answered Noaks, producing a twist of paper from his pocket.

"Don't you think I'd better go and keep *cave* at the

top of the stairs?" whispered Fletcher.

"No," returned Thurston; "Noaks can do that. I'll make the two holes, and you must put the screws in; you're the best carpenter of the lot."

Standing in the cold, dark passage, the work seemed to take ages to perform; but at length it was finished.

"Hist! what are you doing?"

Fletcher had produced a scrap of paper from his pocket, and was seemingly about to slip it under the door.

"I want to make certain that it shall be put down to Oaks," he whispered; "so in case the screw-driver should be overlooked, I'm going to slip this under the door for Grice to find in the morning."

Thurston glanced at the paper, and saw printed thereon in bold capitals the following inscription: -

"BE IN TIME BY THE SCHOOL CLOCK."

CHAPTER XXI.

REAPING THE WHIRLWIND.

Work at Ronleigh commenced with a sort of half-hour's preliminary practice in the various classrooms; the school then assembled for prayers, after which came breakfast. During the progress of this meal on the Friday morning, in the small hours of which had been enacted the scene described at the end of the previous chapter, it became evident that "something was up." The table, at which sat most of the boys of the Third Form, was in a state of great disorder, while the discussion of some topic of unusual interest seemed to be occupying the attention of the prefects. It was not, however, until after the boys had swarmed out of the dining-hall that the reason of this subdued commotion became generally known; and then, like the sudden report of an explosion, every one seemed to become acquainted with the news at the same moment. Mr. Grice had been screwed up in his bedroom! Oaks and Allingford had done it! The doctor had summoned them to meet him in his study!

It was from a member of the Third Form that the Triple Alliance heard the particulars of what had happened. "'Little Grice,'" said this young gentleman, whose own height was about four feet two inches - "'little Grice' never turned up until just before the bell rang for prayers, and then he was simply bursting with rage, and told us all about it. They'd put a note under his door telling him to be in time by the school clock; and besides that, when one of the men went to get him out, he found a screw-driver with Oaks's name on, so it's as clear as day who did it."

This conversation took place in the quadrangle. Travers, the Third Form boy, rushed off to impart his information to other hearers, and the three chums passed on through the archway, and came to a standstill in a quiet corner of the paved playground.

"Well," asked Diggory, "who did it?"

"Who d'you think it was?" retorted Jack Vance.

"Why, some of Thurston's lot, I believe."

"So do I."

Mugford, who was always rather slow at grasping a new idea, opened his eyes in astonishment. "But," he exclaimed, "how about the paper and the screwdriver?"

"Pooh!" answered Diggory, "how about that cipher note that said, 'To-night'?"

"Of course," added Jack Vance, "they'd evidently arranged it beforehand, and that paper was to say when they were to do the trick."

It seems possible sometimes to come by wrong roads to a right conclusion; and though the boys were mistaken in changing from their first opinion as to the meaning of the note, yet in this instance their error caused them to hit the right nail on the head.

"It was one of Thurston's lot who did it," repeated Diggory decisively; "neither Oaks nor Allingford would ever dream of doing such a mad thing."

"I don't see exactly how you can prove it," said Jack Vance thoughtfully; "that one word 'To-night' might mean anything."

"Of course it's no proof in itself," answered the other; "but what I mean to say is, that if the doctor, or any other sensible chap, knew all we do about the cipher, and what they said at their last meeting, he wouldn't doubt for a moment but that it was one of them who screwed up Grice's door. Travers says the doctor has sent for Oaks and old Ally; it'll be an awful shame if they get into a row."

"I don't see how they are going to get out of it," sighed Mugford.

"Then I do," answered Diggory stoutly, with a sudden flash in his bright eyes: "the Triple Alliance can get them out!"

"How?"

"Why, we must tell all we know, and show Dr. Denson the note."

"When?"

"Now."

"Won't it be sneaking?"

"I should consider we were beastly sneaks if we didn't."

"So we should be!" exclaimed Jack Vance. "They've always been jolly decent to us, and it was on our account they had this row with Grice."

"If Noaks finds we've split, he'll send that knife to the police," said Mugford.

"I don't care a straw what Noaks does," answered Diggory boldly. "You fellows needn't have anything to do with it; I'll go and tell Dr. Denson myself."

"No; I'll come too," said Jack.

"So'll I," added Mugford; and off they started. It was always a great ordeal to enter the doctor's study, even in what might be termed times of peace; and now, as Diggory turned the handle of the door, in answer to the muffled "Come in" which had followed his knock, the three friends experienced a sudden shortness of breath, and an unpleasant sinking sensation at the pit of the stomach.

The two prefects were standing at the front of the writing-table. Allingford's face was very white, and Oaks's very red, "for all the world like the Wars of the Roses," as Jack Vance afterwards remarked, though it would be difficult to clearly understand the simile.

The head-master glanced round for a moment to see who had entered the room, and, without taking any further notice of the three juveniles, continued the

Harold Avery

speech he was in the act of making when they entered the apartment.

"I am not going to defend the action of Mr. Grice," he was saying. "We are all apt to make mistakes, and I will tell you candidly that on this occasion I think Mr. Grice was unwise; but it is absolutely necessary that I should uphold the authority of my masters. If boys consider they are not justly dealt with, they have me to appeal to; but the idea that disputes between the two should be settled by practical joking is simply outrageous. This is the first instance of the kind that I ever remember to have happened at Ronleigh, and I tell you plainly that I am determined to make an example of the offenders."

"I assure you, sir," said Oaks, in a low, agitated voice, "that we have had no hand in this matter."

"I am sorry even to seem to doubt your word, Oaks," answered the doctor, "but I think you must own that appearances are very much against you. A screw-driver bearing your name was found in the passage, and this piece of paper, which was pushed under the bedroom door, and which now lies before me, bears a direct reference to the dispute about the school time. As far as I can see at present, the only conclusion which can be arrived at is that this is an act of retaliation which has sprung from your contention with Mr. Grice."

The captain was about to speak, but Dr. Denson held up his hand.

"As I said before," he continued, "I am sorry, Allingford, even to appear to doubt your word; I have always had reason to rely with confidence upon the integrity and honour of my prefects, and believe me, this interview is to me an exceedingly painful one. The matter, however, is too serious to be passed over lightly, and you must hear me to the end. The conduct of the school during the present term has been far from satisfactory: two acts of gross misconduct have already been committed, and I cannot but blame those whom I hold mainly responsible for the order of the school that in both instances the offenders should have gone unpunished. It seems hardly possible to me that such things should happen without its coming to the ears of the prefects who were the perpetrators of the deeds in question. Here we have a third example of the same thing. If neither of you took any actual part in screwing up this door, I am still inclined to think that you must have been cognizant of the act, and I demand to know the names of the offenders. Take time to think before you answer. I warn you once more that I am determined to sift the matter to the bottom."

Once more the two prefects protested that they had not the remotest idea who had played the trick on Mr. Grice.

Dr. Denson frowned, and sat for some moments without speaking, rapping the blotting-pad in front of him with the butt end of a seal; then remembering the presence of the small boys, he turned towards them with an inquiring look.

"Well?"

Diggory's face wore something of the same expression which Jack and Mugford had seen upon it when long ago their friend first distinguished himself at The

Birches by going down the slide on skates. He gave a nervous little cough, and advancing towards the head-master's table, laid thereon the cipher note, at the same time remarking, "If you please, sir, we know who screwed up little - hem! Mr. Grice's door, or, at all events, we think we do."

So sudden and unexpected was this announcement that it caused the doctor to half rise from his chair, while Oaks and Allingford turned and gazed at the speaker in open-mouthed astonishment. They none of them expected for a moment that the three youngsters had come for any more important purpose than to solicit orders for new caps or "journey-money," and this confession came like a thunderbolt from a clear sky.

"What!" exclaimed the head-master, taking the scrap of paper, and glancing alternately from the mystic word to the boy's face - "what on earth is this? Explain yourself."

It would be unnecessary to attempt a verbatim report of Diggory's evidence; in doing so we should but be repeating facts with which the reader is already acquainted. Let it suffice to say that, with many haltings and stumbles, he gave a full account of his finding the first cipher, translating the same, attending the secret meeting, and, lastly, discovering on the previous day the brief note which he had just produced.

The telling of the tale occupied some considerable time, for the doctor had many questions to ask; and when it came to the account of the conversation which had taken place under the pavilion, his face visibly darkened.

"My eye," remarked Diggory, an hour later, "I wouldn't go through that again for something! I swear that by the time I'd finished the perspiration was running down my back in a regular stream."

"Well," said the doctor, turning to Jack Vance and Mugford, when their companion had finished speaking, "and what have you two got to say?"

"Only the same as Trevanock, sir; we - we found it out together."

"Then, in the first place, why didn't you tell me all this before?"

"We were afraid to, sir," faltered Jack Vance; "and we thought it would be sneaking."

"Dear, dear," exclaimed the head-master impatiently, "when will you boys see things in a proper light? You think it wrong to tell tales, and yet quite right that innocent people should suffer for things done by these miserable cowards!"

"No, sir," answered Diggory: "we've come now to try to get Oaks out of a scrape; though we - were afraid - "

"Afraid of what?"

"Nothing, sir."

"Afraid of telling more tales, I suppose. Well, well; the question now is whether the same boys are guilty of having screwed up Mr. Grice's door. Why they should have done such a thing I don't understand, nor do I see how it is to be brought home to them simply by means of this exceedingly brief note."

There was a silence. Diggory glanced up, and received a look from the two prefects that amply repaid him for the trying ordeal through which he had just passed. Jack Vance leaned over to whisper something in his ear, when their attention was attracted by an exclamation of surprise from Dr. Denson.

"Aha! what does this mean? - Look here, Allingford."

Every member of the company edged forward, and looking down at what lay on the writing-table, saw in a moment that the mystery was solved.

The communication which had been slipped under the bedroom door was written on a half-sheet of small-sized note-paper; a similar piece of stationery had been used for the cipher note. The head-master had accidentally brought them together on his blotting-pad and the rough, torn edge of the one fitted exactly into the corresponding side of the other. They had both unmistakably come from the same source!

Even the dread atmosphere of the doctor's study could not restrain some show of excitement on the part of those interested in this disclosure, but it was quickly suppressed.

"Oaks," said the doctor, "go and give my compliments to Mr. Cowland, and ask him to open school for me; and at the same time inform the following boys that I wish to see them at once, here in my study: Fletcher One, Thurston, Gull, Hawley, and Noaks."

To the Triple Alliance hours seemed to pass before a

shuffling of feet in the passage announced the arrival of the Thurstonians. One by one they filed into the room, the door was shut, and there was a moment of awful silence. Even Diggory trembled, and Allingford, noticing it, laid his big hand reassuringly on the small boy's shoulder.

"I wish to know," began the doctor, "which of you boys were concerned in what took place last night? I refer, of course, to the screwing up of Mr. Grice's bedroom door."

No one spoke, but Fletcher turned pale to the lips.

"Had you anything to do with it, Fletcher?"

"No, sir."

"Then will you tell me the meaning of this?" continued the head-master, holding up the cipher note.

"I - I don't know what it means," began the prefect.

"Don't lie to me, sir," interrupted the doctor sternly. "You know very well what it means; it's of your own invention."

Thurston saw clearly that the game was up, and with the recklessness of despair decided at once to accept the inevitable.

"I screwed up Mr. Grice's door," he said sullenly.

"And who assisted you?"

To this inquiry Thurston would give no reply, but

maintained a dogged silence. Gull and Hawley, however, anxious at all costs to save their own skins, practically answered the question by saying, "We didn't," and casting significant glances at Noaks and Fletcher.

What followed it is hardly necessary to describe in detail. The five culprits were subjected to a merciless cross-examination, during which a confession, not only of their various transgressions, but also of the motives which had prompted them to adopt such a line of conduct, was dragged from their unwilling lips. The cloak was torn off, and the cowardice and meanness of their actions appeared plainly revealed, and were forced home even to their own hearts.

"Thurston and Fletcher," said the doctor, when at length, long after the bell had rung for "interval," the inquiry concluded, "go to your studies, and remain there till you hear from me - Noaks, go in like manner to the housekeeper's room. - Gull and Hawley, as you seem to have taken no active part in this last misde-meanour, you may go. As regards your previous misconduct, I shall speak to you on that subject when I have decided what is to be done with your companions."

For the Triple Alliance the remainder of the day passed in a whirl of conflicting emotions. In a very short time the whole school knew exactly what had taken place in the doctor's study, and every boy was incensed at the underhanded meanness of this attempted attack on Oaks and Allingford. It was a good thing for Thurston and Fletcher that they had their studies, and Noaks the housekeeper's room, in which to find shelter, or they would have been compelled to run the gauntlet.

Hawley and Gull, though not found guilty on this particular count, were hustled and abused for their former misdeeds, which it was perfectly evident would be remembered against them during the remainder of their life at Ronleigh.

As for Diggory and his two chums, never were three small boys made so much of before. "What was the cipher?" - "How did they find it out?" - these and a hundred other questions were continually being dinned in their ears, coupled with slaps on the back, ejaculations of "Well done!" - "You're a precious sharp lot!" and many other expressions of approval.

At the close of this eventful day two things alone remained vividly impressed upon their minds.

The first was an interview with Allingford and Oaks in the former's study.

"Well," said the captain, "you kids have done us a good turn. We were in a precious awkward box, and I don't know how we should have got out of it if it hadn't been for you."

"Yes," added Oaks: "I was never more surprised at anything in my life than when Trevanock said he knew who'd done the business. It made old Denson open his eyes."

"So it did," continued Allingford; "and if it hadn't come out, the whole school would have got into another precious row, and there'd have been a stop put to the Wraxby match. I tell you what. You youngsters thought it sneaking to let out what you knew; in my opinion you'd have been jolly sneaks if you'd shielded those blackguards, and allowed everyone else to suffer. Well, as I said before, you've done is a good turn, and as long as we're at Ronleigh together we shan't forget you."

The second thing which lodged in the recollection of the three friends was a look which Noaks had bestowed upon them as he passed out of the doctor's study.

"Did you see his face?" said Diggory. "He looked as if he could have killed us. He's never forgiven us since that time he was turned off the football field for striking you at The Birches."

"No," added Jack Vance; "and then we were the means of old Noaks getting the sack over those fireworks; and that reminds me he's always had a grudge against me for letting out that time that his father was a servant man; and now there's this last row. Oh yes! he'll do his best now to get us into a bother over that knife of Mugford's."

"Of course he will," answered Diggory; "that's what he meant by glaring at us as he did."

"I don't care!" exclaimed Jack Vance, with forced bravado; "he can't prove we stole the coins."

"Of course he can't," sighed Mugford; "but if there's a row it'll rather spoil our Christmas."

CHAPTER XXII.

WHEN SHALL WE THREE MEET AGAIN?

The Wraxby match was played and won. Allingford and his men journeyed to the neighbouring town, so gaming the additional credit of a victory on their opponents' ground; and thus, for the first time for many years, Ronleigh lowered the flag of their ancient rivals both at cricket and at football.

"Hurrah!" cried "Rats," who was in a great state of excitement when the news arrived; "they won't ask us again if we'd like to play a master, the cheeky beggars!"

The same afternoon on which Ronleigh so distinguished herself saw also the melancholy ending of the school life of two of her number. Thurston and Fletcher One went home to return no more; practically expelled, though the doctor, in this instance, did not make a public example of their departure.

Another thing happened on this memorable day which caused quite a sensation, especially among the members of the upper and lower divisions of the Fourth Form.

"I say, have you heard the latest?" cried Maxton,

bursting into the reading-room just before preparation, regardless alike of the presence of Lucas and the rule relating to silence.

"What about?" asked several voices.

"Why, about Noaks!"

"No."

"Well, then, he's run away!"

Magazines and papers fell from the hands which held them, and the usual quiet of the room was broken by a buzz of astonishment.

"Run away! Go on; you don't mean it!"

"I do, though: he's skedaddled right enough, and they can't find him anywhere."

The report was only too true. Afraid to face his schoolfellows, and having already received several intimations, from fellows passing the housekeeper's parlour, that a jolly good licking awaited him when he left his present place of refuge, Noaks had watched his opportunity, and when the boys were at tea had slipped out, and, as Maxton put it, "run away."

No one mourned his loss; even Mouler would not own to having been his friend; and everybody who expressed any opinion on the subject spoke of his departure as being decidedly a good riddance.

The Triple Alliance, however, had cause to feel uneasy when they heard of this latest escapade of their ancient enemy.

"He's got my knife with him," said Mugford; "he may go any day and try for that reward."

For the time being, however, no communication was received from the police-station at Todderton, and none of the three friends was caused, like Eugene Aram, to leave the school with gyves upon his wrists. Whatever evil intentions Noaks might have cherished towards them were destined to be checkmated by a fortunate circumstance, the possibility of which neither side had yet foreseen.

The last day of the term arrived in due course, bringing with it that jolly time when everybody is excited, happy, and good-tempered; when the morning's work is a mere matter of form, and the boys slap their books together at the sound of the bell, with the joyful conviction that the whole length of the Christmas holidays lies between them and "next lesson."

Directly after dinner every one commenced "packing up;" which term might have been supposed to include every form of skylarking which the heart of the small boy could devise, from racing round the quadrangle, arrayed in one of Bibbs's night-shirts, to playing football in the gymnasium, North *versus* South, with the remains of an old mortar-board.

It was at this period of the day that the Triple Alliance proceeded to carry out a project which had for some little time occupied the minds of at least two of their number. The idea was that the little fraternity should celebrate their approaching separation, and the consequent breaking up of their association, with a sort of funeral feast, the cost of which Jack and Diggory insisted should be borne by the two surviving members. Only one outsider was invited to attend - namely, "Rats," whose cheery presence it was thought would tend to enliven the proceedings, and chase away the gloomy clouds of regret which would naturally hang over the near prospect of parting.

The box-room (where such functions usually took place) being at this time in a state of indescribable uproar, it was decided that the banquet should be served in one of the remote classrooms.

"None of the fellows'll come near it," said Jack Vance; "and if old Watford should be knocking round and catch us there, he won't do anything to-day; we shall have to clear out, that's all."

Accordingly, about a quarter to four, the three friends, with their solitary guest, assembled at the trysting-place. Jack Vance carried two big paper bags, Diggory a biscuit-box and a small tin kettle, while the other two were provided with four clean jam-pots, it having been announced that there was "going to be some cocoa."

For the preparation of this luxury Diggory mounted a form and lit one of the gas-jets, over which he and Jack Vance took it in turns to hold the kettle until the water boiled. Sugar, cocoa, and condensed milk were produced from the biscuit-tin, and the jam-pots having been filled with the steaming beverage, the company seated themselves round the stove, in which there still smouldered some remains of the morning's fire, and prepared to enjoy themselves.

From the first, however, the proceeding's fell as flat as

ditch-water. Even the gallant efforts of "Rats" to enliven the party were of no avail; and for some time everybody munched away in silence, Jack Vance occasionally pausing to remark, "Here, pass over that nose-bag, and help yourselves."

The classroom itself, which belonged to the Third Form, was suggestive of that glad season known as "breaking-up." The ink-pots had all been collected, and stood together in a tray on the master's table; fragments of examination papers filled the paper-basket, and were littered here and there about the floor, while some promising Latin scholar had scrawled across the blackboard the well-known words, *Dulce Domum*. These inspiriting signs of a "good time coming" were, however, lost on the Triple Alliance. Their present surroundings served only to remind them of the old days of "The Happy Family," when they had first come to Ronleigh, never expecting but to have completed the period of their school lives in one another's company.

"Well," said Jack Vance, suddenly broaching the subject which was uppermost in each of their minds, "we've had jolly times together. - D'you remember when we made the Alliance, the day you first came to The Birches, Diggory?"

"Yes," answered Diggory; "it was just after we'd been frightened by the ghost. D'you remember the 'Main-top' and the 'House of Lords' and the Philistines? I wonder what's become of them all?"

One reminiscence suggested another, and after exhausting their recollections of The Birches, they recalled their varied experiences at Ronleigh. Only one adventure was by mutual consent not alluded to: their clandestine visit to The Hermitage, coupled with Noaks's threat, hung like the sword suspended by a single hair above the head of Damocles at the feast.

At length, when the paper bags had been wellnigh emptied, Jack Vance intimated his intention of making a speech - which announcement was received with considerable applause.

"Don't finish up your cocoa," he began, "because, before we dissolve the Alliance, I'm going to propose a toast. We've been friends a long time, and both here and at The Birches, as Diggory says, the Triple Alliance has done wonders and covered itself with glory." (Cheers.) "We said when we started that we'd always stand by each other whatever happened; and so we have, and so we would again if we were going to be together any longer." ("Hear, hear!") "I wish 'Rats' could have joined us, but then I suppose it wouldn't have been the Triple Alliance. However, now it's finished with; but before we break it up, I'm going to call upon you to drink the health of Mr. Mugford. May he have long life and happiness, and a jolly fine house, with a model railway, and a lake for boating in the grounds, and ask us all to come and stay with him whenever we feel inclined."

This sentiment was received with shouts of applause, and in honouring it the jam-pots were drained to their muddy dregs.

No one expected that Mugford would reply, for he was decidedly a man of few words; but on this occasion he rose above his usual self, and sitting with his hands in his trouser pockets, his feet on the fender of the stove, and his chin sunk forward on his breast, delivered himself as follows. The room was already growing dark with the early winter twilight, which perhaps rendered it more easy for him to undertake the task of responding to the toast.

"You've always been very kind to me," he began, speaking rather quickly.

"No, we haven't," interrupted Jack Vance.

"Yes, you have. Just shut up; I'm going to say what I like. You made friends with me because I happened to be in the same room at The Birches; but you always stuck to me, and helped me along a lot when we came here first. I know I'm stupid, and sometimes I feel I'm a coward; but I enjoyed being with you, and shall always remember the times we've had together - yes, I swear I shall - always. And now I've got a drop of cocoa left, so I'm going to propose a toast. You must take 'Rats' in my place. I hope you'll have heaps of larks; and you must write me a letter sometimes and tell me what you're doing. Here goes - The new *Triple Alliance!*"

It was customary to laugh at whatever Mugford said, but on this occasion not even a smile greeted the conclusion of his remarks.

Only Diggory spoke. "No, we shan't have another Triple Alliance; now it's going to end."

He turned, and taking something out of the biscuit-tin, said solemnly, "I, Diggory Trevanock, do hereby declare that the association known as the Triple Alliance is now dissolved; in token of which I break this bit of a flat ruler, used by us as a sugar-spoon, into three parts, one of which I present to each of the members as a keepsake, to remind them of all our great deeds and many adventures."

Each boy pocketed his fragment of wood in silence. Jack Vance tried to crack a joke, but it was a miserable failure.

"There was something I wanted to say," began "Rats" thoughtfully. "I shall remember it in a minute. Oh, *bother!*"

"What's up?"

"Why, I know what it was; Mugford's talking about writing to him reminded me of it. I'm awfully sorry, but there were some letters came for you chaps this morning. I took them off the table, meaning to give them to you; but I quite forgot, and left them in my desk."

"Well, you're a nice one!" cried Diggory. "Suppose you go and fetch 'em now!"

"Rats" scrambled to his feet and hurried out of the room.

Jack Vance pulled out his watch, and held it down so that the glimmer of the red light from between the bars of the stove fell upon its face.

"My word," he exclaimed, "it's time we thought about packing!"

"Wait a jiff for those letters," answered Diggory.

A moment later "Rats" came scampering down the

passage. "Here they are," he cried; "I'm very sorry I forgot 'em. A letter for Mugford, and a paper for Vance."

Diggory relighted the gas-jet which he had turned out after boiling the kettle, and proceeded, with the assistance of "Rats," to gather up the remains of the feast. They had hardly, however, got further than emptying the tin kettle down the ventilator before their attention was attracted by a joyful exclamation from Jack Vance.

"What d'you think's happened?" he cried, brandishing the open newspaper. "Why, they've caught the thieves who stole old Fossberry's coins!"

"Not really!"

"They have, though. It was the old woman who looks after the house, and her husband; they're to be tried at the next assizes. They did it right enough; some of the coins were found in their possession, and - Hullo! what's the matter with you?"

The latter remark was addressed to Mugford, who suddenly jumped on a form, began to dance, fell off into the coal-box, scrambled to his feet, and capered wildly round the room.

"He's gone mad!" cried Diggory; "catch him, and sit on his head!"

"No, I haven't!" exclaimed Mugford, coming to a standstill; "but what do you think's happened? Guess!"

"Not that you're going to stay on here!"

"Yes! My uncle says he'll pay for me, and I'm to come back again after Christmas!"

"Well, I'm sure!" gasped Jack Vance; "and we've just dissolved the Alliance! We must make it again."

"No, you shan't!" shouted "Rats;" "Diggory said you wouldn't. I'm coming in, as Mugford suggested, so it'll have to be a quadruple one next time."

"Well, so it shall be," cried Jack Vance, embracing Mugford with the hugging power of a juvenile bear: "next term we'll start afresh."

Diggory and "Rats" promptly fell into each other's arms, and all four, coming into violent collision, tumbled down amidst the *debris* of the overturned coal-box; and after rolling over one another like a lot of young dogs, scrambled to their feet, turned out the gas, and rushed away to complete their packing.

So, as the door slams behind them, they vanish from our sight; for though the renewal of their friendship tempts us to follow them further in their school life, we are reminded that our story has been told. Here ended the existence of the Triple Alliance, and here, therefore, should the history of its trials and triumphs be likewise brought to a conclusion.

www.ingramcontent.com/pod-product-compliance
Lightning Source LLC
Chambersburg PA
CBHW021319250626
47155CB00002B/554